THE NEIGHBOURS

Winner of the Joffe Books Prize 2023

RENITA D'SILVA

Joffe Books, London
www.joffebooks.com

First published in Great Britain in 2024

© Renita D'Silva

Cover art by Nick Castle

ISBN: 978-1-83526-583-3

*For my neighbours, the McKays — Peter, Monika,
Alex, David and Toffi with love and gratitude.*

*We came to this country leaving family behind,
but we've been lucky enough to have found family in you.
Thank you from the bottom of my heart.*

*And for the Bartoszewicz family who made me feel
so welcome and loved when I visited their home in Poland.*

Thank you SO much, Andrzej, Ela, Dorota, Filip and Natka.

NOW

We wake to flashing lights arcing in blue streaks across our dark bedrooms.

The insomniacs among us are already awake and looking out at the darkened world. Our cosy cul-de-sac has turned sinister and unwelcoming in the festering shadows of night, now tinted with pulsing indigo. Neighbours' cats take shelter under parked cars while startled foxes hide among dustbins, their orange eyes bright with unabashed curiosity.

On the road just outside, teenagers stagger past, jostling each other good-naturedly. Snatches of song, conversation and inebriated laughter ring out:

'You didn't!'

'Mate, you're a player!'

Their just-cracking male voices are joined by a chorus of high-pitched female giggling, loud and obscene in the hushed silence, quietening as the police cars approach. They stand straight as they can, glassy, bloodshot eyes in pale, stark faces, suddenly looking their age or younger — children trying to exude bravado and failing. They lean into each other, exhaling in slumped relief as they watch the cars turn into our cul-de-sac one after the other.

1

Muted sirens fracture the secretive quiet. Curtains twitch. More residents gather at windows, sleep-sticky eyes peering out to see what's happening.

An ambulance. Followed by more police cars. So many. Some of them stopping on the road.

The ambulance, where is it headed?

Ah . . .

We saw it coming, we muse, our heartbeats tripping with fear and ghoulish excitement as the paramedics rush in and come back out a few long beats later, hoisting a stretcher.

We don't need to look. We all know who's inside.

No urgency to the ambulance staff. No sirens as the ambulance leaves.

For it is too late, of course.

Far too late for the medics.

But not for the police who now enter the house. It's 2 a.m.

Oh, but wait . . . Listen. More sirens. Yet *another* ambulance. This one with lights blazing and sirens keening, frantically urgent. Why? What's going on? Is it not too late?

And now, we give up any semblance of sleep, putting the kettle on, tea with two sugars just the ticket, our eyes glued to the windows and the goings-on outside.

'We always knew something would happen. Didn't we say it would?' Those of us lucky enough to have partners whisper, shaking our heads, taking long, calming sips of hot, sweet tea. 'We knew it as soon as they moved in. There was just something about them . . .' We pause. Take a breath. 'But we never imagined *this*.' We sigh through pursed lips. But even as we mouth the words, we concede in a secret part of our minds that we always reckoned it was leading up to this.

PART 1

THREE MONTHS PREVIOUS

CHAPTER 1

Sapna

The van Amir has hired veers off the main road as he indicates left and expertly takes the turn into a small street, where stumpy green hedges conceal the houses from the road. Amir brakes abruptly, their possessions rattling in the hold behind, and comes to a stop in front of a long narrow house sharing a wall with its identical twin on the right. The houses in the cul-de-sac are red brick, surrounded by shrubs and rose bushes, and a cherry tree in full blossom rains pink confetti over the grass. The first four houses, including the one they are stopped in front of, do not have any houses facing them, unlike the ones beyond, where the street doubles in on itself.

Cul-de-sac. Sapna looked up the word when Amir showed her the house on his computer, waxing lyrical about it.

'Look at this beauty,' Amir exulted, eyes shining, swivelling his laptop towards her.

They were in the tiny bedroom of the cramped flat in Hounslow that Amir's friend was renting to them for a pittance. The door wouldn't open properly as all available space was taken up by the bed — not even a huge one at that. They'd learned to half open the door and jump into bed, Amir cuddling up to her — the only way the mattress could accommodate two people. When she first saw it, she had wondered how anyone who hated their spouse would manage here and then chastised herself for thinking that way. It felt like they could hear every sound, every sneeze and whisper and argument and secret in the entire block of flats. When Amir kissed her, loved her, he did it in absolute silence.

Even the maids in India had better . . .

Now they were moving on, but somehow leaving Hounslow was like leaving India once again. Sapna had traded her homeland and all she knew and loved, all that was familiar, for a new life with Amir.

When Amir's friend — the same one who let the flat to them — collected them from the airport and brought them to Hounslow, she was shocked by how familiar it felt. If she wasn't so *cold* she could tell herself she was in the poorer, slummy part of her hometown in India. The same shops sold salwars and saris alongside spices and great big bags of rice and chapati flour. The same eye-watering scents of sizzling onions and frying chillies, of smoked garlic, caramelised sugar and over-boiled milk met her nose. Tandoori joints, dhabas and Indian restaurants abounded, as did sweet shops, their windows hosting seductive pyramids of syrupy jalebis, milky pedas and silver-foiled cashew barfis.

She was expecting something completely different, the England she'd heard about, seen on television. Endless green fields and manicured gardens, yellow daffodils and sprawling stately homes, spotlessly clean streets, no litter anywhere in sight. She thought she wanted somewhere a bit more like the cul-de-sac, but now that she's here . . .

She almost misses the flat. Where they kept bumping into each other, she and Amir. It grew on her. There was always something going on, bustle and noise, somebody to eavesdrop on. A quarrel. A visitor. She was never bored.

This tall thin house looks forbidding. She shivers.

When Amir — who had thrown himself into house-hunting from the moment he brought her to England — showed her the house on his computer, she experienced it then. A chill of foreboding.

But Amir was so excited, so very pleased. 'Wow, look at this. A semi-detached home in a cul-de-sac. I cannot believe they're only asking that much for it — that's at the top of our price range but we should just about manage. And it's in such a lovely area too. I do hope we get it. I'm sure there will be plenty of competition.'

She loved the way he said 'our price range' even though he was the only one working. He seemed so happy and hopeful, his whole face glowing with anticipation, and so she didn't share a word of her misgivings.

The next day while he was at work, as a baby wailed in the flat below, a woman's voice raised in agitation, the scent of boiling rice and crisping chapati dough wafting in, she searched for 'cul-de-sac' on Amir's computer. A street with only one exit. Sapna shivered as she looked up the house again — it was saved in the computer search history. All the houses in the cul-de-sac were arranged in a semicircle, the street turning around at the end of the road. The one Amir was keen to rent was the second one in. There were no houses facing it but it was attached to its neighbour on the right. 'They are called semi-detached when they share a common wall,' Amir explained. The house on the left stood proudly unattached to its neighbours — 'detached' was the word for it. She felt claustrophobic just looking at it, this house Amir was so excited about.

She experiences it afresh now as she looks out of the window of the hired van. She is swamped by an urgent, frantic impulse to ask her husband to turn around, drive away. Amir is oblivious to her disquiet, cheerfully enthusiastic, beaming at her while talking non-stop. 'We have a small garden at the back. We can cultivate a herb patch, a vegetable section, even plant some fruit trees . . .'

She sees curtains twitch at the twin house on the right. A face pressed to a window, squashed nose, lined visage, shrewd

6

eyes that meet hers and look away almost immediately. The head moves back from the window. A helmet of silver hair. An old lady, not much to do with her time. Curious. Bored. Dangerous? *Stop this at once, Sapna.*

Amir parks and flashes her a wide smile. 'Welcome to our new home, Sapna.'

She smiles back, reluctant to get out of the van, her heart heavy, beset suddenly by homesickness for a country and a home she couldn't wait to get away from.

* * *

Sapna's mother was in the courtyard supervising the annual plucking of coconuts when she called the previous morning. Her mother took an age to get to the phone and when she did, she was breathless.

'Gopi came late as usual,' Ma grumbled. 'I pay him two thousand rupees to climb up a tree and wriggle the coconuts free and he turns up late and expects breakfast. It's half past eleven now and he's only just started. He was the one who told me the phone was ringing, cheekily asking me whether I was going to answer it or not. He was sitting on top of the tree when I left, fetching beedis out of his lungi pocket — taking a break, no doubt. He wouldn't pull a single coconut if I wasn't there to supervise. He'd be smoking his beedi astride the tree, feet hanging into the abyss below, carefree, king of all he surveys.' She pauses to take a breath, her voice softening. 'Anyway, enough about that. We're all fine here. Your baba and brothers are working in the fields. Your sisters are arguing as usual. How are you, janu?'

Janu, *my life*. Her mother's endearment for her.

Sapna pushes down her upset at what her mother said after, thinking how home is a world away from this not-quite-detached house, and trying to quell the urge for it. The hot sun, blistering gold ire, burning wrath; humid air summoning rivulets of moisture; the baked fields, green blades tinted red with dust; mango, tamarind and coconut trees

7

waving in the occasional breeze; her mother gossiping with Gopi. The sweet, cardamom-infused aroma of tea brewing from the kitchen where one of her sisters is doing the washing-up, clanging the pots with more vehemence than necessary while compiling a list of grievances against the others. The cat would be on a (forever foiled) mission to steal the fish, wrapped in newspaper and waiting to be scaled, chopped and marinated in the spices that one of her other sisters is pounding into a paste with vinegar . . .

* * *

Amir opens his door, jostling her from her thoughts as he jumps out of the van and waits for her to climb out, grinning like a child finally in possession of the new toy he's desired for ages.

Sapna looks at the neat lines of the house, missing the sprawling cottage at home, always full of people and noise. Here the quiet stretches and sighs, still and expectant. She can feel herself being gawped at, pierced by stares: the new neighbours have arrived, an event not to be missed. The air feels thick with freshly minted gossip, rife with rumour pulsing on eager tongues.

'We're moving in at just the right time. Early spring with the promise of summer to come. It's only going to get better. England is best in summer, just glorious, everything in bloom. A season to be enjoyed and celebrated, strawberries and cream in the garden while soaking up the sun,' Amir says, smiling at her.

Still beaming widely — his whole body seems to be smiling — Amir slots the key in the door.

Then, bowing exaggeratedly, 'After you, m'lady.'

Despite her unease, she smiles and her husband laughs gaily with the abandon of a child, bringing to mind wind chimes dancing as they flirt with the breeze, bronzed bells singing in celebration.

The hallway is dark and narrow and opens onto a living room, which leads to a good-sized kitchen with all the mod cons. 'Open-plan,' Amir says, grinning approvingly.

At the other end of the kitchen, a door, framed by glass windows on either side, opens out onto a stretch of weed-infested grass with a tumbledown shed at the far end. Two overgrown trees stand sentinel right by the kitchen, on either side of it. Their branches, budding with new leaves a bright celebratory green, kiss the glass of the windows. The garden is bordered — hemmed in — by a fence on all sides. It appears as if a previous occupant tried to paint the fence panels a bright shade of amber but gave up halfway along, leaving the rest a dull beige. A squirrel sits on the amber side — *Good choice, Mr Squirrel*, Sapna thinks — holding something with both hands and nibbling at it with great concentration, whiskers twitching in delight. Sapna goes up to the glass, presses her face to the pane, cool to the touch, and looks out at the squirrel. It hops away, disappearing in a blinking instant.

The thought arrives out of nowhere: *I wish I could hop away too.*

The hairs at the back of her neck prickle, standing to attention. There, the tree to the left, was that a shadow that moved just now? Someone concealed behind its trunk?

A touch on her shoulder. She jumps.

'Hey, what's the matter?' Amir laughs, his breath sweet and flavoured with mint. She leans into him, her heartbeat gradually returning to normal.

Get a grip. It was nothing. Your imagination is playing havoc with your senses, making you see things that aren't there.

But then why is her skin erupting in goosebumps? Why is her body uncomfortable, not quite able to shake the sensation of being spied on?

Stop it right now.

'Sapna?' Amir plants a kiss on her forehead.

'Overwhelmed, that's all,' she mutters, drawing comfort from her husband's solid arms.

Yet she can't help casting a glance at the garden over her husband's shoulder. No shadow. Not a flicker of movement.

Sapna shakes her head. *Fool.* But she can't quite dislodge the feeling of being watched. She feels strangled, claustrophobic, despite this house being almost four times bigger than the little flat they've come from.

CHAPTER 2

Edith

Edith watches the new neighbours arrive and she feels weary.

A young couple on the cusp of a new phase of life together in their new home. And she at the end of hers. She has lived too long, she thinks as she stretches, trying and failing to rid herself of the aches and pains in her joints, at the centre of her very being.

She has resided here for so many years, seen so many people come and go, not all of them leaving voluntarily, not all of them upright, on their own two feet.

She recalls coming here herself, the cul-de-sac then a rain-churned construction site, only their home fully built and ready for occupation. She was stroking her belly — her firstborn, Tom, now fifty; *where does the time go!* — Jack smiling at her, the paint still drying on the house, no easy access, mud and mulch everywhere. They had to walk on boards to get to the door, the scent of promise prevalent in the wet emulsion. New beginnings.

She had been happy at the first-floor flat they were in before. It was right by the church, practically next door to the shops and a few paces from the local primary school. She had

11

loved hearing the kids walk past each morning and return in the afternoon, their happy chatter, their glorious laughter. She would mark time by the sombre ceremony of church bells, the haunting hymns, the aroma of candles and prayer, the breathy, gossip-winged natter of the Ladies of the Parish council. The downstairs neighbours were kind.

But Jack had talked her round, like he had always been able to do. 'It'll be nice for our children. A garden to run about in. A house of our own.'

These new neighbours are a young couple, like Edith and Jack were when they moved in.

But this couple is not English. Dark-skinned. More and more of them about these days. Nearly all the local shops and most of the ones in town are run by them, it seems. They're nice enough, although hard to understand sometimes.

There's never been one of their kind in the cul-de-sac before. Might ruffle some feathers, especially her at Number 20 on the main road, just before the turn-off. Snooty so-and-so. Gives herself airs and graces, she does, for what reason Edith has never understood. Her house is detached, but then so is Gemma's over at Number 3. Mrs High-and-Mighty at Number 20 might have a bedroom or two more than some others, her garden might be longer and wider too, but that's no reason to act like she's the queen. No, that would be doing the queen a disservice; her royal highness was infinitely more gracious than her at Number 20, who clickety-clacks right past Edith on her high heels (at her age! Serves her right if they catch on the cobbles), nose in the air, without acknowledging Edith (common courtesy, for Christ's sake), even when they both get off the bus at the same stop, Edith dragging her shopper on wheels. Very handy the shopper on wheels, changed Edith's life, it has, what with her dodgy knees.

Edith reins in her drifting mind — it does that more often than not these days, goes off on a tangent willy-nilly — and focuses on the new neighbours.

The girl is beautiful. Thin and small, waiflike, her hair covered by a scarf. But with one of those faces that you can't

12

look away from. She should be happy, excited, and yet there's no sparkle in the girl's eyes. Her shoulders are hunched.

Edith forgets herself, presses her face to the glass. The girl's eyes meet Edith's. Huge cocoa-butter irises, framed by thick, curling lashes, but they are swollen, Edith notes, the whites bloodshot as if from a bout of crying. The girl's gaze appears haunted, Edith thinks. Now where did that come from? Edith shakes her head decisively. She's not usually given to romanticising.

The man with her — her husband? You can't tell these days, what with room-mates and one-night stands and flings and extramarital affairs and what-have-yous; young people changing partners like socks — looks much older. He has the shoulders and build and rugged features of a thug, Edith decides. His walk is a swagger. And the girl, in stark contrast, is a fragile butterfly.

Well, it takes all sorts, I suppose, Edith thinks as she watches the woman — girl, really — get down from the van (reluctantly?); the man doesn't offer a helping hand. She's wearing a patterned dress — silk, Edith supposes — that reaches her knees and shimmers as it catches the light, one of those foreign ones with sequins and mirrors that wink and tantalise seductively. It's the vulgar crimson of blood spilling from a fresh cut, with matching flared trousers and scarf. Her feet are clad in bright-gold sequined sandals, Edith notes (she might be old but her hearing and eyesight is really good for her age; she's been told so, often and enviously and sometimes a tad sourly, by her cronies). The poor girl's feet must be cold, Edith thinks, watching her drag them — there's no other word for it — to the front door, pulling her scarf closer around her face, her dress billowing about her in the racy spring breeze.

I'll bake the carrot cake my boys loved and take it round in a couple of days. Give her time to settle first, making sure to drop by when the man is away, Edith thinks as she puts the kettle on. *Get the lie of the land.*

Will the girl invite her in, Edith wonders as she squeezes the tea bag. She hopes she does. Edith imagines visiting with the girl and experiences a tingle of excitement. She's talked to them but hasn't been inside one of these foreigners' houses before. Will they be set out the same as English ones? Mary, with whom she attends the Silver Surfer computer (and gossip) sessions at the library on Fridays, will be all ears.

CHAPTER 3

Sapna

The morning after they move into their new house, Amir returns to work.

'I have to, my love, otherwise the rent on this wonderful gift of a home will not get paid,' he said as they snuggled together in sleeping bags the night before, when, after finally unloading the van and rooting around the boxes containing all their worldly possessions, they had unearthed their toothbrushes in the one labelled 'Files and Documents'.

When the house move was finalised, they had begun packing meticulously, Amir procuring empty cardboard boxes from the Indian corner shop, Sapna carefully labelling them, surprised at how much stuff they had accumulated in their few weeks together. But by the time moving day came round, their remaining possessions had been chucked randomly into any box that had space, the urgency and inevitability of their move having suddenly dawned on them, especially once the van was booked.

'But you will be tired,' Sapna complained drowsily, spooning Amir as much as the sleeping bags would allow. She couldn't get warm, the night feeling especially chilly after

15

the humid heat of India, something she still hadn't got used to. ('How will you manage in winter then, I wonder,' Amir would say fondly when she complained that it was freezing. And then grinning cheekily, he would provide the answer to his question himself. 'I will keep you warm, my love, don't you worry.')

'Needs must,' Amir said, yawning.

She is still asleep when he leaves for work, planting a kiss on her cheek and piling his sleeping bag on top of hers.

She manages a groggy goodbye. 'Have a good day, try not to fall asleep at work.'

That gets a smile from him; even half-asleep, she hears his chuckle. 'Thanks for the sleeping bag. It will do nicely in your absence,' she adds.

Another chuckle. 'Don't get too used to it. I'm coming back.'

'You'd better,' she mumbles before drifting back to sleep, dreaming of warm sun, green fields, golden paddies, mouth-tingling spices, her mother's laughter, her sisters' teasing, her brothers' jostling and her father, her baba . . .

You are dead to me.

* * *

She wakes with a start, tears on her face, soaking into her sleeping bag.

The new house yawns, vacant and cold and forbidding.

She sits up and shivers, pulling the sleeping bags around her. The room seems empty and bare, despite their boxes of belongings spilling their contents. It screams foreboding — loneliness with an underlying hint of menace.

Stop this, Sapna.

Weak sunlight streams in through the newspaper she and Amir plastered onto the bedroom window the previous evening — a makeshift measure — dancing patterns on the wall opposite. She stares up at the ceiling, an expanse of uniform cream. Not bubbling yellow, stippled with cracks, like at home. Here, there are no lizards flitting between wooden beams, darting tongues on the lookout for flies.

At home, she and her sisters would share a lumpy mattress with Ma, Baba snoring on the wooden bench by the front door. The boys slept in the dining room, which would be swept and mopped after the night's meal. There would be long chats punctuated with laughter, ripostes tossed back and forth between the two rooms before they fell asleep. The boys would place bets on who would be the first to start snoring — almost always their father — composing songs to keep time with his snores, laughing when he stopped for a bit, then started up again in sputtering booms. Her sisters would giggle like little waterfalls twinkling silvery bright among the lush green hills.

Sapna's stomach rumbles loudly, jolting her into the present. She is hungry. Her last meal was a bland chicken sandwich at the service station they'd stopped at on the way here. She will have to go downstairs, dig among the boxes for something to eat. Oh, how she took for granted the luxury of waking up to Ma frying puris in the kitchen, the little rounds of dough puffing up in the hot oil into perfect little balloons. Here there is no sizzle of red chillies and popping of mustard seeds. No golden scent of onions browning, spices roasting. No digging her nails in to watch the air escape.

She sighs, shaking her head to push away the nostalgia, the memories that ambush and overwhelm her.

She stretches, and walks to the window, hugging the sleeping bags to her. She puts her face to the gap between two of the newspaper sheets, curious about the view from this room, and immediately stumbles backward, startled. A woman's face stares, unashamedly, right at her, out of the window of the house next door — the one on the left, not the twin sharing a wall with theirs, which is occupied by the old lady Sapna saw yesterday peering at them through the curtains. Is Sapna dreaming? She blinks, looks again. The woman is still there, still staring. Unblinking. Can she see Sapna? Surely not? Sapna is standing away from the window, only her eyes visible in the chink between the news sheets. Why is this woman staring at the house, *their* house in quite that way? A tad hostile, or is that just Sapna's imagination?

After what feels like an age, the woman turns away and Sapna sees a small face rooting at her shoulder. A baby. It's just a woman rocking her baby while standing at her window.

You really need to get a hold of yourself, Sapna thinks as her heartbeat gradually returns to normal and she turns away from the window. She prepares to explore and get to know her new house.

CHAPTER 4

Sapna

When Sapna goes downstairs, she pauses on the last step for a deep bolstering breath, then, pushing her shoulders back, erect posture belying her frantic heart, she marches purposefully into the open-plan living room and kitchen. Boldly, she strides up to the back door and rests her face against the glass like she did when they arrived.

Nothing. No tingling at the back of her neck; her hair does not stand to attention like it did the previous evening, her skin does not come out in goosebumps.

The garden looks lush in its wild abundance, the grass unkempt, the trees fertile with fresh growth. She lets out the breath she was holding.

I let my imagination run away with me yesterday, and just now, when I imagined that woman rocking her baby was staring into our bedroom.

Sapna walks from room to room, touching the walls, the doors, telling herself, *This is my house, this is my life.*

The silence is deafening and another attack of homesickness washes over her. A longing builds for the home she grew up in, always bustling and filled to bursting with people and

19

yet never feeling crowded or stifling, instead warm and comfortable and welcoming. It overlooked the monsoon-jewelled fields from its perch on top of a hill. The land was flush with fruit trees: mango and coconut, tamarind and guava, lime and jackfruit, the fragrant air scented with ripening fruit and baked earth. It's all so different to this overgrown backyard.

Ma, we have moved into the new house, I think you will love it — it is everything you would have wanted for me, and more, Sapna tells her mother in her head, knowing she cannot call her, not anymore.

Her house-proud mother would have been awed by the gadgets in the kitchen — the washing machine, the dishwasher, the microwave, the oven, the electric stove — no lugging cylinders of gas through the fields, switching them with the empties every month. This kitchen in Sapna's new home, with its pristine work surfaces, is her mother's idea of heaven. So why isn't Sapna warming to it? Why does it feel cold, bereft of heart?

Her mother will never see this house, cook alongside Sapna in this kitchen, sharing gossip and laughter, recipes and stories. Her mother will never be able to participate in Sapna's life.

'What's that sound in the background?' she asked her mother over the phone just after she came to England, standing with her nose pressed to the window of the flat in Hounslow, watching the skiving teenagers' antics. They were taking turns jumping off the wall onto the bins, one of them falling inside, emerging covered in rubbish, the others falling about laughing. Would she ever laugh in such a carefree way again, after everything that had happened?

The sound was a constant thrum, crackle and fizz, loud and brash *like* static but *not* static.

'The monsoons have arrived; everything is muddy, our clothes are permanently wet.' Her mother sighed.

The monsoons, she thinks now, with a great sigh of longing. The air still, heavy, humid, waiting. A crack like the whip Sumitranna uses on his buffaloes and sometimes on

20

his wife, a roar and an angry flash splitting the muggy sky in two. The heavens opening. The curtain of rain so thick you couldn't see anything in front of you, around you. The damp smell of drying clothes. The leaking roof, the *drip-drip-drip* of water collecting in buckets placed in strategic positions around the house. Hot red rice and tart mango pickle eaten to the drumbeat of rain on the tiles . . .

Sapna wanders into the kitchen, stares at all the gleaming appliances. She pictures herself, her mother, her sisters, all working together in this kitchen — a fantastic vision — grinding rice, pounding masala, grating coconut, the hiss of pakoras crisping in hot oil, the nose-tingling, mouth-watering tang of frying spices, the pristine white surfaces anointed with turmeric and vermilion.

She watches television — a talk show blaring angry noise into her too-quiet house. She is transfixed. How can these people air all their shameful secrets so brazenly in public? How can they fight, shout, yell like the fishmongers in the market at home? Aren't they aware that a whole nation is watching? *Wait till I tell Ma about this.*

But . . . she can't. She bites her lip until she tastes blood, digs her fingernails into her palms until the urge to talk to her mother passes.

She looks at the clock. Five minutes after twelve. Too early for lunch. And anyway, she isn't hungry. Too early to cook for Amir. What to do? How to pass the time? She could unpack, but once that is done, then what?

People. She misses people, noise, company, laughter, gossip, the easy camaraderie of family. She yearns for glutinous congee doused in watery buttermilk seasoned with chilli and ginger, with sour-sweet lemon rind pickle on the side. She longs for sun so hot it scalds her head, so humid it plasters her clothes to her body, so blindingly bright it washes away all imperfection in its incandescent gold-white glow. She longs for the song of women planting paddy in the fields, and Baba urging on his bullocks as his plough drags furrows in the wet, fertile earth.

Most of all Sapna misses her mother's touch. Her hands massaging coconut oil warmed on the hearth onto her hair, her voice humming Bollywood songs off-key as Sapna and her sisters lie beside Ma on the mat while, outside, the neighbourhood dogs serenade the moon.

This is home now, the voice in her head chides, yet again. *It will do you good to remember it.*

CHAPTER 5

Gemma

Gemma dreams that she is drowning. Drowning in cantankerous screeches. Loud, plaintive sobs the dismal yellow of melancholy. She shuts her ears hoping the heartrending yells will stop. But they keep on coming, burrowing into her very soul, forcing reciprocal tears from her eyes even as her heart cries, 'Stop, please, enough.'

But they don't pay heed. They are insidious. Demanding. Insistent. Endless. They urge her into action even as they enmesh her with viscous tentacles.

She wakes with a start. Her whole being groggy, head spinning. The room is thick with heat and sleep, the fetid miasma of sweat and nightmares. Beside her, Rob snores loudly, oblivious. She stands, swaying, and rushes from the room to her baby, who screams fit to wake the snoozing world. She lifts Theo from his cot and shushes him, blinking bleary-eyed at the clock: 3 a.m.

She has managed to sleep for forty-five minutes. Deep sleep, with dark edges from which Theo has wrenched her awake. Her baby is warm and trembling in her arms as his sobs gradually judder down to whimpers.

'There, there,' she whispers.

He's not hungry. She fed him forty-five minutes ago and burped him after, so he's not suffering from trapped wind either. His nappy is dry. He just has never been able to sleep continuously at a stretch for long.

When will it change? Will it ever? she wonders wearily, as she paces the upstairs corridor, silent now her baby's cries have quieted to occasional sleepy whimpers, punctured only by her husband's peaceful, undisturbed snores.

How can Rob sleep through their baby's screeching cries? She envies Rob this blessing while simultaneously wanting to wring his neck for being so supremely unaffected, slumbering so deeply.

Edith from up the road promises that it will get better. 'My Tom was just like your bubba. I was so sleep-deprived I didn't know if I was coming or going. One day he'll sleep through and you'll forget he ever didn't.'

Gemma is not quite sure she believes Edith about Theo sleeping through, or about her ever forgetting these dragging, wakeful hours of night, alone with her fretful baby, her desperate thoughts, her tired body arching towards sleep.

Wearily, Gemma rests her forehead against the window-sill at the upstairs landing as her baby snuffles against her. Outside it is quiet. Dark. Not a soul awake.

Once in a while the glimmer of headlights punctures the blanket of black as vehicles drive past on the road outside the cul-de-sac. But here, all is still, peaceful.

Gemma is so tired she could fall asleep standing up. And she must do. For something wakes her, jarring her abruptly into consciousness. Not Theo, who is fast asleep in her arms, but who she knows will wake the moment she places him down in his crib.

A light blinking. In the house next to hers. The new neighbours. The ones who moved in a few days ago. A young couple. She has meant to go round, say hello, but she hasn't had the chance. Theo has been grizzly and cranky — teething, she thinks. He's needed her constantly and she's shattered.

From where she's standing, Gemma can look directly inside the living room of Number 2 and into the kitchen. The curtains aren't in place yet. They have barely any furniture — only a table and a quartet of chairs in the kitchen and a lone stool in the living room, standing sentinel over the cardboard boxes waiting to be unpacked. The view overlooks their master bedroom as well, but they've pasted newspaper on the window in there. Unlike the downstairs windows, which are bare.

Gemma's house is detached, per se, but really only separated from Number 2 by a fence. The houses are so close together that she could, if she wished, reach out through her window and touch the neighbours' wall. But Gemma's house is on a slight bend in the road so it affords her an unparalleled glimpse right into next door, and she takes advantage of this now, holding her baby close, bathing in Theo's warm innocence, his milk-flavoured breath coming out in dreamy little gasps. She wonders why the light was switched on at this time of night. It's usually pitch-black in all the other houses this early in the morning, residents slumbering peacefully while Gemma paces with her fretful infant, deeply envious of their undisturbed nights.

Next door, the woman comes into view as she walks down the stairs. She's angelic. Like a sprite from another world. She stands at the bay window in a long, flowing nightdress and peers out into the night, a wistful expression on her face. Thankfully she doesn't look upwards at Gemma. Nevertheless, Gemma takes a step or two back, standing a little away from her own window.

The woman is silhouetted against her living room window, light framing her face, contrasting with the inky darkness of night. She looks impossibly young — slender and vulnerable, as if a puff of wind will blow her away.

As Gemma watches, the woman shakes her head as if to clear it and walks into the kitchen. She turns on the tap, pours herself a tumbler of water. She drinks deeply. Then she sits at the kitchen table, her back to Gemma, and folds her head into the cradle of her hands. After a bit, her shoulders start to shake.

She is crying, Gemma realises, with a shock of surprise.

Although she feels like the worst kind of voyeur, spying on this woman's pain, Gemma can't look away. This is the first time Gemma has seen anyone else awake at this time of night in any of the other houses in the cul-de-sac. There are women with school-age children, even some with babies in the houses that have been converted into multiple flats further down the cul-de-sac, where the street turns in on itself, but Gemma has never noticed any lights on in there at this time of night. Their babies must be those well-behaved ones who adhere to routine, sleeping for a solid five hours or more at a stretch. How she envies them, those smug mums who blithely say, 'Oh, my Marcus is a textbook baby, out like a light at 9 p.m. and waking at 5 a.m. bright and ready for a feed.'

But now, here is someone else moving about in the small hours alongside Gemma. And right next door too. And even if it is a woman indulging in private sorrow, oblivious to Gemma watching her, it eases Gemma's loneliness a tad. It is as if the sobbing woman is expressing what Gemma herself is holding back, has been since Theo arrived — her mixed feelings about her child. She loves Theo with all her heart but there are times when she wants to scream just as loudly or even louder than him, to yell, *I don't want this. I didn't ask for this. I want to sleep. I want my body, my life, my time back. I want to once again be the woman I was before I became this weary zombie.*

Gemma stands there for what feels like for ever, watching the other woman cry. Then, she turns away, carries her baby to his cot. Gently, Gemma lays Theo down and waits a beat, two. Theo stirs, his face crumpling, but he doesn't wake. Gemma counts to ten. Her boy sleeps, his hands thrown up above his face, his teddies arranged like sentinels around his cot keeping a steady watch.

Gemma tiptoes back into the bedroom she shares with Rob. The light is still on downstairs at Number 2.

Gemma pauses once again, transfixed, glad to hide among the shadows of her own house. The woman's shoulders have stopped shaking. She stands up, blows her nose

26

and makes her way from the kitchen to the living room, her steps weary, as if carrying a weight almost too heavy to bear. She looks out, up at the sliver of moon that has just made an appearance. The light peeks tantalisingly from behind a glower of clouds, illuminating the woman's face, her young body, and then she slowly makes her way up the stairs, the silver anklets wrapped around her ankles catching the ghostly light and glinting seductively, the last to disappear from view.

As Gemma slides into bed beside her husband, breathing in his dreamy fug of sleep, she promises herself that she will visit the woman later this morning, with some biscuits and the offer of conversation and welcome. She is, obviously, quite lonely. And it will assuage Gemma's guilt for rubbernecking inadvertently on her secret pain.

CHAPTER 6

Sapna

Sapna and Amir seem to be arguing every day, all of the time, since they moved here, their first fight on their first full day in the house. She complained about him getting home late, which kicked it all off.

'I haven't even set foot inside the front door yet, and you are complaining. Can't it wait?' He sighed, his face irritated in a way she hadn't seen before, lines of tiredness and annoyance surrounding his eyes.

She knew she should keep quiet but her upset burst from her unbidden; it had a mind of its own. 'I've been all alone and counting down the hours to your homecoming. It's dark now. I was worried. Where were you?'

'Working, my love.' But there was no love in the endearment at all, just waspishness.

'I was scared,' she cried. 'You didn't return my calls.'

'No signal underground,' he said shortly.

She knew he was irritated, that she should stop, but she was angry too. Incensed at all the useless hours of worrying and wondering. 'Before then—'

He did not let her finish. 'I hadn't charged my phone, all right? Forgot to, didn't I, in all the hassle of moving. I don't know where the charger is. Can't remember where I put it.'

'But . . .'

'I went to bed at three, got up at six and have been either commuting or working non-stop since then.' He ran a hand down his face, the gesture weary. 'When I finally finished work for the day, I missed the train home by a minute. So can you please stop with the nagging?' he snapped.

The tone of voice he used, as if she was a nuisance, unwanted . . . She couldn't help her tears.

Instead of consoling her, he walked off without eating the food she had so carefully prepared and kept hot, although she had had to reheat it a few times as the hours of evening dragged on with no Amir in sight. She had worried that something had happened to him as 6 p.m., when he used to get home in Hounslow, came and went. Her calls to him wouldn't go through. She had panicked when darkness fell, thick and heavy and unremitting, with no sign of Amir. She had imagined all sorts, him in an accident, lying somewhere, unconscious.

What will I do? She had fretted. *I know nobody here.* She had wondered if it was too early to start calling hospitals. She had looked at the houses on either side of her, glimmers of light angling through chinks in drawn curtains. One belonging to the woman with the baby Sapna had thought was spying into their bedroom, and the other to the old woman who had been peering out from between the curtains when they moved in. Which one to approach?

Please, she had prayed, *let Amir come home safe.*

Just as she was about to knock on the old woman's door, deciding she was less likely to be put out at this late hour, eschewing the lady with the baby for it might be the baby's bedtime, Amir had arrived home. She'd been so relieved — her prayers answered, her husband safe and well and home with her. And yet, instead of throwing her arms around him in welcome, her mouth had flooded with angry bile, her hours of panicked worry making her lash out, whine, chastise, even before he was inside the house.

That night, following their first full day in their new house, he did not hold her — he inched as far away from her as possible, the sleeping bags helping to put distance between them. She cried herself to sleep.

In the morning when she woke he was gone. But his sleeping bag was on top of hers. Had she dreamed the kiss she was sure he planted on her lips when he left for work?

She resolved to be nicer the next evening but as the solitary hours dragged on, misery took precedence, and try as she might, she just could not dredge up the smile he needed when he got home from work. Instead her emotions ran close to the surface, so even a disappointed look from Amir was enough to make her burst into tears.

Truth is, she is immeasurably lonely with nothing to fill in the long hours when Amir is at work. She loves to read but her beloved books were left at home as there was only limited space in their luggage when travelling to England. She can read English only passably, translating each word in her head as she goes. She is determined to rectify this and so she occupies some of her time painstakingly reading articles from the local newspaper that someone shoved through their letterbox, looking up words she doesn't understand in the Hindi–English dictionary she found in the Cancer Research charity shop near their flat in Hounslow. She imagines telling Ma, 'Can you believe it, here even the newspapers are free *and* delivered to your door?' She pictures Ma's gasp of marvel and she hurts, aching for her mother's touch, the sound of her voice, her infectious laughter.

At the flat in Hounslow, Sapna could watch all the Indian channels on television — Amir's friend had set that up before they moved in. So she was able to keep up with the soaps she had watched with her mother and sisters after they completed their chores, sitting or lying down on the cool cement floor, or propped up against each other, sharing roasted groundnuts and heated opinions about the characters' actions. One of her sisters, usually Sunita, who loves anything to do with hair, would massage their heads with coconut oil, plaiting their tresses, the breeze scented with ripe mango and fried onions dancing in through the open door.

During her first few weeks in England, watching those soaps while Amir was at work helped to pass the time, and although alone in the flat, she could pretend she was with the family she'd left behind. Later, she'd discuss and dissect the soaps with her mother over the phone during their long conversations. But now there are no more phone calls. And here they are yet to install the TV provider that streams Indian channels.

Perhaps there *is* some truth to the hurtful accusation Amir had flung at her the previous night, his face distorted with anger, so he looked like a ghastly stranger. 'You are never happy — you always need to pine for something, be upset about something.'

She thought she wanted to escape her childhood home. She thought she hated the flat in Hounslow. And now she misses them both with a vengeance. She misses the girl she was at home in India and the woman she became in the flat in Hounslow. The couple she and Amir were then . . .

Although it was barely a week ago, it feels like a lifetime. It seems as if they have both changed irrevocably in the short time they've spent in this house. Sapna is sure they're no longer as close as they were just a few days previously. The distance that has sprung up between them is acrid with recriminations, foul with festering resentments.

She rubs her arm viciously. Has *she* changed or has Amir? Or perhaps it is the both of them? No. Her instincts tell her it's neither. It's this house.

Take the easy way out and blame the house, why don't you? her conscience taunts.

But she's not making it up, this house . . . there's something *evil* here. She senses it.

She wraps her hands around herself, rubs at her arm again. Closes her eyes and pushes away the hot scald of pain. She has burned her bridges with her family, moved across the world with Amir. And now it feels like her husband, her only link to this alien country, this unfamiliar world, is at cross purposes with her.

The house mocks her with its brooding emptiness. Its echoing hollow walls. Its seething silence.

As if to contradict this, the doorbell goes just as Sapna is getting out of the shower. She recoils, scared and stumped for a few flabbergasted minutes, wondering what the noise is, where the vaguely sinister music is coming from. She's not used to the chimes.

She stands there, water droplets clinging to her and making her shiver as they cool on her body. She thinks of the warm, steamy, woodsmoke-scented mugs of water she would pummel onto her body in the bathroom at home. The heat from the embers that had been used to boil the water in the brass pot stinging her eyes — the scent of Lifebuoy soap and fiery ash and clean skin and wet logs.

She aches for home and yet when she was there she could not wait to get away. And now she can't go back, can't even call to chat to her mother . . .

'You know how stubborn your baba is,' her mother had said during their last conversation the morning before she and Amir moved home. 'He found out, janu, that I've been talking to you and he's not happy. He's banned me from speaking to you. I will find a way around this, but let's stop telephoning each other for now. Janu, you're always in my thoughts, you know that. Take care.'

Is that why Sapna is so unsettled? Why she cannot warm to this house? Does she, irrationally, illogically, blame this house for what she did, her mistakes, her stupid choices?

The doorbell goes again. Quickly, she slips on clothes over her wet body, and, wrapping her dripping hair in a towel, pads downstairs.

At the door she pauses. Peers through the keyhole. A woman with a baby, holding a small cardboard box. Her next-door neighbour, the one she caught looking into their bedroom.

She plasters on a smile and opens the door.

'Hi,' the woman says. She looks wan, washed out, circles under her eyes, like she has not slept for days. The baby is impossibly small and fast asleep on her shoulder, shaped like a question mark.

Sapna feels a pang as she thinks of her littlest brother, whom she and her sisters used to take turns looking after. He is fifteen now and thoroughly spoiled. A menace, not above yelling at the top of his lungs if he doesn't get his way. Their fault, of course. Their cosseting has turned him into the cheeky brat he is now. That's how it is with all the boys in the family — hopelessly indulged and made to think they run the world. Small wonder it goes to their head.

She shakes her own head to clear it. She really must stop slipping away to a home and family no longer hers. *If you keep on moping like this, looking backwards to all you have lost, how will you move on? No wonder this house seems unwelcoming when you're pining for another a world away.*

'I'm Gemma and this is Theo,' the woman is saying, indicating the sleeping cherub, little gasps escaping from the half-open mouth squashed onto the curve of her neck. 'I live at Number 3.' The woman nods her head to indicate the standalone — *detached* — house next door.

She must be in her mid-thirties, Sapna thinks, judging from the lines crowding her eyes. As old as her oldest sister. Another sharp pang of ache. *Stop this at once.*

As old as Amir. She rubs her arm and flinches, biting her lower lip.

'I'm Sapna. Come in, please.' She smiles. 'I'm so sorry, I was in the shower.'

'Here.' The woman holds out the box. 'Sorry, I didn't have time to bake anything. Just shop-bought chocolate cake. Good old M&S.' Then she looks worried. 'You don't have any allergies or food intolerances, do you?' She shakes her head ruefully. 'I didn't think to check.'

Sapna scrunches up her nose. Food intolerances?

'You're not allergic to gluten?' the woman clarifies. 'You eat wheat?'

'Oh yes,' Sapna says, thinking of her mother's chapatis, hot off the hearth, glistening with the ghee Ma would dab liberally on top, deliciously soft and melt-in-the-mouth.

'And dairy?' the woman is querying.

Sapna pictures herself and her sisters taking turns milking their cows and goats as dawn rises over the sleepy fields, coating them in a mellow rose-gold glow.

'And you like chocolate cake?'

The woman's voice jolts Sapna into the present. 'Yes, I do like chocolate cake, thank you. But there was really no need for it,' Sapna says.

'Oh, no one ever *needs* chocolate cake, but you must have it. It's one of life's great delights, in my humble opinion.' The woman — Gemma — laughs gaily. 'I for one should eat a bit less of it,' she adds, nodding to her stomach. 'But not quite yet. I'll start being good once I've polished off the piece I have waiting at home — I bought one of these for myself too, of course. Any excuse.' She shifts the baby from one shoulder to the other. The child lets out a little snuffle, eyes aflutter, then goes right back to sleep on his mother's shoulder. 'Sorry, I'm rambling. Since Theo was born I don't get to interact much with adults, you see, so when I do get the chance, I don't stop talking. Just tell me to shush any time, please.' She takes a breath. 'Anyway, what I wanted to say is, welcome to our neighbourhood. I meant to come earlier but Theo has been grizzly and I—'

'Thank you.' Sapna takes the box she's been holding out. 'You shouldn't have, but we'll enjoy it.' Then, stepping aside, 'Come in,' she says again.

'Please sit.' Sapna pulls out the stool that is the only piece of furniture in the living room. There's a table in the kitchen-cum-dining room but she's loath to invite Gemma in there, knowing that she hasn't cleared up from dinner the previous night. Although Gemma can see the mess from where she's standing, of course.

Sapna feels ashamed and awkward for having dawdled over the unpacking — it gives her something to look forward to, to fill the long hours before Amir gets home — then irrationally angry at her unexpected visitor for making her feel so.

'Sorry,' she says, indicating the cardboard boxes littering the room and perching on one as the woman — Gemma, Sapna really must remember her name — lowers herself, gingerly, with the baby, onto the stool. 'I haven't finished unpacking yet.'

'Tell me about it!' Gemma rolls her eyes. 'I still have boxes to unpack from when I moved in, *years* ago.' She smiles wryly, a dimple peeking out from her left cheek like the tantalising glimpse of a secret. When she smiles, her face lights up and she looks much younger and a lot of fun.

The baby stirs, and a small moan escapes his rosebud lips.

'There, there,' Gemma says, patting him, and he gently falls back into sleep. 'Wish he would do this at night.'

'Doesn't he sleep well, then?' Sapna asks, knowing it's expected of her. Mothers everywhere are the same, she thinks. Her older sisters love nothing more than fondly complaining about their babies.

Enough. Stop dwelling. You're becoming a right old misery guts, she chides herself, although it is Amir's voice she hears in her head.

'Wakes every half hour like a wound clock. If I'm very lucky, I get forty winks, literally.' Gemma sighs but there's affection lacing her voice, like Sapna knew there would be. 'So, are you settling in okay? How are you finding it here in our little cul-de-sac? Too quiet for you?'

'It's all right. I like it.' Again Sapna says what she knows is expected of her. But she can't help adding, apologetically, 'I think I'll feel better once I've unpacked.' *I hope so.*

'Do you know your way around — the bus stop, the train station, where the shops are?'

'Yes, my husband brought me on a tour before we moved in. When we came to sign the rental, we acquainted ourselves with the area and he pointed everything out.'

'Your husband's at work?'

She nods. 'He works in the city. Takes the train.'

'Like mine. They might bump into each other.' Gemma smiles.

'Sorry, where are my manners? Would you like some tea?' Sapna stands.

'No, I'm fine. Please sit back down. I just came to say hello and introduce myself, that's all.'

'We could have some of the cake?'

'No, that's for you and your husband. Like I said, I've one for myself and Rob — not that there will be much left for him by the time I'm through. I had a great big slice with my morning cup of coffee before I came. My not-so-healthy breakfast.' Gemma grins again.

As Sapna sits back down, the sleeve of her kurta catches on one of the boxes piled beside her, the hem riding up as she disentangles herself. She is aware of Gemma's eyes focusing on the bruise on her arm.

'Ooh, that looks sore,' Gemma says with raised eyebrows and a concerned frown.

'Ah, it's nothing. Appears worse than it is.' Sapna rubs her arm, trying not to wince, making light of it. 'Just bashed it when I was moving one of the boxes.' Her voice is carefully bright and airy.

The woman's gaze is shrewd as it meets Sapna's.

'I'm a nurse — on maternity leave now, of course. Do you want me to take a look?'

'It's fine.' Sapna's voice comes out sharper than she intended.

Gemma flinches at the same time as Sapna does.

'I . . . I'm sorry, I . . . I'm really okay,' Sapna stammers.

Gemma nods shortly, her lips pursed. She stands up, gently holding on to her baby. 'I better get going before this little one wakes up and starts making a right racket.'

Sapna nods, not quite meeting Gemma's eye.

'If you need anything, do knock,' Gemma says.

'Thank you,' Sapna says. 'And for the cake. You're very kind.'

'A pleasure,' Gemma says. 'As I say, do pop in for a cup of tea. Don't hesitate. I could do with some adult conversation, to be honest.'

'Thank you,' Sapna says again, eager now to see the back of her neighbour, preferring the hostile silence of her new home to her neighbour's calculating gaze.

CHAPTER 7

Sapna

Sapna shuts the door behind Gemma and rests her head against it, the cool wood a balm for the headache that's looming. The simple act of trying to navigate the minefield of polite conversation appears to have wiped her out.

Silence settles around her, ominous, seething with . . . something unpleasant. She shudders, her gaze going to the garden. It is still. The grass unkempt. The trees with new shoots, bright green. Nothing stirs. There is no breeze. The sky is grey with a hint of blue. No shadows moving stealthily, no prickle at the back of her neck. Nobody watching. So why does she sense this insidious throb of peril, unease clogging the back of her throat?

Her thoughts veer to the noisy bustle of the flat in Hounslow with its semblance of busyness, the roar of planes flying overhead every other minute. It felt like every plane that passed swooped lower still, and the horror of it crashing into the building, all of them wiped out in a flaming second, felt very real. When she voiced her fear, Amir laughed and kissed her soundly. 'You and your wild imagination,' he said, eyes sparkling, then gathered her in his arms for another kiss that went on for longer . . .

Then, Amir had time for her anxieties. But now . . .

She shivers, hugs herself, rubs her arm where the bruise throbs with a dull, persistent ache.

In Hounslow, there were people always popping in, borrowing something or coming to complain about someone, stopping by for a cup of tea and a chat. They accepted her as if she had always been there and she felt welcome. Although she had been disappointed at first with the size of the flat, she came to feel like she belonged. Gemma was profuse in her welcome too, so why doesn't she feel accepted, why does she feel like an outsider, why does she think Gemma didn't really mean it? Is it because she's white? There's not a brown face among her immediate neighbours, or the cluster of mums from the flats further down the cul-de-sac who walk past each morning and afternoon, pushing babies and toddlers in buggies and nattering among themselves even as they keep a beady eye on their school-age children racing past on scooters and bicycles. Even the people living in the houses on the main road are white, at least the ones Sapna has seen. She's yet to notice any signs of occupancy at Number 4, the house next to Gemma's.

Amir counts this as another point in the house's favour. 'I don't want to live in Hounslow where everyone we encounter is from our own community. We need to mix, integrate. And that's another reason why this house is perfect.'

This woman. Gemma. Sapna thinks of her assessing look. 'I'm a nurse,' she said with that knowing glance directed at Sapna's arm. It was clear she hadn't believed Sapna when she told her how she came by the bruise. She was judging them, her and Amir, and Sapna didn't like it one bit.

How dare she? What right does she have? Just because she's a nurse, it doesn't mean she can make inferences about people . . .

And there it is. The thing about Gemma that has grated on Sapna most of all. She is *jealous* of the woman, with her noble profession and her beautiful child. This must be why she's unsettled, uneasy about the woman's neighbourly gesture.

Sapna has often mused about where she would be if she had been allowed to continue at school. She had loved learning but had had to stop when she matriculated even though she had come top of her class. Her teachers' forceful rejoinders to Sapna's parents that their daughter had a bright future if only she were allowed to continue her schooling fell on deaf ears. If permitted to study further, she could have become an author perhaps — her secret, cherished wish, for she loves reading, writing, making up stories, escaping to different worlds. 'That imagination of yours will get you in trouble one day,' her mother would chide fondly when Sapna concocted wild and fanciful scenarios from snippets of conversation or gossip she'd overheard. But there was no use speculating for the only thing Sapna and her sisters were groomed for from birth was marriage. How to keep a tidy home, how to care for and bring up children, how to be good wives — all drilled into them so they were conditioned not to think of, or hanker for, anything else.

And now here she is, trying to be a good wife and failing, despite all her mother's and older sisters' diligent lessons and examples.

In the first charmed days of her marriage, she and Amir had felt like a strong, happy unit. She was far away from her country and her loved ones, but she had her husband with her, so she could deal with the homesickness, the longing. But now, it feels as if she and Amir are on opposite sides of a great divide and she doesn't know how to bridge the gap. Everything she tries seems to only push him away further. Her mother's and sisters' wisdom didn't cover this aspect of marriage and she can't even call them to ask. It was kind of Gemma to say she could pop in any time for a chat, but Sapna can't see herself confiding in this confident, assured white woman. A nurse and mother, who clearly did not believe Sapna's explanation for the bruise on her arm.

Amir. Sapna pinches her arm again, right where the bruise is. The pain masks briefly the bigger throb of hurt pulsing inside her as she thinks of her husband's face this morning. Anger hardening his features into a cruel mask, his eyes glinting sparks directed at her. Pulling the door shut behind him so hard that it felt like the whole house rocked on its foundations. Leaving behind the lunch she had carefully packed for him. Ignoring her when she opened the door, called out to him, held it out. Walking away from the plea in her voice as it stumbled over his name.

CHAPTER 8

Edith

Edith is getting the carrot cake out of the oven when she hears the shouts.

Her eyes go to the radio, but it isn't on. She forgot to switch it on this morning. Oh dear. She didn't even notice. More and more things are slipping from her mind nowadays.

She likes to have Radio 4 on in the kitchen. Having been born at the end of the war and brought up amid the austerities after, she's not one to leave the TV on when she isn't there to watch it. Although she must admit she likes the noise, the illusion it provides — that there is another person, *someone* with her in the house, temporarily dispelling the miasma of loneliness that has settled in these rooms since the children went their own ways.

More shouts. Tinny as if coming from a distance, which is why Edith thought it was the radio at first. Now she understands that the sounds are echoey because they are wafting in from her neighbours' house — Number 2, with which her own house shares a wall.

These flimsy houses, it's a wonder they've stood so long. She can hear everything that goes on. It was the same when the Shaws and their kids were next door. She knew about the Shaws' plans to divorce almost as soon as they did — she had heard it all. Oh, the secrets she could spill about the lives lived next door all these years.

This is why when she and Jack argued, they always made sure to do it in their bedroom, away from the side that adjoins Number 2.

More sounds from next door, louder, harsher, intruding aggressively into Edith's musings. Raised voices, a throaty masculine growl clashing with, talking over a high-pitched feminine whine. Anger thrumming through both voices.

Number 2 was empty for weeks and quiet before then as old Mr Shaw spent most of his time in hospital anyway. There's been no life in the house until now. This is why the sounds are so jarring and she couldn't quite place where they were coming from at first. She's got used to the silence.

When she saw the young couple move in, she thought, *Good. The house needs youthful energy to rejuvenate its tired old bones.* But *this* — fire and ire — is not what she expected. Or perhaps it *was*. Why else had she felt weary and resigned instead of enthusiastic? She had disliked the man on sight, thinking he had the demeanour and bullish swagger of a thug as soon as laid eyes on him. And the woman's swollen eyes in that beautiful face . . .

This is why she has waited a few days before baking the cake to take round to Number 2. She doesn't want to meet the man. Edith has taken against him and she is quite a good judge of character — now. She wasn't when she was the girl's age, of course. She had to learn the hard way.

She saw Gemma from Number 3 visit next door with that little cherub of hers, was it yesterday or the day before?

Gemma and Theo pop round to Edith's for a cuppa and a natter sometimes.

'I'm climbing up the walls, desperate for some adult conversation, Edith. I just had to get away. Hope you don't mind me calling by unannounced,' Gemma says every time she turns up at Edith's door, jiggling Theo from one shoulder to the other.

'Of course not, my dear, you're always welcome,' Edith is quick to reassure.

And Gemma *is* welcome. The girl is a dear and her little one — oh, he's an absolute angel. The smell of an infant, innocence and milky sweetness, there's nothing quite like it.

It makes Edith feel ten years younger just being around little Theo. He reminds her of when hers were young. Long, exhausting days and endless sleepless nights that couldn't go past fast enough. Then, she had resented every dragging, sleep-deprived minute. But now . . . oh, what she wouldn't give to have those days back!

Her boys are scattered around the world and it has been absolutely ages since she's seen them. Billy is in Australia — married to an Aussie girl, Kelly, brash with big hair and sun-tanned skin. They have two girls, Joanna and Grace, whom Edith met during their one visit here when they were five and three. They haven't come to England since; they must be ten and eight now, where has the time gone? Billy invites Edith to their home in Melbourne every time he calls. Billy says it's hard for them to make the trip to England because of school, jobs and so on. Much as she'd like to see her grandchildren, she is too old and, to be honest, apprehensive at the thought of travelling all that way on her own. Jack was always the one who organised their holidays and they never went further than France — and Spain that one time. Billy and Kelly send Christmas cards with photos of the girls getting bigger each year, grinning out of the two-dimensional card. She tenderly traces their profiles, wishing she could reach into the photo, hug them, hear them laugh, call her *Nana* in their sweet Australian accents. Their features are etched into her memory and every year she updates them, touches up her memory with the changes she notes on the latest picture. The cards are all on the mantelpiece, lined up in chronological order. Although her children and grandchildren are always on her mind, sometimes she looks at their faces and they feel as unreal and removed as the people on TV.

Tom is in Scotland but he might as well be on the moon — he rarely visits or calls. He's divorced with grown-up children he rarely sees and she has a feeling he's depressed. She invited him to come and stay here with her when his marriage broke up — she'd never liked his wife, Angela, who was as far from an angel as you can get — but he upped sticks and moved to Scotland instead.

Her youngest, Jamie, is travelling the world, showing no sign of settling down, either in a country or with a partner.

She misses her boys, but she tries to shrug it away, busies herself with dusting, cleaning, baking. She attends church regularly. She's a member of the choir, welcomed heartily despite her thin, reedy voice (which has now acquired a quiver — are there no limits to the indignities of ageing?). Then there's the knitting group on Tuesdays and Silver Surfers on Fridays, both at the library. She and Mary sometimes have lunch at the café opposite the library after. They do nice sandwiches with freshly baked bread — nice and chunky, unlike those thin, processed slices the texture and consistency of paste — and plenty of filling. Both she and Mary like to feel they've got good value for their money.

Edith keeps herself busy but even so . . . Oddly, it's when Gemma visits that Edith feels it keenest. Loneliness, rearing its ugly head, biting at her. Ironic really, to realise she's lonely when she has company. A child cooing one minute, wailing the next, smelling of new life and talcum powder and promise and the future.

The couple of hours nattering with Gemma go quickly and she doesn't mind missing *Antiques Roadshow* for it, not at all. After all that's happened with Gemma, it's nice to see her happy. Great to see she's landed on her feet.

Edith can't picture herself being friends with the woman next door, not like with Gemma. Not that Edith is racist, not at all. People are people, no matter what race or colour. Some good, some bad, most a little bit of both.

Am I good or bad? She shivers. That's a question she shies away from, even in church, especially in church. 'Our Lord is a forgiving God; lay your sins at his feet,' the pastor drones. *Will you forgive me my sins, Lord? Or will I languish in hell for ever?*

And yet she goes to church, religiously, accruing brownie points, she hopes. Ha!

No, she's not racist but she has an inkling that this woman — girl — next door will never be as close as Gemma is to her. Odd, their friendship, given the age gap. But Edith was there for Gemma when she was going through her bad patch and that has forged a bond.

This girl just moved in to Number 2 — she's closed up, that's the impression Edith gets. She seems one to keep herself to herself, not interested in gossip, or even a good old chinwag. One of those silent broody types (although not all that silent right now, the way they're banging on at each other next door). But . . . she *is* Edith's neighbour and it is only polite to go round, introduce herself, welcome the girl to the neighbourhood. Good manners cost nothing. Hence the carrot cake she's just baked — and she has to admit it's one of her best. The house is infused with the aroma of caramelised sugar. She'll take it over when that thug of a husband is definitely not around. Offer friendship and welcome and a listening ear, and then it's up to the woman. Judging by her swollen eyes that day when they moved in, and the fiery goings-on bleeding through the wall right now, the girl will be needing it.

A huge thud next door reverberates through Edith's house — they share the wall after all. Edith nearly drops the cake in shock. Now, that would have been a disaster, especially as it's come out so soft and moist, and in any case, Edith hates waste.

She sets the cake to cool on the rack on the kitchen counter, wipes her hands on her apron and goes to the living room window — it looks out onto Number 2.

The man has pulled his front door shut hard enough to wake the dead and now he is charging outside, walking too fast, not looking where he is going. The front door of Number 2 opens again and the woman stands there, her eyes brimming and spilling over onto her lovely cheeks. She is a picture in her long flowing clothes. Like an otherworldly sprite. Edith glances towards Number 3 and, sure enough, Gemma is upstairs at the window, rocking her babe at her shoulder even as she peers avidly down. She must have heard the commotion at Number 2 as well — the slamming door must have woken the baby. God knows he sleeps little enough. How annoying for poor Gemma.

The house next door to Gemma's, Number 4, is occupied by a businessman whom the other occupants of the cul-de-sac hardly ever see. His work requires him to travel so he's rarely home, and when he is, he leaves for work early in the morning, returns late at night and is away at the weekends, racing the sports cars that he collects and keeps in a garage down the street. It's his hobby. She managed to corner him for a chat once, did Edith. She likes knowing the goings-on in their small part of town.

The houses beyond Number 4 in the cul-de-sac were bought by a property developer two decades ago. He converted each house into multiple flats and rents them out so tenants are always coming and going. Edith used to make an effort to keep track of the residents before, welcome them with cake and a warm smile but now she's too old and weary to bother. In any case, by the time she's got to know them, they're moving on, so she's given up. Gemma complains about the mums letting their kids run wild, making a noise outside her window just as she's put Theo down to bed. Edith must say she doesn't approve of the children plucking the flowers in the beds across the street that separate the cul-de-sac from the main road. In her day, mums told their children off for defacing public property. Nowadays anything goes.

'Amir!' the woman next door calls, her voice plaintive.

Edith would have thought no man could resist that cry.

Except for the thug.

He turns towards the girl slumped in the doorway of Number 2 and his eyes spit venom, so much so that Edith, safely inside her house (but with a bird's eye view of the goings-on, of course), rears back, a hand upon her heart. His voice, trembling with rage, carries in the otherwise peaceful quiet as he hisses, 'You are never happy. Nothing satisfies you,' and walks away.

47

Oh dear, Edith thinks as the woman's tears cascade down her face unchecked. She watches her man disappear down the street and, taking a juddering breath that seems to rock her entire being, she turns around and shuts the front door. Quietly. Gently. In complete contrast to the man's brute display of force, his unnecessary, belligerent, attention-seeking violence.

CHAPTER 9

Gemma

Theo starts to wail as soon as the drama that has unfolded next door reaches its inevitable conclusion, even though Gemma is holding him.

Forty minutes. And she has been rocking him the whole bloody time; as soon as she stops, he sniffles, preparatory to waking. The time that Theo sleeps at a stretch gets shorter and shorter. What is she doing wrong?

She gathers him closer to her, rocks him more vigorously. His snuffly warmth, his hot, sweet breath. His body shuddering with sobs that slowly quieten and then still. She is so tired. She can barely keep her eyes open. Increasingly she feels as if she is going through the motions, a zombie. What has happened? Just a few weeks ago, although it feels like a different world now, she was a competent nurse, admired in the wards by doctors and nurses alike, feted by patients as nothing fazed her. But a tiny little being, her very own, has brought her to her knees, reduced her to a blubbering mess. Sometimes — often, to be perfectly honest — when Theo wails, Gemma wails right along with him.

Rob is oblivious. He comes home happy, enthusiastic, full of energy, trailing the seductive aura of the adult world she is no longer part of, the intoxicating perfume of smoke and conversation. 'How are my two favourite people in the world today?' he coos and Gemma wants to club him. To keep hitting him until he understands just what she has been through that day: the highs — when Theo slept for longer than half an hour at one time and she actually got a load of washing done, although every nerve ending was screaming for sleep — but, mostly, the desperate, desolate lows that have characterised her day. And yet, paradoxically, when she's holding her baby in her arms is when she is most at peace and everything recedes into the background. There is just this moment. Her child, who needs her, and herself.

She shifts Theo from one shoulder to the other as she stands at the window. It offers an unhindered view right into Number 2's entire downstairs area. *These houses must have been designed by a voyeur*, Gemma muses. Since having the baby she's spent unprecedented amounts of time at windows longing to be part of the competent adult working world again. It's not her fault is it, if Number 2's curtains are still not up? All she's doing is standing at the window rocking her child to sleep . . .

The woman — 'I'm Sapna,' she'd said, her voice musical, the accent tantalising, her huge eyes moist brown like a muddy lake with hidden depths — is sitting at the kitchen table with her back to the window, her shoulders shaking. It seems to Gemma that every time she sees the woman, she's crying. Last night too, when Gemma awoke to attend to Theo, she saw Sapna in tears downstairs, her husband presumably asleep upstairs. Again, like before, even as she battled guilt for spying on the woman's private sorrow, Gemma couldn't stop. It made her feel strangely less lonely to see another person awake — and miserable — at this ungodly hour.

She knows Edith next door to Sapna has a history of insomnia, but Edith doesn't come downstairs at night, and in any case, Gemma can't see into her house. She finds herself wishing Number 2 never put their curtains up.

Stop it, Gemma, the woman is upset.

Should she go over? She's not dressed — what's the point of changing when she'll just get dribbled on again? Her nightdress is stained with milk and there's sick down the back of her shoulders from burping Theo, she knows.

And anyway, Sapna is not the most approachable of women. When Gemma went round to introduce herself, she looked like a deer caught in headlights. A particularly beautiful deer. Even dripping wet, with her hair in a towel, she was stunning.

And that bruise on her arm. Gemma has been a nurse long enough to know she did not get it from bumping into a cardboard box.

She was so evasive, her eyes swollen, even though she'd just had a wash. 'I'm sorry, I was in the shower,' Sapna said when she finally came to the door after Gemma, debating with herself, had rung the doorbell a second time — she knew the woman was in there, she'd seen her ten minutes ago!

What *is* going on in the couple next door's marriage, exactly?

But she can't do anything to help unless Sapna asks for it herself and Gemma knows the police can't either, even if she called them with her suspicions. There have been women coming into the hospital where she worked with broken bones and improbable excuses, unable, no matter how many times they ended up in the same sorry situation, to utter a word against their partners. Gemma had tried to get the police involved once or twice but it was always: 'Unless the victim lodges a complaint against her partner herself, we can't do anything, sorry.'

Gemma watches Sapna for a few more minutes. Then she turns away from the window, goes into her bedroom, pulls her own curtains closed and lies down on the bed, still

messy from Rob, infused with his scent of mint and musk —
she hasn't had time to make the bed. Then, settling her baby
beside her, ignoring the instructions not to take your child
into bed with you, just this once, Gemma closes her eyes and
gives in to the alluring draw of sleep.

CHAPTER 10

Edith

Edith stands outside the door to the new neighbour's house and rings the bell, hearing the chimes merrily sounding inside. The doorbell is new — there's not been one at Number 2 before. She wonders when it was installed. The Shaws never bothered to have one, they were not a family who entertained. They kept themselves to themselves, a lot like this young couple here now, although the Shaws were always very civil to Edith and Jack. And their little ones were friends with Edith and Jack's boys of course, all of them attending the local primary and secondary schools together. There were the usual little spats and fallings-out and makings-up, and once grown, the children all flew the nest. The adults have left the world altogether. Except for Edith. She's still hanging on. *For what?* she wonders sometimes. Goodness, but she feels ancient.

Times change. Life goes on for some and stops for others. Lord Almighty, she is in a melancholy mood today! Must be the effect of standing at the door of this new couple moved into Number 2. Well, they've got a lot going on, haven't they — always quarrelling when the man is back from work. Even in the morning sometimes before he leaves to get the train.

Raised voices filtering in, shattering the hard-won peace and quiet of Edith's house, audible even above the noise of her television or radio, when she's cooking and when she's in bed, waking her from sleep with the harsh, angry reverberations of a real-life nightmare.

Edith didn't take the carrot cake she baked over that day when the man stormed off, banging the door violently behind him, leaving his wife — well, Edith guessed they were married, although she knows you shouldn't make assumptions in this day and age — in a flood of tears. Edith didn't want to intrude. She did dither as to whether she should knock and ask the girl, who had looked dreadfully upset, if she was all right. But then she talked herself out of it.

You don't know them, she heard Jack chiding in her head. *You can't just barge in there and offer comfort to a woman you aren't acquainted with.*

She looks ever so upset, Edith parried to her husband in her head. *If she was my daughter, I wouldn't have liked* . . . A shaft of pain as she recalled the miscarriage after her boys. So many years had passed and yet it still hurt. She still dreamed about her, her daughter — for she was sure the child had been a girl — who never got the chance . . .

Well, she isn't your child, Jack said in his gruff, no-nonsense, end-of-conversation voice and Edith turned to look at the armchair where he had always sat — with a pint and the telly on loud as sin — to check if he was there; he had sounded so real just then.

You're getting fanciful in your old age, she scolded herself, brushing off the shiver tingling her spine.

In the end she took the cake over to Gemma and they had a good old natter.

'Ooh, carrot cake, just what I felt like today. You are a mind reader, Edith. You know, no one makes carrot cake quite like yours. So deliciously moist and melt-in-the-mouth. The Marks one doesn't come close,' Gemma gushed, cutting herself a nice, large piece. Taking a huge bite, she closed her eyes and mouthed, 'Heavenly.'

Edith turned quite pink with pleasure. 'It's the cinnamon. That's my secret ingredient, don't let on, will you? Gives it a nice kick, it does.'

'Thank you, Edith, but you really shouldn't have,' Gemma said, taking another huge bite. 'You know I can't resist your cake and I need to be watching my waist.' Looking rueful as she gathered the bit of stomach not quite fitting into her jeans in her hands.

'Ach, you're fine,' Edith said. 'You've just given birth. And you need sustenance, you're breastfeeding the bubba.'

'You know just what to say to make a girl feel better, Edith.' Gemma smiled at her fondly while taking another nice big bite, her whole face lighting up with pleasure as she chewed. 'You're a good friend.'

Edith glowed, even as she mused that there was no greater satisfaction than seeing someone enjoy the food you had cooked. She recalled the days when the boys were still at home and how they all — and Jack, when he returned from work on time — would sit around the table for their evening meal (she had insisted on this) and tuck in. Everyone silent as they enjoyed her food. She missed them, those days she had ardently wished away. But, if granted a second chance, she would do things very differently, of course.

Edith's house echoes with memories; it is stamped with impressions of the boys' younger selves. This is why, despite the bad things that have happened there, Edith hasn't moved away, although the boys urged her to when Jack died: 'Downsize, Mum. Move to a cottage or a house better suited to you. Start afresh. Leave the past where it belongs.' But she couldn't. How to explain to the boys what she felt? That it was more than just a house — it was the receptacle of memories, every nook and corner holding a story, a recollection. It had watched Edith change and grow from young wife and hopeful mother-to-be to lonely old woman. It will still be standing, God willing, when she is gone, bearing the imprint of the lives they lived within its walls long after Edith's own memories have turned to dust.

Don't wish your time with this one away, Edith wanted to tell Gemma. *It goes so quickly. Blink, and they've flown the nest.*

But Gemma must have heard this selfsame refrain a thousand times from a thousand different old ladies, so Edith was silent as she took a small bite out of her own slice of cake that Gemma had set down beside her. She had to admit, it was one of her best efforts yet. Perhaps she would make it for the church over-seventies dance next week, not that she could dance with her knees. She couldn't decide what to bake for it — if they couldn't dance, they might as well eat — carrot cake or lemon drizzle, another firm favourite.

'This is better than your lemon drizzle, I think,' Gemma said, as if she had followed Edith's thought process. 'How do you make it so deliciously moist? I do so love your cakes, Edith.' Gemma sighed, chewing dreamily.

The little fellow was fast asleep in his pram. 'I took him for a walk, he's been a bit grizzly and upset today, and the fresh air settled him, lulled him into sleep. I didn't have the heart to take him out; he looks so angelic, doesn't he? That's the longest he's slept at a stretch in . . . Oh, I can't remember how long. He obviously needs it. Why doesn't he do it at night?' Gemma spoke quickly, not pausing to take a breath, the sentences rolling into each other in a giddy rush. It was as if she had been starved of conversation and now she was making up for it, getting her money's worth, worried Edith would leave or Theo would wake and interrupt before she had said everything she wanted to.

'One day he will and you'll miss that time with him, just you and him, in the lonely small hours of night,' Edith couldn't help saying.

'It's not been just me and him lately. That girl from Number 2 has been awake and sitting at the kitchen table downstairs, crying.'

'Sobbing on her own at night?' Edith queried, her heart going out to the girl.

'Yes,' Gemma sighed.

'What do you think of them, then?' Edith asked, feeling bold now the topic was out there, Gemma having brought it up. She seemed as eager to discuss the new neighbours as Edith herself.

'They don't get on, do they?' Gemma met Edith's eye knowingly, and Edith could see that she too, like Edith, was thinking about the argument conducted in full view of the neighbours.

'Our cul-de-sac has always been quiet and largely peaceful,' Edith said, 'despite the comings and goings over at the flats, and even when my boys and the Shaws' kids were teenagers. Never any carry-on like the to-do the other morning.'

'Yes well . . .' Gemma began, but whatever she was about to say was drowned by her little one's wails as he woke up hungry and distraught.

'Here, hold him a minute, please,' Gemma said, lifting him from the pram and thrusting him onto Edith while she went to heat up his milk.

And Edith held the baby to her, her old body instinctively shifting to accommodate him, swinging in rhythm as she shushed him, humming a sweet melody from long-ago boys' bedtimes, suddenly arriving perfectly formed in her head, and breathing in deeply the sweet smell of new life, innocence and purity.

'What's the matter, Edith?' Gemma asked, her voice spiked with worry as she tested the temperature of the milk on the back of her hand before taking her boy from Edith.

Edith wiped eyes she did not even know were leaking and sniffed. 'Nothing, pet. Got a cold looming, is all. I better go before I give it to both of you.'

Gemma nodded tiredly as her son's cherub lips closed around the bottle's teat. 'Thanks for the cake.'

* * *

Edith moves the freshly baked cake to her other hand and rings the doorbell of Number 2 again. The girl must be home. She's always home. Edith hasn't seen her going out since she and her partner moved in. Of course *he* comes and goes as he pleases.

She tries the door with her free hand and is surprised to find that it is unlocked.

She raps sharply on the door and when there's still no response, daringly pushes it open. 'Hello?' she calls.

Nothing. Silence in the hallway.

She pops her head into the living room.

Not a soul.

Where *is* the girl? A tendril of fear slithers down Edith's spine. Has something happened to her? Has her thug of a husband . . . ? Is that why the door was open? Oh dear.

Decisively she walks into the living room. 'Hello? I just dropped by . . .' The words die on her lips. They are in the kitchen. *Both* of them. Alive and well, thank goodness.

You let your imagination run away with you, that's your problem, says Jack's censorious voice in her head.

But . . . she has interrupted *something*. A ball of dough is drying, abandoned, on the kitchen counter, cracks on its surface, like the photos of the human brain she's seen on the telly. The man is dressed in his work clothes. He's standing beside the woman, menacingly close. She has flour on her hands and her face; he must have interrupted her in the process of kneading the dough. She's facing him, her features contorted — in fear? — and splashed with tears. His hand is raised. They turn to look at her as one. The man's gaze is so angry that Edith flinches.

'I . . . I . . .' Edith finds herself stammering, her mouth dry with dread as she is transported into the past.

She takes a breath, and with it, a firm hold of herself. *You are not that woman anymore.* And with that, she stands as tall as she is able — not very, what with her bad hip and uncooperative knees — and looks right at the man, facing his barely suppressed rage head-on. 'Hello there, sorry to intrude. I rang the bell but nobody came. I tried the door and it was open . . .'

She watches as, with difficulty, the man wipes the fury from his face and tries on a smile. It doesn't reach his eyes, which are hard as flint and radiating angry sparks. The woman turns away from Edith and wipes her eyes with the sleeve of the flowing dress she's wearing.

'I must have forgotten to lock the door when I got home from work. But it shouldn't matter, should it, as we were told when we signed the rental that this is a safe area.' His words and eyes issue a challenge even as his lips curve upwards.

She gives as good as she gets, steadily meeting his gaze. 'It is. I should know. I've lived here for half a century now, and counting.'

'I'm Amir.' He extends his hand, even as a muscle works in his jaw and his gaze remains unforgivingly steely, giving a lie to his smile.

No matter. Edith still takes it as a win that he backed down first, although she notes that he makes no move to introduce his wife, acting as though she's not right there beside him in the kitchen.

His hand is cold. Like his eyes. When he smiles he looks quite charming in a thuggish sort of way, Edith thinks. Edith can see right through the charm to the rotten core it is hiding, but she can also understand how a certain type of girl might be taken in by it. Lord help her, Edith herself might have been taken in once upon a time. Edith feels for the poor delicate beauty beside him discreetly trying to rid her face of the sheen of tears but only serving to make a damp, flour-streaked mess.

'And you are . . . ?' The thug queries.

'Oh sorry, in all the palaver I quite forgot to introduce myself. I'm Edith. I live next door. I baked a cake. To welcome you to our neighbourhood, you see. Sorry it's late, but I thought better late than never.' She holds out her offering.

Stop blabbering, woman, Jack orders from inside her head. *You always do that when you're nervous, it's a dead giveaway.*

Go away, Jack.

She doesn't want to admit it but Jack is right. Despite giving herself a stern talking-to, Edith is, nevertheless, quite shaken by her proximity to this man with his barely held-in anger, and by what she thinks she might have interrupted.

She wants to go home. It breaks her heart afresh that for the poor girl, this place, with this man, is home.

Her hands tremble as the thug reaches for the cake and she hopes he doesn't notice, or if he does, that he'll put it down to old age. Or he might be *pleased* she's scared.

What is he *doing* here?

It's his house, woman, Jack wisecracks in her head.

Oh for goodness sake, Jack, she snaps back in the privacy of her head. *Why have you taken up residence in my mind? In any case, I saw him go out this morning*. To work, she'd assumed, as always. He'd walked briskly, arms swinging, without a backward glance. Usually, once he's left for work, the thug returns late in the evening. Not that she's voluntarily kept abreast with his movements — she's been forced to, for that's when the shouting next door usually starts. Now, it's only just past 4 p.m., teatime. She had hoped the girl would invite her in and that they would have a chat and Edith would then gently prise the truth about what was really going on in her marriage out of her, offer help and support. This man has put paid to that fantasy — it's as if he had a sixth sense Edith was going to pop round today and decided to foil her plans.

'Thanks so much.' The man nods, flashing another smile at odds with the forbidding look in his ebony eyes, displaying too-white teeth in a rugged face, the hint of a beard shadowing his chin like the suggestion of threat, dark with menace. The woman sniffs quietly but she does not turn towards Edith nor does she utter a word.

'Nice to meet you. I'm sure we'll see you around.' The man ushers her through the living room and to the front door. Before she knows it, Edith is outside again, gratefully gulping in greedy mouthfuls of the fresh spring air, and she can hear the key being turned in the door, the man making sure to lock it this time.

Feeling quite perturbed, and sorry for the woman, Edith goes back into her own house, turns the key, double-checks to make sure the front door *is* locked and then sits with the telly turned off, her ear to the wall. She sits like that all evening, phone in her hand, ready to call the police if she hears anything.

That slender girl, so small and delicate — she doesn't deserve to be treated that way.

But there is only silence from next door, no angry shouts, no hissing venom of violence.

Just . . . nothing. The absolute calm scares Edith, she realises. She doesn't know, cannot determine if the silence is worse or better than the raging fights usually sounding from next door.

She can't think when a neighbour has affected her in this way. *If anything happens to her, I'll feel responsible.* She debates telling Gemma, but that girl has enough on her plate what with the baby not sleeping at night. And so Edith sits and frets and, in the end, makes herself supper — just baked beans on toast, she can't stomach much else. She switches on the telly and eats while watching her usual show but is unable to lose herself in it, turning the volume up, trying (and failing) to put the couple next door out of her mind.

CHAPTER 11

Sapna

Sapna is chopping onions as she prepares supper for Amir, and wipes her tears with the shawl of her churidar. She hears her mother's voice in her head, threaded through with fond laughter. *How many times have I told you not to use your shawl to wipe your face? It will get dirty. Here, use this clean cloth. I make sure to have one ready when you are chopping onions, just for this very purpose, knowing your tendency to cry a river.* The onion-induced tears are in danger of turning into real ones, when she becomes aware of a sinister prickle at the back of her neck, the creepy conviction that she is being watched.

It hasn't occurred since that first morning when they moved in. Not even when she wakes at night and can't go back to sleep again, worrying about her fraught relationship with her husband, wondering how to fix it. It feels, then, like she is the only person in the world. She hasn't felt watched, spied upon. No prickly sensation of discomfort.

So why now?

She looks out the kitchen window. Dark shadows everywhere; thick, melancholy, brooding. During the day she likes the light filtering in, the naked, curtainless windows giving the illusion of space, of company.

And usually, when she comes downstairs in the middle of the night, she doesn't mind the dark, occasionally punctured by pinpricks of light as a car vrooms past on the main road, a sudden bubble of noise bursting the melancholy silence. But now . . . She shivers. She feels exposed, vulnerable. The kitchen light is on and she cannot see outside clearly (or at all, in actual fact) because of the glaring reflection — her eyes huge and startled — but she understands that anyone looking in can see her. Anybody could be hiding among the shadows watching her and she wouldn't spot them. They really should get curtains, although the only living things that can spy on her are the foxes that daringly root around in their unruly patch of garden. Aren't they? Or is there something more menacing out there?

Is the ominous shadow she thought she saw on her first day here slinking behind the tree for cover . . .

Stop.

She goes back to her cooking. She is marinating chopped chicken breast in tandoori spices when . . . *Tap-tap-tap.*

She jumps, a scream, stifled by terror, escaping her suddenly dry mouth.

She turns round. Nothing. Just shadows, thick and persistent.

And then, as she stands rooted in stupefied panic, the tapping sound comes again.

Ah. Mystery solved. Her heartbeat gradually steadies.

Tree branch silhouettes waving ghostlike, rat-a-tatting against the kitchen windows when a gust of wind blows through them.

Get a grip, Sapna. Trees brushing against the windows, that's all it is.

And yet, there's the insistent prickly warning of danger, the hairs at the back of her neck standing to attention . . .

To distract herself she thinks about foxes. She had not seen foxes before she came here — she never thought they

63

looked like this, so small, like ferrets. She had expected bigger animals, but perhaps she had mistaken foxes for wolves in her head. She has also seen a cat in the garden a couple of times, a fat ginger furball. It had wandered all the way up to the kitchen door and given her a fright, like the trees did just now — she does scare annoyingly easily.

She thinks of home, evening falling over the fields, the paddy waving in the darkness, the fragrance of jasmine and night and cooling earth and spices. Fireflies twinkling. A canopy of stars. Dogs howling. Mosquitoes buzzing. Insects whirring. Frogs croaking. Crickets chattering. Her younger brothers arguing. Baba and her older brothers chatting in low voices while sharing toddy and fried fish on the veranda. Sapna, alongside her mother and sisters, slapping dough into chapatis, boiling rice, peeling vegetables, grating coconut, grinding spices, stirring pots, talking all the while. Banter and love and warmth.

Here, loneliness is like a second skin and she has to work at shrugging it off. Here the sky is a brooding grey premonition. Gloomy and sullen.

Amir is working late. Again. 'Someone has to work to afford to pay the rent on this house, which you have done nothing but complain about since we moved in,' he said. Yelled. 'I don't know you anymore, Sapna.' Rubbing a hand wearily against his face. 'I thought you wanted a fresh start. Away from everything.' All the heat leaving his voice, so he sounded spent, resigned.

She preferred the yelling to this: his voice so very beaten.

'I do . . . I . . .' she began, but she was speaking to his back and then to an empty room.

She puts a pan on the hob, pours a tablespoon of oil and when it is hot, adds mustard seeds. Once again, that prickle. The horrible sensation of being watched.

She looks outside. Shadows. Thick and seemingly impenetrable. Nothing else that she can make out. Nothing moving. Not even the trees at the window or the grass. All is still. There is no breeze like there was a few moments ago.

The mustard seeds start to sputter in the hot oil and Sapna shivers. With effort, she turns her attention to her cooking, adding the chopped onion, ginger and garlic to the sizzling, spitting mustard-flavoured oil.

She is reaching for the chopped chicken when . . . at the corner of her eye, movement. Imperceptible. But . . . *there*. She turns. A glimpse of a face pressed to the glass. Leering, grotesquely squashed features. Familiar? A flicker of movement, a hand waving.

Real. Definitely so. Then just as surely . . . gone. Blending in with the shadows. One with the dark.

Sapna opens her mouth. She screams and she screams as the onions burn and the smoke alarm goes off and Amir, thankfully, arrives, dropping his bag and gathering her in his arms, begging her to please tell him what is wrong.

'A fff . . . ff . . . face . . .' she stutters. 'Th . . . there.' She points to the kitchen window with a shaking hand. She can't seem to stop trembling.

Amir's concern drops away, replaced by weary resignation. 'You must have imagined it,' he sighs.

His casual dismissal makes her mad — she can still see the distorted face when she closes her eyes, leering at her. Why does he not believe her?

She takes a breath. And another. If she shouts at him, they will have another argument. Right now, she wants, needs him onside. Whoever it was that she saw, they'd come to the kitchen window from the garden. That fleeting moment when she thought she recognised . . . Could it be? No. No. 'Please could you just check the garden out?' She says in what she hopes is a level enough voice, not giving her anger, her fear away.

Amir grits his teeth in frustration, his face creasing with irritation. 'Sapna . . .'

When did he start getting so vexed with her, as if she's someone he has no choice but to put up with? It hurts. 'Please, Amir,' she begs.

He sighs deeply but puts on his shoes and goes outside.

As soon as the kitchen door closes behind him, she wonders if this is a mistake. What if there is someone lurking out there still? What if they hurt Amir? She paces up and down, too scared to go outside herself, call Amir back, and hating herself for it.

What if the person at the window is who she suspects it to be? Her heart lurches in terror. But how is it possible? And if not him, and it can't be him, then who? Sapna knows nobody apart from Amir in this country, and his friends in Hounslow only vaguely. They wouldn't do this . . . would they?

A rattle at the kitchen door.

She jumps.

But it's only Amir — he's safe, thank God.

The flare of relief she feels is snuffed out by her husband's expression. It's grim as she's ever seen it. 'One of the fence panels is loose. I'll fix it at the weekend.'

She shivers. A part of her had been hoping she'd made it up. It would have been the less scary option. But she can't resist saying, 'See, I told you—'

'That doesn't mean—'

And now, she can't stop her anger from showing. All the upset and fear coming out as a raging shriek. 'Why don't you believe me?'

They go to bed not speaking to each other, lying side by side but apart, careful not to touch the other, Sapna's hot tears silently escaping down the sides of her cheeks and soaking into her pillow. She has never felt more alone than with her husband right beside her, fast asleep, soft snores escaping his open mouth, oblivious to her pain.

CHAPTER 12

Sapna

To give Amir credit, he fixes the fence panel the very next morning, knowing Sapna won't relax until it is done, and perhaps feeling guilty for not believing her.

She hates the way her husband's gaze hardens when he looks at her nowadays, a mixture of disdain and scorn and impatience, the way his features settle into a sneer when she shares her worries, the way he pooh-poohs her fears. Perhaps he would like her to be smarter, like the white women she sees walking past her window. Like Gemma next door. Confident and independent, despite being a new mother and permanently sleep-deprived.

Sapna could take the bus, go into town, like Amir has suggested. And one of these days, she will conquer her nerves, her shyness, and do it.

In Hounslow, the high street was just two blocks away. She could walk there. And most of the people she encountered were like her, brown-skinned, wearing churidars or saris or burqas. They talked in Hindi or Urdu or one of the other myriad Indian languages. She felt at home there. Here she's yet to see another brown face. Her clothes stand out.

She needs to buy what she thinks of as 'Western' clothes, get used to wearing them. Perhaps then, dressed like the white women, she will gain some of the confidence that appears to come so naturally to them? Perhaps then Amir will look at her with pride and love instead of irritation and impatience?

But she's reluctant to stop wearing the churidars her mother helped her pack as she was leaving, tears streaming down both of their faces. They are her last connection to home. A part and parcel of her identity. Who is she without the clothes she's grown up wearing? And although she's washed them multiple times since coming here, she still fancies they bear the imprint of her mother's touch as she neatly pressed and folded them into Sapna's suitcase. When she wears them, it is as if her mother is reaching across the oceans separating them to embrace her, imparting her love.

Sapna cooks Amir's favourite dinner — chicken biryani — as thanks for repairing the fence. She resolves to be less melancholy, more cheerful and loving when he comes home. Maybe that will fix their marriage? Amir is all she has — her one familiar in this unfamiliar land. She is estranged from her family. She cannot afford to alienate Amir too.

Nevertheless, the day drags along, and although she plasters the kitchen windows with newspaper like in their bedroom, she just cannot shake off the creepy sensation of being watched however much she tries to convince herself there is no way anyone — him, the person she thought she recognised? — can get in now the fence is fixed.

As soon as it starts getting dark, she sits in the living room with the lights off and waits for Amir. The windows face onto the road and she hasn't covered them with newspaper here. She likes it open so she can watch for anyone entering the cul-de-sac or walking past on the main road. But even so, she feels seen, the hair at the nape of her neck standing to attention.

But how? How could it be . . . ? She has asked herself this over and over. But to no avail. She believes she saw him. But he cannot be here. So she must be going mad. This house . . . . *Stop blaming the house.* Perhaps it *is* her, like Amir says.

When Amir gets home, she tries to reheat the chicken biryani — she prepared it earlier, when it was light, afraid to be in the kitchen after dark even with newspaper sealing the windows — but it burns. She can't help but burst into tears, and Amir's features are pulled down by the now familiar frustrated frown, the light going out of his eyes.

'If you didn't want it to burn, you shouldn't have cooked it before. Biryani is meant to be prepared fresh!' he snaps.

'I . . . I was afraid . . .'

'Of what? The fence panel is fixed. Nothing can come in, not even a fox, let alone anybody else.'

She hates the mocking tone to his voice. 'I did see someone at the—'

'I don't have time for this,' he sighs. 'I'm tired. I've had a long day at work.'

'Why don't you believe me?'

'Because, Sapna, you're paranoid,' he flings at her. 'Your imagination is out of control.'

Amir had claimed to love her to the exclusion of everything else when he married her. How has the love soured so quickly? How can they fling hurtful words and accusations at each other so casually, curdling the affection that was once the firm foundation of their marriage?

Before, Amir would have listened to her fears, he wouldn't have emitted that mirthless chuckle, which is somehow even worse than his scowl, and called her 'paranoid' — she's looked that horrid word up in the dictionary. She loathes it and loathes the way Amir's eyes narrow and his lips disappear when he addresses her so.

Before, he would have hugged her close, said, 'You've nothing to fear when I'm around.' Not anymore. She cannot believe it has taken such a short time for them to drift apart, rub each other up the wrong way. What happened? She happened. She does this, brings upset wherever she goes.

She's a whore. Her brothers' voices reverberate in her ears. Her own brothers — they had been talking about her, hadn't known she was listening. She shuts them out, pressing her palms to her ears as if that will make the voices, the agony, stop, even as once again she cries into her pillow while her husband sleeps beside her, not touching, a barrier of sheets between them.

CHAPTER 13

Edith

Edith is watching *Bargain Hunt*, a mug of tea and a couple of the jam tarts she made earlier on a tray beside her, when there is a knock at the door.

'Coming,' she calls as she digs around for the remote, which has, typically, fallen down the side of the sofa and under it, just out of reach so she has to go on all fours to fetch it, murder for her poor knees. After scrabbling around for a bit, she manages to reach it and mutes the telly — she isn't missing much, it's all been tat so far — and shuffles to the door. She wouldn't wish old age on anyone. Everything is so much harder now. Getting up in the morning, her joints feel so stiff and it takes her an age to stand upright after lying down. She has to sit up first, which is a production in itself, and then work her way up to standing. Goodness.

It's the girl from next door, holding out the plate Edith had taken round to Number 2 on which she'd placed her carrot cake. One of her 'good plates' from the set she'd bought with her Green Shield stamps, accrued after nearly a year of diligent scrimping and saving. She still has all the plates from that set, and they're as good as new — they just don't make quality like that anymore, an absolute shame. She had dithered about whether to use one of the good plates (like she does with Gemma, who knows how much they mean to Edith and always returns them, washed and sparkling), or one of the cheap plastic ones she gets from the pound shop. She takes her offerings to the over-seventies socials on those, then she doesn't mind if they don't come back. You get a set of six for a pound, so if one or two get misplaced, it's no big hardship. Although, having said that, more than a few have gone missing this year — must be Mrs Riley, the newest member of the club. 'I thought I'd give it a try seeing as I've only just turned seventy,' she's fond of saying. Edith and Mary are keeping tabs on how much longer she can keep it up — she joined at the beginning of the year and if she's still going on about it at Christmas, well, that *would* be pushing it. Mrs Riley is notorious for taking things that don't belong to her, especially husbands. What she did to the first Mrs Riley, who's now 'poor' Miss Franklin, having reverted to her maiden name after the messy divorce, is just plain shocking.

In the end, Edith had decided to take her cake round to Number 2 on one of her good plates. It made the better impression. She'd give it a good three weeks, and if the girl didn't return the plate in that time Edith would ask for it back. Who knew how these foreigners did things; they might not know the convention, might assume that everything gifted to them was theirs to keep, including the plate.

But here she is, the girl from Number 2, with the plate. It now holds a pyramid of shiny burgundy-gold globules. The girl appears wan, washed out, and Edith fancies she's lost weight, that she's thinner even than when she first arrived. Like she's shrunk. She looks impossibly young.

'Come in.' Edith smiles. 'Sorry I took so long. Old bones don't cooperate as quickly, not like yours.'

The girl hesitates, but Edith ushers her through, and after a bit, the girl steps inside.

As Edith closes the door, she sees the curtains on Gemma's upstairs landing — which has the best view of her door — twitch and wonders if she's watching.

'Thank you for the cake,' the girl says. She speaks slowly, enunciating each word carefully, and Edith understands, as she watches the girl's forehead scrunching in concentration, that English is not her first language and that she is translating what she wants to say from her mother tongue into English in her head before speaking out loud. 'It was delicious. I . . . I made some gulab jamuns.' She points at the balls, which glow with a sheen of syrup.

'Thank you. I'm sure I'll love them,' Edith says, although she's not sure of any such thing. They don't look like something she would eat, to be completely honest.

The girl stands just inside Edith's living room and looks around.

'Please sit. Would you like a cup of tea?' Edith asks.

In her long, flowing dress, her ethereal beauty, Edith's visitor looks like an exotic bird, out of place in Edith's living room. And yet, something about this girl, her slender neck, her acute vulnerability, that haunted look in her caramel eyes, speaks to Edith, reminding her of herself a long time ago when she was a young bride starting out, more than a little lost and out of her depth.

'Your house is exactly like ours and yet ours looks so empty. Yours is lived-in.' She pauses for a moment, thinking hard as she searches for the right word. 'It is *cosy*.' Something like awe colours the girl's voice, even as she smiles triumphantly at having found the word she was looking for.

Edith glows with pleasure, touched by the compliment. She must say, it is nice having someone appreciate her house, see it with new, admiring eyes. It offers Edith a different perspective of her tired old home.

'Houses 1 to 4 in this cul-de-sac are exactly the same, apart from the fact that Numbers 3 and 4 are detached,' she says. 'All the rest around here have been converted into flats.

'Do you know, my dear, my husband Jack and I were the first ones to move in here when it was a brand-new development. The other houses hadn't even been built yet. Only ours, this corner house. Because of the building work and the constant rain, the whole area was a mud bath. We had to enter the house by walking on planks, like pirates!'

'You were the first ones here? You've been here since they were built?' Marvel and wonder colour the girl's musical voice sunlit gold.

'Yes, my dear. There have been plans over the years to build houses opposite us, where we now have the flower beds that bloom so gloriously in summer, but thankfully they've been vetoed every time. We live nearly on top of each other as it is, and further down the road, at the turning of the cul-de-sac, where there are houses on both sides, it's awfully cramped.' Edith takes a breath. 'I've seen families come and go, too many to count. Yours was occupied by the Shaws. They moved in at the beginning of the eighties. What a decade that was!' Longing and nostalgia for her boys, babies and toddlers, for whom, then, she was the centre around whom their world revolved.

'Wow,' the girl says.

'Come through to the kitchen. I'll put the kettle on. I made some jam tarts this morning. Have one, here.'

But the girl doesn't appear to have heard. She is standing at the kitchen door, looking out into the garden. Overgrown now Edith can no longer work to keep it in order. As it is, just pulling out the occasional weed does her in.

'Do you ever get the feeling someone is spying on you?' the girl asks, hugging herself as if she is cold.

'Oh no! My dear, whatever gave you the idea? Never in all the years I've lived here have I felt watched.' *The real monsters are inside the house, not outside. You've got one of those, I see.* Edith has more sense than to say what she's thinking out loud.

The girl shivers.

'Are you cold? Should I put the heating on?'

'No.' The girl appears flustered. And again, she says, 'No, thank you. I'm fine.'

74

She looks anything but fine, in Edith's opinion.

'What's your name, dear?'

The girl colours becomingly. 'Oh sorry, I should have said. I'm Sapna.'

Edith has never come across the name before. 'Sapna,' Edith says slowly, hoping that if she does it will stay in her memory, which is so whimsical these days — she recalls things from years ago but not what happened the previous day. The two syllables had sounded lovely in the girl's sing-song accent, not so much in her quivering old-lady timbre.

'It means "a dream",' Sapna says, offering a small smile.

'Ah, I see.' The name suits her, Edith thinks. The girl does project a dreamy fragility. 'And I'm Edith. But I'm afraid I haven't a clue what my name means, my dear.'

Sapna smiles widely now, a proper grin, and it is a rainbow, a bouquet of flowers. She really is beautiful.

'Do you take sugar?'

'Pardon me?'

'In your tea?'

'Yes, please.'

'How many teaspoons?'

'Oh. In my house, we just boil the tea leaves with cardamom and cinnamon and ginger and plenty of sugar and milk . . .' She bites her lower lip. 'Sorry, I mean, where I come from, my mother . . .' Her eyes sparkle with sudden tears.

'Oh, child.' Edith says. She wants to reach out and pat the girl's back, offer comfort. But she doesn't know how she will take it. 'It must be hard,' she says instead, 'living so far away from all of your loved ones.' Her voice is thick with empathy as she remembers how she herself had felt coming to London as a young bride, leaving everyone behind in Liverpool. How different it all was, how scary.

The girl sniffs. 'It is.'

Edith is generous with the sugar in the girl's tea. She hands her the mug.

The girl takes a sip and smiles at Edith, her eyes still bright with tears. 'Thank you. It is very nice.'

Edith is gratified. This girl, she has that delicate vulnerability about her that makes you want to protect her, to try and keep her happy. 'Have you just come to this country, my dear?' Edith asks.

The girl nods. *What's her name again? Sapna, yes. I must remember.*

'So where is home, then?' Edith asks.

'India.' Sapna whispers the word, wistfulness and longing.

'I've never been but I've heard it's beautiful.'

'It is.' She sniffs.

'You must get terribly homesick.'

'Sometimes.' Her voice is small and hollow. Lost.

'You don't have family here?'

'No.'

'And friends?'

'Amir has friends.'

Amir, her thug of a husband. Edith suppresses a shiver as she recalls the barely held-in rage on the man's face, glittering menacingly in his eyes. How he shut the door in her face.

'Oh, that's a shame,' Edith says. 'But you will make your own friends soon, my dear, I'm sure. Until then, well, if you need anything at all, I'm right next door.'

The girl's eyes well up again and Edith once again resists the urge to touch her, pat her back, squeeze her hand, and offer comfort. She's not had this impulse since the boys were little and needed her. Not even back when Gemma was going through the wars. With Gemma, Edith feels on equal footing, despite their age difference. They're friends, sharing confidences and gossip. This girl arouses her maternal instincts. Makes her feel fiercely protective.

She's just your neighbour. Don't get too close.

But . . . This slip of a girl, looking so lost, trying so hard to be brave . . .

'I understand,' Edith wants to say. 'I really do.'

But she keeps her counsel, like she has learned to, over the years.

'Thank you,' the girl says, her voice heartfelt, eyes sparkling as she smiles wanly at Edith. She sets down her empty mug and says, 'I better go.' But she doesn't move.

I understand, Edith thinks again. *Loneliness clings to you too. A dress you don't want to wear but which wears you.*

The girl stands — reluctantly, it seems — and walks to the door.

'Goodbye, my dear. I meant what I said, you know. If you need me, I'm here.'

The girl nods and then, impulsively, she leans forward and squeezes Edith's hand. 'Thank you,' she says again. She smells of rosewater and exotic spices and that all-too-familiar ache.

Edith stands at the door and watches until the girl lets herself into Number 2. Upstairs, at Gemma's, the curtains twitch again.

CHAPTER 14

Gemma

'Have you seen the new neighbours?' Gemma asks Rob, casually.

He's home early-ish for a change and they've ordered a takeaway as Gemma hadn't got round to even thinking of dinner — the breakfast dishes are still in the sink and it will not occur to Rob to stack them in the dishwasher. Theo has finally settled down for a nap and Gemma is rushing around finishing off the most pressing chores, which cannot be put off any longer while they wait for their food to come.

'A couple of times, yes,' Rob says, as he takes a generous sip from his glass of red.

'Isn't the woman pretty?'

'Well, I suppose so,' Rob says, rubbing his chin thoughtfully, 'if you go for that sort of thing.'

'What sort of thing?'

'Small and vulnerable. I like my women tall with a little flesh on them.'

Gemma does not know whether to feel pleased or patronised.

'Come here,' Rob says. 'You've got milk and sick and Lord knows what else on your clothes and hair, but you're the most beautiful woman alive, the only woman for me.'

'Get over it,' she sighs. 'Can't you give me one compliment which is genuine instead of barbed?'

'What do you mean?' Rob looks stumped, a frown crowding his brows.

'Milk and sick on my clothes, a bit of flesh . . .'

'I like that. You're real. Strong. Comfortable in your skin. Unapologetically, wonderfully yourself. I like a robust woman, me.'

'There you go again.' But Gemma can't help smiling. Her dolt of a husband just doesn't get it. And, to be honest, even if it goes against her feminist leanings, even if outwardly she protests, secretly she likes that — likes how clueless, yet earnest, her husband is. Rob loves her, all of her (well, the versions of her that she lets him see), his love uncomplicated and undemanding. After everything she's been through, it's just what she needs and so she'd said yes when he proposed and she's tried hard ever since to be the woman she sees reflected in his eyes. He makes her strive to be her best self, unlike . . .

Don't go there.

'Come here.' Rob gathers her to him, his eyes taking on that soft look that means he is about to kiss her.

She allows him to, shutting her mind off to other kisses, old flames that had blazed bright and incandescent, nearly destroying her.

* * *

Afterwards, as they are tucking into their curry, Rob says, through a generous mouthful of pilau rice and peshwari naan, 'Babe, I've got a release coming up. It will mean a few late nights.'

Gemma, who's been shovelling down food knowing Theo is about to wake up any minute as he's due a feed, stops eating the chicken balti that she'd been enjoying flavoured with upset and weary disappointment. 'But . . .'

'I know it's not a good time. I know you're shattered, babe.' Rob reaches across and covers her palm with his.

She fights the urge to pull away and bites down on her lower lip instead. The dinner that she'd looked forward to is ruined by his announcement. As it happens, she's already doing almost all the baby care and household chores herself. But nevertheless, she waits eagerly all day for the evenings when Rob gets home and bathes Theo, practically his only contribution towards looking after their child — Gemma's fifteen minutes of peace to freshen up, get some quality time to herself, to drink some wine and relax if possible.

Now that too will be gone. If Rob's previous releases are anything to go by, then Gemma knows that something will go wrong and the few days will stretch to weeks.

'I've no choice, what with the recession, the job climate. If I don't agree, I'll be the first to go in the next lot of redundancies. Look, before the madness starts, I'll take Theo round to my mum's for the weekend and you can have the house to yourself. What do you say?'

She closes her eyes, briefly savouring the thought of an entire weekend to herself. Two whole days to do what she likes. Sleep undisturbed for more than a few minutes at a stretch. Who would have thought she'd be salivating at the thought of a good night's sleep, she who'd never baulked at four night shifts in a row?

She looks across at her husband. His familiar features, his eager gaze. For all his faults, he does care, knows what she would like the most. She has to give him that much.

'Deal,' she says, and his worried frown relaxes into a smile.

He leans forward and kisses her. She is starting to respond, experiencing a spark of desire for the first time in what feels like for ever, when there is a cry reverberating from the baby monitor and she pulls away, standing up tiredly to attend to their son.

CHAPTER 15

Sapna

Sapna pulls the front door to Number 2 — she struggles to think of it as her house — shut behind her, locks it, making sure to check that she has her keys.

Yes, they are in her pocket. She lost a set recently and Amir, with depressing predictability, raged at her. 'That's it, now I have to spend money we don't have cutting a new set for you. And I don't know when to find the time to do it, as you complain if I'm even slightly late through no fault of my own — I can't help it if trains and buses don't stick to their schedule.'

She teared up at his tone, frustration and impatience laid bare, as if she was a naughty child he had no choice but to babysit, and he huffed even more.

Now, she sniffs, and determinedly wipes at her eyes with the shawl of her churidar. It is nippy outdoors, so she drapes the shawl over her head, covering her ears, even as she inhales great gulps of air that is cool and smells clean, of grass and flowers, so very different from home.

Not your home. Not any longer.

The air here does not have the slap of humidity, the kiss of moisture, the taste of spices and dust. It feels rarefied, with a hint of ice. No warmth to it. No scents of cooking emanate from nearby houses. No noise except for the occasional vehicles whooshing past on the main road outside their cul-de-sac. It is quiet, still. Not a soul in sight. Not even Gemma at the window with her baby, her face framed there as if begging for escape, for deliverance, her eyes bloodshot. Like a prisoner. Like how Sapna feels here.

She is tired of sitting indoors and feeling stalked. Scared of every perceived movement. She has no way of proving it but she feels watched, she feels exposed, despite having covered the kitchen windows with newspaper and cooking only during the daytime, when it is light.

Sapna shivers. She is cold despite the so-called warmer weather. 'The warmest spring we've had, they're saying on the news,' Amir had told her. 'And you're shivering even with your coat *and* my coat on!' Laughing fondly, back when he still laughed, was still fond.

Where has that Amir gone? She misses him.

The sun is out — and in this country that is not guaranteed, she's learned, not in spring and not even in summer. Its appearance is always cause for celebration. Celebration or not, the sun here is weak, Sapna thinks, not harsh and unforgiving like in India. Like her baba, who made it clear she was never welcome home again.

She pushes away the tears that threaten, that are never far away. *You will never be happy, will you?* Amir's voice tells her. *You always need something to whine, complain, cry about.*

She shivers again and this time it's nothing to do with the cold. She's had enough of these voices going around and around in her head. This is why she's ventured outside. She needs a respite.

Sapna fingers the money, the unfamiliar coins and notes, in the purse in her pocket. She will buy some vegetables — brinjals, peas, carrots — and some yoghurt. She will make a vegetable pulao with baingan bharta and raita. There are gulab jamuns in the fridge from the batch she made for Edith, for afters. She will make an effort: set the table nicely, dress up for Amir. She will smile until her cheeks hurt.

She looks back at the house. Without curtains at the windows, it looks bare, soulless.

Stop.

She and Amir need to go shopping at the weekend. Buy curtains and some furniture for the living room. Perhaps even buy the set-top box so they can stream Indian channels on TV. But Sapna has a feeling that when the weekend finally arrives, Amir will be working — again. He's taken every shift going, working non-stop, seven days a week since they moved in. The rent on this house, although very good for this area, is still barely affordable for them. She could go into town herself. But Sapna can't get the things they really need — the curtains and the furniture — on the bus. Amir needs to hire a van or a car or they must order it for home delivery.

Now, she is at the shops. The Parade, it is called. Four small businesses with striped awnings — a laundromat, a grocery, a video rental which has a closed sign and a butcher's — set in a semicircle around a small green, bordered by a cornucopia of flowers. 'Pansies,' Amir had told her, when showing her around. 'We'll get them for our garden.' But of course it hasn't happened as all they do nowadays is argue.

But they will not argue today, Sapna resolves. Today, she will be different. She will not give in to emotion. She will rise above it. She will not mention her fears, instead she will ask Amir about his work. This evening will be all about him.

A few benches are set on paths intersecting the green. Beyond this, a road with cars zooming past, and beyond that, fields. But these fields are not like the paddy fields at home — not home any longer, of course, she remembers. These fields are profuse with wild grass and dotted with daisies and dandelions waving in the frisky breeze, a few dogs running among them, their owners following with jangling leads and indulgent smiles. In the far corner, horses graze, their bodies the same shade of brown as a plucked coconut, their manes the shaggy orange of coconut coir. The other corner has been fenced in and made into a playground, sporting two swings, a slide and a roundabout. A preschool girl sits on the swing, her golden hair flying in all directions, a shimmering halo, asking her mum to push her 'higher, higher, pleeeease!' Her delighted laugh carries up to where Sapna stands, making her wistful, igniting a poignant ache for a different, more innocent time.

A shaggy black dog comes up to her and sniffs at her feet, which are clad in the sequinned sandals that she brought from India. A gift from her sisters.

Sapna smiles at the dog. The owner calls the dog to heel sharply and the dog obeys, tail between its legs. 'Sorry,' the man says to Sapna, concentrating on putting the lead on his reluctant pet.

'It's fine.' She smiles.

He nods shortly, offering no smile in return, and walks away.

She goes into the grocery shop. The selection of vegetables is limited. She is debating whether to buy courgettes or green beans — she has never cooked courgettes, but they look like marrows; the beans come in sterilised packs and are small and even, not wild and curly like the ones at home — when someone bumps into her.

'Move, bitch,' the man snaps, pulling off his headphones and glaring at her. 'Why are you standing in the middle of the aisle taking up all the space?'

She staggers backwards, nearly falling among the vegetables, too shocked to say anything.

'Bloody Muslims, everywhere you turn. Why don't you go back where you came from?' the man mutters, as he walks away.

She's shaking as she sets the beans she was considering buying carefully down, and stumbles out of the shop, retracing her steps, walking very fast, so that she is almost running towards home.

Edith opens her door as Sapna fumbles with her key.

'I was at my window and spotted you running past. Whatever is the matter, my dear?' She sounds genuinely concerned.

'The . . .' Sapna cannot get the words out, she is so upset. 'That man, he said . . . Go back to your country. He . . .'

'Oh dear, that was very rude of him. You've had such a shock. Come to mine, my dear. I'll make you a cup of tea. It will do you the world of good, I promise,' Edith says.

Sapna allows the older woman to lead her into her house, to sit her down in the lounge smelling of old memories and even older ghosts.

She sips the sweet tea Edith brings, and finally her tears subside.

Edith is so kind. The cake she brought across to welcome Sapna and Amir to the cul-de-sac was delicious. Sapna ate almost the entire thing; Amir had only a tiny slice.

'Nosy cow,' he'd said after she'd left.

But Sapna, who had been mortified by the encounter, wondering what Edith had seen, worrying about it, had felt sorry for the hunched old lady. Thinking about her grating carrots for the cake with those claw-like hands made Sapna immeasurably sad. She had been brought up to respect her elders. And consequently she'd felt terrible about the way Amir had treated Edith, nearly pushing her out the door and deliberately locking it behind her when she'd barely crossed over the threshold. Sapna had felt so rude for not talking to her when she came in, keeping her head turned away. But she'd been too choked up to face the woman.

Amir had forgotten to lock the door behind him when he came in from work — early for once — and they were caught up in their own drama when the bell rang.

'Someone's at the door,' she'd cried.

'They'll go away,' Amir had snapped.

But the bell had rung again.

Sapna had flinched. Amir's eyes had hardened to flints. They'd both waited a beat and just as Amir had turned to her . . .

The door had opened and there she was. A tiny old woman. An apparition bearing a cake.

Sapna made gulab jamuns to take round to Edith as thanks — not from scratch, of course, she didn't have all the ingredients. She used the instant mix she'd got from the Asian shop in Hounslow before they left, imagining cooking for Amir and enjoying leisurely and languid three-course meals with him. Ha! They'd never materialised.

The elderly lady invited her in, refusing to take no for an answer. Her house had a sweet, musty smell, infused with years of family meals and nostalgia-tinted memories. It was very dark but cosy, packed with knick-knacks and photographs of her three boys from infancy into adulthood, two with smiling, happy families of their own, one without.

Sapna saw the tray beside the sofa, in front of the television (on top of which were balanced more photographs of the boys), holding a cooling cup of tea and the jam tarts she'd offered Sapna. It broke her heart.

Edith insisted on making her tea. She walked very slowly — shambled, really. Her knees must give her trouble, or perhaps it was her hip. Her hands shook as she switched on the kettle, rooted around for the tea bags, milk and sugar.

Somehow, sitting with Edith, drinking her tea — very weak, too sweet; Edith with her rheumy, kind eyes that seemed to see right through her — Sapna felt comforted for the first time since she had moved into the cul-de-sac. She'd finished her tea too quickly it seemed, although she'd taken tiny sips. She didn't want to leave. The conversation didn't require effort. Edith reminded Sapna of her long-dead grandmother, although her grandmother, with her sharp bark of a voice, her constant nagging, could not have been more different. Something about Edith spoke to her. Perhaps it was the fact that she was surrounded by photographs — they couldn't replace reality, couldn't fill the void. The woman knew loneliness, was on intimate terms with loss, pain, aching, longing.

Gemma from Number 3 aroused Sapna's envy, raised her hackles, made her feel inadequate. Was it because she had a career, a baby? She seemed confident, accomplished. She knew what she wanted from life, whereas Sapna . . .

Sapna was floundering. She thought she wanted to escape her home and her past, the wrong choices she'd made. But she was fast realising that you couldn't escape yourself. She was the problem, not everyone and everything else . . .

* * *

'Well, my dear, that man was terribly rude,' Edith says now, lowering herself into her armchair with a wince and an audible crack of her joints. 'But we're not all like that. You mustn't get the wrong impression.'

'Why did he think that I was Muslim? I'm not. Amir is, but he doesn't practise.'

'Your scarf, perhaps?' Edith says.

It is only then that Sapna realises that her shawl is still wrapped around her head. 'I only did that because I was cold. If I cover my ears, I feel noticeably warmer.'

Edith nods. 'I'm the same, my dear. Never leave the house without a hat.'

The older woman's kindness loosens something in Sapna and she asks the question that has been in her head since that man . . . His look of loathing and disdain . . . 'Why do they hate me?' She doesn't know who she is referring to. The man just now? Her brothers? Her baba? Even Amir, at times? Perhaps all of them.

'It's not *you* they hate,' Edith sighs. 'People are scared of change, anyone different. It makes them defensive. They need targets for their fear. You were an easy one.' Edith sighs again, deeply. 'It takes all sorts. When we first moved here, they used to make fun of my Northern accent.'

'You have a Northern accent?'

Edith smiles. 'It's not as pronounced now.'

And for the first time that day, Sapna smiles as well. 'Thank you,' Sapna says. And she means it. This old woman is the closest thing to a friend she has here.

CHAPTER 16

Gemma

Rob is working late. Again. And the release he said would require him to stay longer in the office isn't even underway yet. Lord knows how much later he'll be once that starts . . .

Gemma bathes Theo, wraps him in his towel and brings him into his room.

Downstairs, she hears the key in the lock, Rob's voice: 'I'm home.'

'There's leftovers in the fridge,' she calls.

He doesn't reply but she hears him coming up the stairs.

'I already ate, love,' Rob says, wrapping her in a hug, leaning over and pecking Theo on the cheek. Rob is cold. He smells of sweat and smoke and the nippy outdoors. 'A few of us went to the pub.'

All right for some, she thinks sourly.

He kisses her — he tastes of beer and something spicy.

'I'm shattered,' he says.

She bites her tongue to stop her retort from escaping: '*You're* shattered? You don't know the meaning of it.' Instead she pulls away from him, saying shortly, 'I've got to see to Theo.'

After Rob leaves to have a wash before bed, she sets Theo down in his crib with his bottle. He's a bit snuffly, his nose is blocked, and she goes to the cabinet to search for the Olbas Oil that helps him breathe better. The cabinet is beside the window, the curtains not drawn yet. She goes to pull them shut and is aware of movement in the garden below. Not in their garden but the one next door. The new neighbours, although they're not very new now. Yet still no curtains. And the girl crying at her kitchen table every night, unaware of Gemma watching. It seems to be a ritual. Sapna coming downstairs, getting a glass of water, sitting and crying and drinking and then wiping her eyes and disappearing upstairs again, her gait as weary as Gemma feels.

Gemma peers into Number 2's garden, taking care to keep out of the way. Hidden. She's not quite sure why. It must just be a fox. Although she could have sworn it looked like a person — a brief, shadowy glimpse of a human silhouette.

Their houses are arranged in such a way that, on one side, Theo's bedroom window and theirs peers out into the gardens, while on the other, their windows look out into the cul-de-sac and inside Sapna's house. Before Theo was born, Gemma didn't give the arrangement of the houses a second thought, but now she thinks that whoever designed them must have been either nosy or careless. Her house, on a slight bend in the street, is pitched to have a direct view into Number 2. She had got to wondering if Number 4 on their left could see into theirs. But Number 4 is angled slightly away so the occupants can't see into Gemma's house the way Gemma is able to snoop into Sapna's, which is a relief. Of course, Gemma has nothing to hide. Well . . . not anymore.

Theo is silent, drinking his milk, his eyes closing. Sapna's garden: grass growing wild, weeds having a 'field' day, a tumbledown shed that has clearly seen better days, its ragged tarpaulin roof dancing in the breeze, and two trees by the kitchen, also overgrown. Wait. What *is* that? Something not quite right behind the looming shadows cast by the tree nearest the kitchen. A thicker shadow that doesn't gel. Is her sleep-deprived mind making things up? She edges back, making sure, once again, that she is well out of sight, camouflaged among the curtains, and focuses on the tree and its surrounds, concentrating hard. The shadow behind the tree beside the kitchen — yes, there definitely is something, someone, there. Hidden, carefully, deliberately out of sight.

She shakes her head to clear it, closes her eyes, opens them. Whatever it is is still there, casting too long a shadow to be a fox. The darker shade of black, menacing. She shudders.

Who or what is it? Gemma watches until Theo finishes his milk and starts to cry. When she has soothed Theo into sleep, after having liberally applied Olbas Oil to his pillow, she looks again. No darker shadows anywhere. No hidden menace. Nothing out of place in any of the gardens.

Whoever it was is gone. Or was it — were they — there at all?

Gemma shivers.

She goes into her bedroom, taking Theo's monitor with her. Rob is fast asleep, small snores escaping his open mouth. She slips under the duvet beside him, hugging his slumber-soaked warmth. But she is still cold, the chill nothing to do with the temperature and everything to do with what she thought she saw. *Is* someone spying on the neighbours? Should she tell them what she thought she saw? Did she see it at all? She has roughly half an hour before Theo wakes again, forty-five minutes on a good night — and she has a feeling tonight is not one, what with his cold. Normally she would fall instantly into sleep — she has trained herself to do so, making the most of these short spurts. But now she can't sleep, no matter how much she lectures herself. She's spooked by that shadow.

She tosses and turns and finally gives up. She stands at the window of the bedroom she shares with Rob which looks out into the gardens. The gardens — both hers and that of Number 2 — look calm and undisturbed. Peaceful.

Theo wakes, predictably, half an hour after she put him down. She soothes him, standing at the landing window, and watches Sapna's husband arrive — after a late shift, perhaps. Gemma shivers again. This means that Sapna was alone in her house when Gemma thought she saw something — someone — in their garden.

Sapna's husband looks tired. His shoulders sagging. He appears to be working all hours. Gemma has noticed him go to work on weekends too. He is thinner than he was when they moved in here, she thinks. When he reaches his house, he stands at the doorstep for a minute as if loath to go in.

And then he turns and looks up, directly at Gemma. She is hidden behind the curtains and yet, it is as if he can see her. She blushes and moves away from the curtains.

You have done nothing wrong, she tells herself as she puts her sleeping baby back in his cot and, clutching the baby monitor, finally falls asleep.

CHAPTER 17

Sapna

Sapna is in the kitchen, heating up the rice and dhal left over from the previous evening to have for lunch, when the doorbell goes.

It is Gemma, with her baby in a stroller.

'Can I bring it in or leave it here?' she asks.

The baby is sleeping peacefully and Sapna notes the plea in Gemma's eyes. If she takes him out, he will wail and they will not be able to have a conversation. It is tempting. Sapna doesn't feel like talking to this woman — there's something about her she doesn't quite trust, her every instinct screaming warning. Also, she feels exposed. She knows the woman might have judged her when she came before — Sapna hadn't been at her best then. That bruise on her arm . . .

'I'm a nurse,' Gemma had said suggestively, leaving the sentence hanging.

You are living here now, you need to make friends. You can't afford to be standoffish.

If Amir was party to her thoughts, he would scoff: *You have a* feeling *about her, do you? Like you have a* feeling *about the house?*

94

Gemma is waiting. The dark circles around her eyes, her messy hair, her clothes with their milk stains . . .

I will need her help in the coming months, Sapna thinks.

'Come in, please, and bring the buggy in,' Sapna says and Gemma smiles.

And again, like she did when Gemma visited before, Sapna thinks, *When she smiles, she looks much younger and really quite beautiful.*

'I won't stay long. Theo will be up soon and will need his feed. I just . . . went to the shops with him and . . .'

Sapna shudders inwardly as she recalls her one aborted attempt at going to the local shops. She hasn't stepped out again, asking Amir to get the shopping on his way home.

'You really need to start doing it, Sapna. You can't hide for ever,' he'd huffed, frustrated.

'But what if that man is there again?' His snarling face. His horrible words . . .

'Whatever happened was a one-off. If you're so afraid, take the bus into town.'

Sapna knows she can't stay in for ever, especially now that . . .

But her thoughts are interrupted by what Gemma is saying, sounding uncharacteristically hesitant, at odds with her usually confident manner.

'I thought I'd pop in to tell you that I *think* I saw something strange in your garden the night before last.'

Sapna's hand goes to her stomach, even as her whole being stills. The woman is a snoop, she remembers thinking when she was startled by Gemma looking into their house, their *bedroom*, that morning when she woke up, her first in the house. But she supposes there are benefits. 'What do you mean you *think* you saw?'

Gemma colours. 'Well . . . I've been debating whether to tell you, but on balance, I decided you should know. I'd want to, if I was alone at home . . .'

'You think you saw something when I was alone at home?' Sapna asks, feeling a shiver electrify her spine.

Gemma colours even further, her entire face turning bright red. Although chilled by Gemma's words, Sapna is fascinated. She's never seen a person turn this shade before. Brown faces just turn darker, becoming more flushed. This is something else.

'Well, I . . . Later that night when I was up with Theo, I saw your husband returning home. So . . .' She shrugs as if embarrassed.

She was right, the woman is a terrible snoop, Sapna thinks, experiencing a flare of anger alongside the fear that has taken her captive. 'What did you see?' she manages to ask. She wants to know and she doesn't. She wants her suspicions that someone is watching her validated if only to prove she isn't going mad . . . and she doesn't.

'Theo was unsettled. A cold, you see. I was with him in his room. His bedroom window looks out into our gardens — yours and mine — and I thought I saw something . . . someone . . . in your garden . . .'

'Oh, oh, oh . . .' There's a prolonged moan and it is only when Gemma looks worriedly at her, standing up and reaching out as if to comfort her, her hand hovering above Sapna's shoulder, hesitant, that Sapna realises it is coming from her.

She tries to stop it but she can't. She is bent double. She cannot seem to catch a breath.

Gemma appears to make up her mind. She squats beside Sapna, her arm around her shoulder, saying gently but firmly, 'Deep breaths. In. Out. There, that's better.'

Sapna is able to breathe again thanks to Gemma. The panic is still there though, a stranglehold on her throat. She was right. And yet, what she saw, how could it be . . . ? How is it possible? Then again, why is it not? People escape all the time. They disappear from where they are meant to be and reappear somewhere else. *No, please* . . .

'Did you . . . did you see who it was?'

'I don't even know if there definitely *was* someone there. I just . . . I didn't want to frighten you, but it didn't sit right with me, not letting you know, just in case . . .'

Sapna nods, swallowing down her fear with difficulty. Deep breaths. 'Thank you,' she manages.

'Are you . . . ?' Gemma's concerned face hovering above her, wavering, fading in and out.

'Um . . . I don't feel very . . .'

'Sapna . . .' she hears from far away. 'Sapna!'

Then nothing.

CHAPTER 18

Sapna

Her mother is holding her and she is comforted. Soothed.

'Sapna?'

Oh. *Oh.*

Crushing disappointment. Not her mother. No. A stranger.

Fleshy arms. The smell of sweat and baby powder and curdled milk. Anxious eyes the colour of the sea on a summer's day. The fine hair on top of strawberry lips glowing gold.

Not a stranger. Well, not quite. Her neighbour.

Shame swamps her, a tidal wave.

'Sorry,' she manages, sitting up (she has been lying on the floor, she must have fainted), her throat hoarse as if she has been screaming aloud all the pain hidden within. Sitting up, she is level with the buggy. The little boy, Theo, sleeps, his breath escaping in soft gasps, his chubby hands folded into fists and curled up on either side of his angelic face. A flaxen-haired cherub.

For the first time in a long while, looking at the baby, despite everything that has happened, Sapna feels hope unfurl, sweet as barfi in her stomach.

'No, *I'm* sorry,' Gemma is saying. 'I shouldn't have . . . Are you okay?'

'Yes, thank you.'

'Please don't thank me. It's the least I could do after the fright I gave you. Look, it's probably nothing . . .'

'It's *not* nothing,' Sapna says. 'I saw him too.' Giving voice to what she saw doesn't make it any less terrifying, if anything more so.

'You saw . . . *him*?' Gemma's eyes grow wide and round with surprise.

'I . . . I think it's a man.'

'Well, I only saw a shadow. I couldn't determine anything. I told Rob, but he laughed it off. I'd made up my mind not to tell you, having convinced myself that I'd imagined it, but I was walking past just now and I . . . I just . . . If it was me in your position, I'd like to know. That decided it,' Gemma is saying.

But Sapna is not paying attention, having heard very little beyond *I told Rob, but he laughed it off*. She suddenly feels a kinship with this woman, despite her earlier embarrassment, despite her instincts warning her to be wary. This woman has been nothing but kind to her, and now, what she's said, it *speaks* to Sapna.

'Amir said I was paranoid,' Sapna says, her relief at finally being understood overriding her fear at what Gemma is telling her and loosening her tongue.

Amir . . . And now she realises what has been niggling her. It's as if her fainting spell has finally made things clear. When Amir saw the *welcome to the cul-de-sac* cake Gemma had brought round — untouched, as Sapna had not had the inclination to tuck in — he'd exclaimed, 'What have we here! Chocolate cake, from Marks too. My favourite.'

This was news to Sapna. 'I thought you were more of a savoury person.'

'Except when it comes to this particular chocolate cake from M&S.'

'One of the neighbours brought it round.'

99

'Gemma?' Amir asked as he went to cut himself a slice.

'Yes,' Sapna said. 'You can have it all, I don't feel like cake, but wait until after dinner, please. If you have some now, it will ruin your appetite. I made onion bhajis and saag aloo with peas pulao.'

All that evening, she felt uneasy, knowing there was something obvious that she was missing.

Now, it's as clear as her reflection in the stainless-steel plates it was her job to wash at home . . .

'By the way, do you know my husband?' she asks Gemma, and she can hear the steely ice in her voice, sharp enough to cut flesh.

The woman blanches, going very pale. 'Pardon me?'

Sapna is quite sure Gemma heard her but she repeats the question anyway, intrigued by this woman's reaction. 'Do you know Amir?'

'No. Why would you think that?' Gemma fiddles with her necklace, a simple heart-shaped pendant.

'He called you Gemma as if he knew you.'

'I . . . I might have met him when he came here to look at the property.'

As far as Sapna is aware, Amir never actually came to look at it without her. They came once together and accepted the rental, and after, Amir had showed Sapna around, pointing out the shops and the bus stop and so on. But how can she be certain? She realises that she barely knows her husband at all, having married him so soon after they met. He can be loving one minute and the next . . . Well, not that he has been loving at all since they moved in, but that's her fault, what with all her moaning and complaining. She doesn't want to do it, but can't seem to stop herself. She knows it irritates Amir, but *she* is irritated by his mocking dismissal of her fears, her upset, his constant working, his never being home.

Whenever she brings it up, he yells, 'I'm doing it for *you*! You were disappointed with the flat we were renting!'

'I never said—'

'You didn't have to. Your face said it all. And now you have a house of your own which I have to work every minute of every day to afford and you're not happy here either!'

Now, she looks at Gemma, her mind whirring. She is older and taller than Sapna, and with striking features. Slightly overweight and scruffy, but that's what having a baby must do to you. *How do you know my husband?*

Gemma is not meeting her eye. Sapna is sure she's hiding something.

This woman is not your friend. You cannot trust anyone, a voice in her head warns. And another, at odds with the first, sounding very much like her husband: *You really are becoming paranoid. What's the matter with you?*

The smell of burning assaults her nostrils — the leftovers she was heating up. She left the flame on the lowest setting when the doorbell went, but even so, they've had it.

She goes to stand, but is giddy and stumbles. Gemma helps her, holds her.

'Look, are you okay?'

'No . . . I mean yes . . . I . . . I'm just . . . I'm pregnant.' The words are out of her mouth before she can stop them, take them back. Maybe it's seeing the baby sleeping so peacefully in the stroller, pure innocence. Maybe it's because she's been wrongfooted by the woman's reaction to her questions, as if she's hiding something. Or perhaps it's because she's feeling unsettled about the fact that Gemma too saw someone in her garden — that her conviction about someone spying on her is not unfounded. But why oh why did she have to go and blurt out something so personal to *this* woman of all people? And as always when she says something she shouldn't, she keeps on babbling to disguise her embarrassment. 'You're the first person I've told. I just found out. I have suspected for a while, but now I'm sure. I haven't even had the chance to tell Amir yet.' *Stop. Now. Remove yourself. You have an excuse.* 'I have to go to the kitchen, switch off the gas,' she says. The smell of burning is intensifying as she speaks.

Gemma's face is absolutely colourless, in stark contrast to before, when her skin had flooded red.

It is Sapna's turn to ask, 'Gemma, are you all right?'

'Yes, yes. Sorry, I need to get my little chap home. He'll be up and hollering for his feed any minute.'

But she doesn't look all right at all, Sapna thinks.

'Congratulations, by the way. Exciting times,' Gemma says.

Is Sapna imagining it, or does it take a supreme effort for Gemma to mouth the words, like she doesn't mean them at all? 'Oh. Yes. Thank you.' She smiles.

She switches off the gas and comes to the door to watch Gemma make her way to her own house, manoeuvre the buggy in and wave to Sapna.

Strange woman, she thinks as she goes inside, locking the door behind her. *But kind with it.*

It is only when she is alone again that the significance of what Gemma said truly sinks in. Someone standing outside her kitchen, even with the windows plastered with newspaper. Not . . . ? No . . . But that face she thought she saw . . .

I thought I could get away. I was wrong.

CHAPTER 19

Gemma

Gemma holds her baby close, kissing the top of Theo's downy head, smelling sweet, of innocence and 'no tears' shampoo, trying to ground herself in the present. Her child. Her husband. The here and now.

But the past beckons. Suddenly more immediate, more demanding, more urgent than the present. The past she has relegated to a corner of her mind, shut away — or so she thought. Now it's jarred awake by the next-door neighbour's question: *Do you know my husband?*

Carefree days at uni, laughing, drinking, daring each other into mischief, falling in love . . .

Her shattered heart that she had wilfully, and with great difficulty, glued back together, shaken by the young girl's admission. *I'm pregnant.*

She holds her baby close, wraps him up snug in her arms. For once he's not crying, even as his wispy hair is anointed by *her* tears.

CHAPTER 20

Edith

Edith gets off the bus at her stop, manoeuvring her shopper off the step with effort — she got some really good bargains at the market today, she's pleased as punch, but she has to admit the shopper is a pain to handle when full to the brim.

She's looking forward to a nice, strong cup of tea and a slice of the Victoria sponge she baked this morning. It's heavenly, fit for royalty, even if she says so herself. She's been generous with the jam, and the sponge is melt-in-the-mouth soft. The recipe is from Delia's *How to Cook*, which Edith received as a Christmas present one year from Marge, Jack's sister. It was meant as a slight — even years into Edith and Jack's marriage, Marge never stopped trying to show up Edith's unsuitability as a wife for her beloved brother. She thought he could do much better, the cow went to her grave convinced of it. Well, the joke's on her. She's dead, and Edith's still here, enjoying delicious cakes. Delia never disappoints.

The bus arrived on schedule for once and Edith is pleased; she'll be bang on time for *Gardeners' World*, although she can't do much gardening anymore, what with her dodgy hip, her uncooperative knees, her arthritic hands — oh dear, the list of complaints gets longer every day. But she does like Monty Don — a sight for sore eyes, that man. And he loves his dogs; she must admit she has a soft spot for anyone who loves animals. She wouldn't have minded a pet or two over the years, and Lord knows the boys hankered for them, but it wasn't to be. And now she's too old to look after another living thing, plant or animal — she struggles some days to get by herself. And tempting though it is, especially when she sees those ads on the telly, those poor mistreated pets with their huge, wet, pleading eyes, it would be cruel to get one, there's nothing worse than your animal outliving you . . . Well, she supposes there are worse things, but still—

'Excuse me.'

Edith starts at the well-bred voice pulling her out of her ruminations.

Mrs Snooty So-and-So, from Number 20 on the main road just before the turning into the cul-de-sac. She was on the bus, come to think of it. She got off before Edith, swanning regally past as Edith stood up — taking ages, what with her hip locking at just the wrong time — and tried to drag her unwieldy load along to the door without stumbling. No offer of help, mind, but Edith had got a noseful of Mrs Snooty's posh perfume — something expensively flowery.

But now . . . Is Mrs High-and-Mighty deigning to talk to *her*? Well, well. Wonders will never cease.

'Yes, dear? Did I drop something?' Edith asks.

It's entirely possible. The bus pulled away with a grinding of gears even before Edith had properly stepped off, jolting her and sending spasms through her already complaining joints. She understands that the driver must have been tired of waiting, but goodness, nobody has any patience nowadays!

The jaunty air brushes Edith's face as she checks the pavement for the bananas or eggs she packed right at the top of her shopper.

'No,' Mrs Snooty says, the word rolling out of her pursed lips in a short, snappy burst.

'Well, that's a relief.'

The woman brushes her words away, waving her hand like there's a pesky fly in front of her face.

'I was wondering if you've had anything to do with the foreigners who've moved into your close,' the woman sniffs.

Oh my, Edith thinks, *she sounds just like the queen.* The same plummy tones as if she's sucking on a lemon. But the queen *never* sounded quite this disapproving on telly.

'They're a young couple, just starting out. And, well, I've talked to the woman.' Her brief encounter with the thug doesn't count, Edith decides. 'She's ever so young, a girl really.' What was her name again? It's gone, Edith cannot remember it for the world. Another disgrace of old age. There are so many she can't keep track. Ha! 'They're from India, I think she said.'

'My dear, it's a real pity. Before you know it, our lovely village will be overrun by them. This is how it is with their lot. My friend Margaret had to move away from the town she'd happily lived in for nearly fifty years. First one moves in, then hordes follow. Next thing, there will be spice shops and foreign voices and coloured faces everywhere you look, bringing down the tone and the house prices. And like poor Margaret, we too will have to move. I've already started looking.' The woman speaks without taking a breath, her voice getting more nasal by the minute.

'Oh dear.' Edith thinks longingly of her Victoria sponge and tea. She wants nothing more than to rest her sore hip in her armchair with her legs propped up on the stool in front of her. The trip into town and back is murder on her hip, not to mention her knees. 'The girl . . .' What *is* her name? 'She seems ever so nice, although her husband . . .'

'Just you wait,' Mrs Snooty says grimly, 'very soon you won't be able to move for all of them.'

Edith thinks of the poor girl, how she had sobbed her eyes out after being insulted at the shops. 'When you get right down to it, they're just like us, really, aren't they? And in any case, they've as much a right to be here as we do.'

106

'I don't know about that. Most of them are here illegally, you know. But, well, you seem to be taken in.' Mrs Snooty's face is like a shrivelled prune, her voice not much better. 'Keep your belongings under lock and key is my advice. You can't trust that lot.'

'I don't think that's true of *all* of them. There are good and bad eggs everywhere, mind.' And Edith knows this better than most. Speaking of eggs, will she ever get home?

'Don't say I didn't warn you. Cheerio.' And with what passes for a smile — a minuscule lifting of her sour lips — Mrs High-and-Mighty opens her gate smartly and click-ety-clacks up the drive to her house.

Edith has never been happier to get home, settle on the sofa with a builder's tea and a liberal helping of her Victoria sponge, which is even better now it's had time to sit for a bit (longer than expected, thanks to Edith being accosted as she got off the bus). She resolves to take a slice round to the girl — now what *was* her name again? — after *Gardeners' World*, if only to spite Mrs Thinks-She's-the-Queen.

CHAPTER 21

Sapna

Sapna is in the shower when she hears the knock on the door. Urgent. Pounding.

Why does everyone decide to pop in during the five minutes when she's in the shower?

'Coming,' she calls, thinking it must be Gemma or Edith. Couldn't they have just rung the bell? Perhaps they did and she didn't hear it above the clamour of the water.

She runs downstairs, looks out the curtainless window. She can't see anyone.

She opens the door. Nobody there.

Strange.

She was pretty sure she heard knocking.

She goes to the kitchen, deciding to make herself some tea the *proper* way. Thinking how she and her sisters would sit on the stoop with Ma, enjoying a mid-morning break from their chores with sweet, spiced tea and snacks. Gossiping and laughing and teasing each other. Companionship, warmth, love. So effortless she took it for granted.

She wipes her eyes with her pallu as the water boils. She adds tea leaves and cardamom, crushed ginger and cinnamon

108

bark, hearing her mother's voice in her head, talking her through the steps: *Not that large a piece of cinnamon — you don't want it overpowering the tea. Yes, you must crush the ginger to release the flavour.* As she's adding milk and sugar to the spitting spiced tea, a knock. And another. And yet another, right on its heels. A staccato beat.

She's irritated. What's with the pounding? Haven't they seen the doorbell?

She flings open the door.

Nobody there.

But then, a sound. Footsteps, hurried. Someone running. She just catches sight of their back as they exit the cul-de-sac onto the main road. A gait at once familiar and scary.

She locates her phone, calls Amir — her hands, her whole body shaking. It's Saturday but he's working. Of course. Always.

'To pay the rent,' he says, but she knows it is, partly at least, to get away from her. Lately, he would rather work than be at home.

It's a vicious cycle. She's homesick and lonely and scared, feeling spied upon — it's constant now, that creepy sensation of being watched — and so when he comes home worn out from work, even though she promises herself otherwise, all her pent-up emotions are released in a big, messy stream. He's tired and doesn't have the patience to deal with her anxieties; he thinks she's imagining things that aren't there. She's upset that he doesn't take her seriously. He thinks she's unhappy, dissatisfied. He takes it as a personal failure. And so he stays away more, for longer. And she feels even more lonely, upset and resentful. Which pushes him away further . . .

She's been waiting for the right time to tell him about the baby. But it's *never* the right time. If she's honest, that's not the only thing holding her back. She could always make time. And she will have to, very soon. It's not fair that Gemma knows before him . . .

Oh *why* did she have to tell Gemma? It just came out, and she's regretted it ever since.

A baby on the way would make Amir so happy, despite their money worries, she knows. In the first heady, happy days of their marriage — a fast-fading memory now — he'd whisper in her ear after they made love, 'I hope we create a child that is the image of you.'

Now, she strokes her stomach with the hand not holding the phone. Her hands are shaking. Her whole body is shaking.

It goes to voicemail. She leaves a message, trying not to show how afraid she is, trying to keep her voice composed. 'Amir, it's me. Please call back.'

But he won't as she's done this once too often, calling for the 'silliest' of things: a movement in the garden, a sound she can't place coming from upstairs.

I'm sick and tired of your paranoia! his voice cries.

In the kitchen, the tea boils over with a gleefully malicious hiss and she spends the next twenty minutes cleaning the stove.

CHAPTER 22

Sapna

Sapna can't stop shivering, shaken by who she thought she saw running away from her house, this place that is supposed to be her haven and her new start, this place that gives her the creeps, this place that even her mother doesn't know she's moved to. At the end of their last conversation, they were both sobbing: 'Your baba found out, janu. No more phone calls for a bit, until I find a way to get around him. Only for a while, my janu, not for ever.' She sees her baba's forbidding face as he turned away from Sapna with great finality: 'You are dead to us.'

She sits in the living room, looking outside. The cul-de-sac is silent. Still. Not even the bushes stirring. No traffic. No people. No curtains twitching at Gemma's window. She wonders what Edith is doing. She pictures her sitting in that living room thick with memories of the dead, the missing and the long gone, the damp, mouldy scent of the past permeating the house. She is tempted to visit her, have a cup of tea. She understands Edith, feels a bond with her. Like Sapna, she too is lonely, it comes off her in waves.

But Sapna decides not to in the end. She doesn't want to rely on the old woman too much. After everything that's happened, she's afraid to trust even Edith, who is essentially harmless, with her fragile, papery skin, her lined face, her quivering voice, her delicious baking.

Sapna is reminded of her grandmother again, who died when she was ten. Dadima had been scary, but Sapna was not deterred. She'd ignore the woman's sharp voice, her paan-stained face, her witch's cackle, and climb into her roomy lap. Sapna had been Dadima's favourite. Sapna was *everyone's* favourite, her brothers', her baba's — until, of course, she wasn't. Even the strict nuns who ruled the village mission-ary school with an iron fist loved her. Sapna was universally adored — 'You are irresistible, my minx,' her grandmother used to say — but her beauty was also a curse. Only her mother was wary. Only her mother understood that Sapna's beauty was a double-edged sword. Her mother's eyes would widen with fear whenever she saw people looking at Sapna, men and women alike — the men leering, the women assess-ing. Her mother was right to be anxious. This beauty has brought Sapna nothing but trouble. If she could trade her looks with someone else, she would do so in an instant.

She does not want to go to Edith for another reason. What if Edith, whose living room also faces the road, saw nothing, nobody, just now? What if Edith, like Amir, dis-misses her fear as nonsense, thinks she is paranoid? She couldn't bear it if the person she considers her one ally derided her. *Is* she paranoid? Is she seeing things? Is she going mad?

Gemma has been kind in her way, but, try as she might, Sapna can't quite trust her. There's something about her . . . And the woman is tired, yes, but she's not lonely. Not in quite the same way Sapna is, aching for home and relatives so far away. Edith understands. Her sons, she told Sapna, are scattered around the world, her husband long gone.

Sitting at the window, scared out of her wits, waiting for Amir to come home, Sapna thinks of the choices she's made and unpicks them — she imagines a different life, one where she is back home, within the folds of her family and not ostracised, but happy. She sighs. What's done is done. She has to face the consequences. She rubs her stomach gently with trembling hands. *I don't regret you. You are innocent in all of this. I love you, my heart.*

She is startled out of her musings by the shrill ringing of the house phone. For a minute she sits motionless, her hands on her stomach.

No, she thinks, as dread ambushes her, pushing rational thought away.

Breathe.

She does, slowly and deeply, but nothing can shift the panic that has gripped her with icy tentacles, rooting her to the spot.

Stop this. It's just someone calling.

But *nobody* knows their landline number. The house phone has not rung since they moved in. *Perhaps Amir gave the number to someone.*

The phone stops ringing and she heaves a sigh of relief. That's one decision taken out of her hands.

You had better become strong before the baby arrives, her voice of reason chides. *Your babe does not deserve a nervous, dithering mother, unable to make even a simple decision about whether to answer a phone call.*

The ringing starts again. Whoever it is is insistent. She wants to clap her hands to her ears and ignore it.

You are not a child. You are a grown woman, set to become a mother in a few months.

She stands on shaky legs and walks to the phone.

She picks up the receiver, cradles it under her right cheek. 'Hello?'

Nothing. Just static. Crackle. Hiss. Like a cobra in the moment before it springs. She checks the caller display. It says *withheld.* She goes to replace the phone when she hears loud breaths echoing down the line. A sliver of fear. *Could it be . . . ?*

'Miss me, Sapna?' a voice whispers. Deep. Throaty. Familiar.

No!

How did he get this number? How? Winded, she leans against the wall, phone still pressed to her ear.

'You thought you could run away, didn't you? You thought you could start again.'

Oh no.

'Are you happy in your little world? Are you? Tell me. Speak to me.'

Please, she thinks.

'You don't *look* happy.'

She swivels round so abruptly she pulls a muscle in her neck. The kitchen is still, the window opaque, panes overlaid with news sheets spouting faraway tragedies. Is he standing behind there, watching her? It *was* him she saw at the kitchen window that day, and just a few minutes previously running away from her front door . . .

She is *not* going mad. This is happening. It is real. But how?

'Why do this? Why, Sapna?'

Please. Leave me alone.

'I am coming for you.'

The disconnect tone is loud and ominous in her ear.

Her knees give way and she slumps down onto the carpet, the phone emitting a keening noise.

How?

Slowly, very slowly, after what seems an age, she replaces the phone carefully onto its holder. Then she stands and makes her way to the door, opens it, steps outdoors, breathing in huge gulps of fresh air. It does nothing to calm her. She closes the door behind her and locks it, in a vain effort to keep the monster away — but it is too late now. He is already here.

CHAPTER 23

Gemma

Loud banging on the door. It just won't stop. The knocking feels like someone hammering persistently on her skull. Why isn't Rob answering the bloody door? Then it comes to her. Rob is away. With Theo. At Rob's mother's. Which is why she is spending the day in bed, luxuriously sprawled across the whole mattress.

Bang, bang, bang. Each thud tears into her skull.

Theo. Something must have happened to him.

Suddenly all sleep escapes her, replaced by instant and absolute dread. She bolts out of bed, heart thundering, squinting blearily at the clock: 12.15 p.m. She grabs the phone next to her.

But there are no messages from Rob or his mother. Her baby is safe. Rob would call if anything was wrong. He wouldn't be hammering on the door like Death come calling.

The knocking is showing no signs of stopping. If anything, it's getting louder. She'll have to answer it.

She scrabbles under the bed for her slippers, determined to kill whoever it is making all that noise. Why can't they use the doorbell like any other sane person? The doorbell has a pleasant chime that normally irritates her, but right now she would give anything to hear it over this pounding.

'I'm coming!' she yells. She stomps down the stairs and swings the door open. 'What on earth? Are you trying to break the door down?'

There's nobody there. She looks up and down the street, shifting her weight impatiently from one foot to another. But their cul-de-sac is quiet. Nothing stirs except a crisp packet fluttering in the springy breeze.

Who was causing all the noise, then? Has she been hallucinating? Did she dream the sounds of mutiny at her door? She could have sworn she saw a hand just now as she pulled the door open. She blinks.

Then a noise, a pained whine, like a wounded kitten, comes from near her feet. She looks down. Someone is slumped in the doorway.

Gemma doubles back, shocked. She certainly wasn't expecting this — a woman flopped against the front doorway, appearing as if her legs gave way suddenly, not having the strength to hold her up.

A woman wearing a colourfully patterned dress. Sapna from next door.

Her pregnant neighbour.

She looks pale, ill.

'Please,' she says. 'Please help me.'

Her voice is breathless, coming in loud gasps. 'I tried Edith but she isn't home.'

Worry shoots through Gemma, even as her nurse's training kicks in. Is the woman having a miscarriage? She squats beside Sapna, puts an arm around her, says, gently, 'Edith takes the bus to the farmers' market in town on Saturdays.' Then, making sure her voice is kind but reassuring, the one she'd regularly use when working, she asks, 'What's the matter? Is it the baby?'

'No,' Sapna whispers.

116

That's something. But if not the baby, then . . . 'Are you not feeling well?' Gemma asks.

'It isn't that.'

'Then what is it?' Gemma coaxes gently.

'. . . Help me,' is all Sapna says.

She's evidently had some sort of shock.

'Would you like to come indoors?' Gemma asks, and her neighbour nods meekly, allowing Gemma to lead her into the living room, sit her down on the sofa.

'I'll get you a drink,' Gemma says once the girl is ensconced on her settee, red-eyed and swollen-gazed and yet so beautiful — the perfect mixture of vulnerability and loveliness. Gemma fetches a glass of water from the kitchen, making sure to stir in a liberal couple of tablespoons of sugar — good for shock — and hands it to the girl. 'Drink it all up. It will help, I promise.'

Sapna obeys, and when she sets the glass down, Gemma notices that she's no longer quite as wan, some colour returning to her face.

'Now, tell me, what's the matter?' Gemma asks.

The girl bunches her dress in her palms, looking at Gemma with wide, fearful eyes. 'He . . . He's coming to get me.'

'Who? Your husband?'

'No! Why would you think that?' Sapna looks wounded and shock colours her voice.

Because you have been fighting in the street. Because you sob in your kitchen every night. Because of that bruise I saw the first time I visited.

'You're upset. And I've seen you with swollen eyes a couple of times before,' Gemma says evenly.

Sapna blushes. 'Oh, that! I have very sensitive skin and I'm allergic to something. I haven't been able to determine what yet.'

She is clearly lying, fiddling with her shawl, not meeting Gemma's eye.

117

And now she's sure the woman is not sick, that she's no longer in shock, that her is baby fine, Gemma's worry eases, irritation taking its place. This is Gemma's weekend off, the first since Theo was born, and God knows she's earned it. It's her time away from babies and pregnant women and husbands and neighbours. Time for herself. And every second she wastes here is taken away from her time to recover, so she can be a good mum instead of a zombie going through the motions for Theo.

Gemma is annoyed now. 'And what about the bruise on your arm I saw that day?'

The woman flinches as if Gemma has hit her. Gemma experiences a twinge of remorse.

'It was as I said. We hadn't unpacked properly and I bumped into one of the boxes.' She sounds defensive; she's biting her lower lip.

'It didn't look like that type of bruise,' Gemma says firmly. Now she's started, she might as well see it through.

Colour rushes into Sapna's cheeks. 'Amir wouldn't . . .'

'That's what they all say, and I've seen plenty in my line of work. What's more, Edith said she saw him raise his hand to you and only stopped because she barged in—'

'When?' Sapna's nose scrunches in befuddlement, then recollection. 'Oh! That time she came in . . . He was going to move the hair from my face as my hands were covered in flour. I was kneading dough.'

Gemma believes this excuse as much as she did the last one — not at all. Her eyelids drag down as a yawn escapes. She needs more sleep.

'Edith told you that?' Sapna looks even more upset and hurt if it were possible, as if Edith has betrayed her.

'Yes. She was worried about you. She wondered if she should do something, say something. We both did. She said she hears the two of you arguing all the time.'

The girl bites her lower lip even harder. She'll be drawing blood soon. Dwarfed by Gemma's comfortable black sofa, she looks very young. How old is she really? Is she even in her twenties?

'I . . . I am missing home and have been lonely. It is hard on Amir as I keep bursting into tears — because of the pregnancy, I think. My emotions are all over the place. I miss my ma and baba, my sisters and brothers. At home there was always noise, people to talk to but here . . .' A sob in her voice. 'And then there is . . . You saw yourself . . .'

She shudders, her eyes huge with fear, and Gemma knows she's thinking of the man she thinks is spying on her, not helped by Gemma telling her she thought she saw something in their garden. If Gemma had known it would have such an adverse effect on the girl, fuelling her already rampant panic, she wouldn't have mentioned it. She should have heeded Rob's advice and let it go.

But right now, the girl appears to have had a shock. She clearly believes someone is out to get her. And so, Gemma says, briskly but kindly, 'Look, I've been keeping an eye out and I've not noticed anything since, all right? That shadow I saw — thought I saw — I'm sure it was just my imagination. I've not been sleeping and . . .'

Gemma stops mid-sentence for the girl is shaking her head vigorously, her shawl dancing, even as she curls deeper into the sofa, a small, terrified ball. 'No, I . . .' She cannot get the words out. With effort, Sapna swallows. 'It *wasn't* your imagination,' she says in a burst of fierceness. And just like that, her spirit deflates like air from a punctured balloon and she slumps dejectedly again, looking spent, as if that small show of defiance has taken everything out of her. 'Amir doesn't believe me. He wants me to be happy, and when I'm not, he gets upset . . .' She doesn't look at Gemma but at the shawl of her dress, twisting it round and round her fingers.

'And then he loses his temper and hits you?'

'No! I'm leaving.' She stands up so suddenly that she sends the little basket of potpourri on the coffee table in front of her flying. Yellow, blue and violet flakes scatter everywhere. Gemma catches a whiff of lavender. She winces. Now she'll have to spend time cleaning this, time better spent sleeping. God, what an absolute nightmare!

'I'm sorry.' Sapna is flustered. 'Coming here was a mistake.'

'Look, is there anything I can do?' Gemma asks, feeling bad for having rubbed her neighbour up the wrong way, perhaps not completely unintentionally. What if there *is* something genuinely wrong?

Sapna doesn't respond. She's almost at the door, tripping over the buggy, when she turns and asks, 'Where's your baby?'

'My husband has taken him to his mother's, to give me some time alone.'

Another blush spreads across the woman's cheeks. 'You were sleeping, weren't you, when I knocked?'

Knocked! It was more like a barrage!

'Yes, I was. Next time, please use the doorbell.'

She looks mortified.

'I will. Sorry for having disturbed you,' she says again.

'What did you want?' Gemma tries again, feeling she should. 'What happened to make you so upset?'

Even more upset than you normally are, every time I've met you. I don't think I've ever seen you smile, not even when you told me about your pregnancy.

Sapna's face falls again, fresh tears erupting in her eyes. She seems to be one of those ultra-sensitive women who cries at the drop of a hat. Must be hell living with her — not that Gemma is condoning abuse, of course. There is *no* excuse for that. Yet still . . . Rob would go crazy if Gemma turned on the waterworks like this every time he even raised his voice — not that he does, bless him.

'I had a phone call . . .' Sapna hiccups.

Gemma waits. Sapna does not say anything else. Oh for God's sake, does she have to do all the work here? 'And?'

'He's coming to get me.'

'Who?' Gemma sighs. She dare not add, *if not your husband*, for the girl will look incredulous again, as if Gemma has been blasphemous in a holy place.

Sapna starts shaking. She can't seem to stop. She looks terrified, her face contorted. Whatever it is has thoroughly spooked her.

Gemma reaches out and pats her shoulder. Sapna looks up at her. Huge, watery eyes the colour of espresso, slanting upwards slightly at the corners. She says a strange thing then. 'Have you ever done something you've regretted? Something really bad, in your past, and it's come back to haunt you after?' Her soft Indian accent brings back memories Gemma would rather forget.

She blinks, pushing them away. 'Why do you ask?' She is defensive, her voice harsh. Then, understanding dawns. 'Is that what's happened to you? Your past catching up with you?' But what past can this slip of a girl have? She's barely out of her teens, if that . . .

Sapna reaches out, clamping her tiny hand around Gemma's wrist. 'I don't know what to do.'

She wishes the girl was not holding on to her, looking at her with such imploring eyes. What is she supposed to do? 'So what's happened exactly?'

'I had a phone call. Someone from my past. He said he's coming for me.'

'Where is this person?'

'The last I knew he was in India, but . . .' She swallows. 'I think it is him you saw in the garden, my garden. I think he has been stalking me, spying on me.' Sapna starts worrying the hem of her shawl with her free hand. 'What shall I do? Oh, what shall I do?'

'If you're that scared, if you're sure this person has been stalking you, and is harassing you on the telephone, I think you should tell your husband and call the police. Stalking is an offence and they will—'

'I . . . I can't tell Amir. He . . . he doesn't know what I did.'

121

Well, well, this slip of a girl is keeping secrets from her husband? 'I'm sure your husband will understand once you explain.'

Her face blanches. 'I don't think so . . .'

'Well, then don't tell your husband. But do call the police. They will get to the bottom of this.'

'I . . . I'll think about it.'

Gemma can see that she won't. She saw the fear on the girl's face at the mention of the police. The same look as when Gemma suggested she tell her husband. But, well, what can she do? She's tried, been neighbourly. She will look out for her, but she can't do any more than that. 'Oh, and don't answer any phone calls. What did the caller display say?'

'Withheld.'

'Just don't pick up any calls from a withheld number. He'll get tired of calling and stop. And I'll keep an eye out to see if he's hanging around.'

Sapna keeps on staring at Gemma in that pleading way, her eyes glistening. What more is she supposed to do, for God's sake?

'What if . . . ?' Sapna begins, her voice a whisper, and then she tails off, face crumpling, shoulders heaving.

Gemma waits for her to finish her sentence. When she doesn't, she says, aiming for an even tone, 'Look, he knows you scare easily. If he's watching like you say and sees you react like this every time he calls . . .' She rubs a hand across her aching forehead, her words swallowed by a huge yawn taking her unawares. Her body has decided it wants to catch up on sleep and is determined to do so. Her bed beckons. 'If you don't pick up his calls, he'll stop.'

Sapna's nails press into her palm. 'I know him. He won't stop. Please help me, please.'

'What more do you want me to do?' Gemma asks coolly, patience exhausted. She wants her bed, pillow on her face, oblivion.

'He's going to come for me.'

122

God, she's had enough, every last vestige of neighbour-liness shredded to bits by this woman's clinging. 'When he does, come get me,' she says, dispassionately. 'Now go home, have a stiff drink and a lie-down before your husband gets home.'

CHAPTER 24

Sapna

Sapna paces the living room, mortified. Her fear and upset made her do something she shouldn't have, throwing herself at the mercy of a woman who was enjoying some rare time off from being a mother and wife. Gemma was catching up on precious sleep and Sapna disturbed her. And not only that, but why oh why did Sapna have to behave in that needy and weak manner? Her excuse — pathetic, she sees now — was that she was panicking. She still is, while Gemma comes across as strong and capable, someone to have on your side.

But Sapna has only made things worse, alienated her neighbour. And she is doubly upset because she understands she cannot trust Edith either. Edith, whom she considered a friend, has been discussing her with Gemma. They have been talking about her, comparing notes.

'She was worried about you,' Gemma had said.

Was that true? Or was she someone to be gossiped about — those Indians next door, quarrelling like nobody's business.

She can't shake the feeling of being watched. And then, in a burst of defiance, she stands up straight, looks right at the kitchen window, thinking, *Watch me. I don't care.*

The long drowsy hours of afternoon fade into evening. She watches Edith return, pulling a trolley with one hand, holding a shopping bag in the other, stopping every other minute to shift them around. Sapna resists the urge to run outside and help her — Edith will offer tea and sympathy and Sapna will not be able to stop herself from sharing her woes.

No. Enough of being weak, running to others for help with her problems. It's time she sorted them herself.

But how? She's trapped, in a bind she cannot see a way out of. She thought she could escape by moving countries, coming here, far away from home. But she can't. She never will, perhaps.

How to manage this? She could come clean to Amir . . . But no. *No.* It will devastate him. How to tell Amir that he was but a means to an end? That she used him?

She wants to talk to her mother. Just once. Then she will never contact her again. Then she will be strong. She will stop giving in to despair, relying on others for help. She will face this, whatever it is, to the bitter end.

She picks up the phone. Amir has put international minutes on it — just in case, he said. Sapna gets so upset with him when he doesn't acknowledge her fears, when he mocks her 'paranoia'. But . . . her husband has also been so kind to her, making sure she has the means to call home any time she wishes. He works all these long hours for them, so they can afford this house. It would do her good to remember this.

'I'm sure your baba will forgive you eventually,' Amir has reassured Sapna in the past, during the early days of their marriage before it was soured by arguments. But Amir doesn't know her baba. He will *never* forgive her.

Her baba loves completely, and he hates with even more vigour than he loves.

Her fingers hovering over her ma's number, Sapna makes the calculations. India is four and a half hours ahead. Her ma will be home, cooking supper. She hopes none of her married sisters are visiting.

With each ring her heart perks up, thudding noisily, drumming a rhythm of hope and desperate longing in her chest.

On the fourth ring, her mother picks up, her voice slightly breathless. 'Hello?'

'Ma.'

'Sapna.' Her name whispered. A prayer and an apology. Soft with her mother's tears. 'You are not to call. If your baba found out . . .'

'*He* called me, Ma. He somehow managed to find my number. He is here, I think. Watching me. Biding his time.' Sapna doesn't have to specify the 'he'. She knows they are on the same page.

Silence. Thick and pulsing with so many things unsaid.

'Your brothers said he had got out.' Her mother's voice is taut with the same terror that has a stranglehold on Sapna's neck. 'Stay strong, janu, I'm sure he won't dare do anything with Amir there . . .' She's trying to sound confident but wavering.

'Yes,' she sighs, knowing her mother doesn't believe what she's saying, and neither does she.

'I'll see what I can do here, all right?'

'Yes, Ma.'

'You'll be fine, janu.'

'Yes, Ma.' Both of them choose to believe the other's lies. What else can they do?

The hand not holding the phone strokes her stomach, and because Sapna can't help it, it slips out. 'I'm pregnant.'

The pause goes on for ever. Then, her mother whispers tentatively, 'Is it . . .'

'I don't know.'

When her mother speaks, Sapna can hear the tears in her voice. 'I wish I was there, janu, to help. Better still, I wish you were here.' Her mother sighs deeply.

'I know, Ma,' Sapna says, inserting brightness into her voice. 'I'm fine. Don't worry. He can't do anything.'

'Your brothers will call their friends, make sure to keep an eye on him,' her ma promises, her voice tremulous with pain.

During their last phone call, when her mother asked Sapna not to contact her again until she had convinced Baba to forgive his daughter, Ma cried that this was worse than losing her child — knowing her child needed her, wanted her, but being unable to do anything about it.

'Love you, Ma. Love to everyone. I won't call again.' If her baba discovers that Ma spoke to Sapna, her mother will be punished and that will punish Sapna. It's best not to call, as this way she can keep the hope that her mother is always just a phone call away alive. If her baba finds out, that too will be destroyed.

'I wish things were different. I'm working on your baba,' Ma whispers. 'Take care of yourself and the bubba.' Ma's voice is thick with longing and love. 'You will be fine, janu. You are stronger than you know, my beloved girl.'

And then her mother is gone and she is alone again. Except for him. Her stalker. Unwanted. Unwelcome. But always there.

CHAPTER 25

Sapna

Day two of her resolve to be strong, to rely on no one but herself. She is making chicken biryani, Amir's favourite, wearing an apron she found in one of the kitchen cupboards, left behind by the previous owners: pink with sunny yellow flowers dotting it. She knows that she doesn't have much time until her past catches up with her. Until then, she will be the best wife to Amir that she can possibly be.

Her resolve to be strong, to not give in to emotion, worked the previous day. What she had feared and dreaded had occurred. Somehow, even though she knew worse was to come, this feeling of deadly inevitability gave her courage she hadn't found before. She did not say a single word to Amir about what had happened, for where would she begin? Instead she smiled valiantly, she urged him to take second helpings of the bhindi bhaji and the rajma she had prepared, she enquired after his day, she pretended to listen. And it worked. She hadn't realised it would be so easy to fool her husband into believing she was okay when she was actually in pieces.

Although she was adept at keeping secrets — growing up in a large family meant you had to be shrewd at carving

128

out a private space, keeping some things to yourself — when it came to emotions, Sapna had not learned to dissemble, to say everything was fine when it was not. There had never been any need, and even if she *had* tried, someone in her family was guaranteed to see right through her. She and her siblings had shared everything — food, love, laughter, gossip, feelings. At home her parents, brothers and sisters all said whatever they were thinking, showed any and all emotions they were experiencing — there were arguments and dramas, loud and messy, and just as quickly resolved with hugs and tears. There was always someone to offer comfort, a solution. There was always someone on your side. In her family, everyone had a role; Sapna was the 'sensitive' one, and they would all make a huge fuss of her the moment her face crumpled. Sapna had played up to this moniker until she didn't know when she was acting and when she was genuinely upset. This is why she had been so open with her emotions with Amir, showing all she felt, expecting him to comfort and coddle her like her family had done all her life. She was spoiled, she saw that now. Completely and thoroughly indulged and naive with it. That's why she had gone running to Gemma.

You are not a child anymore. You have made your choices; you are the architect of your problems. Nobody is coming to rescue you. You have to deal with them yourself.

And so, when Amir came home, she smiled until her cheeks ached with the effort, and Amir smiled back, looking relieved. He was so very tired, she saw, so thin and worn out from working. He took her in his arms, and she kissed his worry lines away. He was fond and loving. It felt almost like their first few days together, back in that cramped flat.

She opened her mouth to tell him about the baby but she lost her nerve, the words evaporating somewhere during the journey from her mind to her mouth.

'I'm sorry I have to work tomorrow,' he said just before drifting off to sleep. 'But it's too late to cancel, palm off my shift to someone else. I promise I won't work next weekend and we can go out, into town, do some shopping, get the curtains finally, what do you say?'

'Yes,' she replied. 'I would like that.' In her heart she wondered what would happen between now and then, whether she would be allowed this stab at a normal life, what with the man from her past very much present and bent upon letting her know it.

She woke late, having lain awake into the early hours, gnawing on the worry she had tried to hide from Amir. Her husband had already left for work. She peered through the chink in the newspapers covering the bedroom window, saw Gemma at her window and stepped back, although she knew Gemma couldn't see her, mortified afresh by her behaviour of the previous day. From now on, the old Sapna was dead, she resolved anew. She would never behave like that again — weak, tearful, dependent on others, disturbing their privacy, infringing upon their hard-earned free time. She had finally uncovered the secret to being an adult — pretending to be okay even though you weren't.

An urgent knock on the door. Just like the day before. A series of knocks increasing in intensity, like the ones she inflicted on Gemma's door after the phone call the previous day.

It must be him. Her heart seizes up in dread.

CHAPTER 26

Sapna

Now, thanks to her cooking, the house smells of fried onions and roasted cinnamon, warm and welcoming. The knocking on the door goes on. And on.

She is aware of the irony as she feels anything but warm or welcoming — for she will be opening the door to her past once again, the past she ran away from. He is not going to go away, and she is all alone in this country, no brothers to protect her, nobody coming to the rescue. Amir doesn't know about her past, and she can't bear to tell him, so he can't help. And in any case, he's not here. Sapna has no choice but to make good her resolve, to deal with her problems on her own, face him herself. She will do so bravely, reason with him. And she will keep the door wide open at all times, so anyone walking past, Gemma or Edith looking out their windows, can see and take note, bear witness, so he won't be able to try anything. Taking a deep, bolstering breath, she pushes the stifling dread firmly away, and flings open the door, one hand behind her back trying to undo the knot on her apron.

She finds herself staring at a bouquet of bright scarlet roses, her favourite.

'Amir?' She's confused. Her terror is pushed down by incomprehension. Did he forget his key? Why has he decided to surprise her in the middle of the day with flowers? He has never bought her flowers — they can't afford them. But perhaps after their reconciliation last night — that's what it felt like — he's making an effort.

But then the bouquet moves and Sapna is staring at features she has tried so hard to forget.

'Sapna,' he says softly. 'Have you missed me?'

He is across the threshold before she can protest or shut the door on him, so close that she can smell his breath, warm, sour, and she is back again, in the lane behind Sumitranna's house, hemmed in by mossy walls. She is back in the jacaranda copse, the taste of flowers and fear.

She had expected him, had tried to ready herself for him to be at the door and yet . . . *nothing* can prepare her for the horrible reality. He is here. Intruding into her new life, which she chose at great cost in her desperation to escape him. She thought she had succeeded.

She staggers back. Please let it be a nightmare. In a moment she will wake in Amir's arms and everything will be fine.

And then he is upon her, right there in the doorway, kissing her cheeks, her eyes, saying, 'Oh Sapna, my beautiful Sapna, how I have missed you.' The scent of roses is suffocating, choking the breath from her.

This can't be happening. But it is. It *is*.

With all her might she pushes him away, one hand protectively spanning her stomach. 'Please, I'm married.'

That stops him, thank God.

He takes in her turquoise silk salwar dotted with shimmering sequins, the apron she's wearing over it, and then, closing the front door behind him for all the world as if it is his own, he sets the bouquet down on the carpet, sinks to the floor right there in the hallway, cradles his head in his hands and sobs. 'Oh Sapna, what shall we do?'

The 'we' scares her more than anything. She cannot believe this. What she and her mother have dreaded is happening. She wants nothing more than to push him out, shut the door, extricate herself from this nightmare. But she can't. He is too big, too strong for her. And it won't stop him even if she might succeed this time. For she knows exactly what he is capable of, what he can and will do.

This big man is crying in her hallway like a toddler having a tantrum. She hopes curtains are twitching in Gemma's house. That Gemma is watching. That Edith is. That they will come to the rescue. But the door is closed — they can't see inside. And he's blocking the door.

Please let them come anyway, knock right at this moment, needing something, wanting a chat. Please.

All her resolve to be strong, to rely on herself alone, evaporates and is replaced by terror. Sapna knows better than anyone that he might cry like a child but he can also hurt, plunder, destroy like a monster.

How will she come out of this unscathed? Can she? He is blocking her escape, is settled squat against the door. The house phone is in the living room. Her mobile is in her purse in the kitchen. Too far away for her to retrieve either without him noticing. Why didn't she bring it with her when she came to open the door? Why didn't she *think*? Because, until now, everyone else has always done the thinking for her.

She wants her husband. *Amir, please come. Rescue me.*

Why did she open the door, invite the past right back into her life, giving it free rein to invade the present, sully the future she — futilely, she sees now — hoped she would create without him? But she had no choice. For he would have kept on knocking, phoning, stalking, until she gave in.

She massages her belly where her baby grows. *I must protect you.*

And somehow this thought pierces through her panic. This precious, vulnerable little miracle is reliant on her. And just as, the previous day, when she spoke to her mother, she tried for light-heartedness, injecting false brightness into her voice knowing her mother needed it, now, knowing her child, this tiny collection of cells, is dependent on her for protection, gives her strength she did not know she possessed, calms her hysteria.

The worst has happened. She will deal with it. She will protect her child.

'Why are you here, Sanjay? How did you get here?'

He looks up at her, tears glistening on those long eye-lashes she once admired. He looks like a lost child, that same look that persuaded her eight-year-old self to befriend him, thus irrevocably sealing her fate.

He stands, crowding her, still blocking the doorway.

'Turn around,' he says.

'No. You have no right to order me around,' she says, her voice a weak cowering thing even as she pushes the words out, her heart thudding desperately in her chest.

She sees his eyes darken dangerously at her insolence.

Please. Don't hurt my baby.

His hand whips out and she flinches. He smirks, grip-ping her shoulder, swivelling her around as easily as if she is made of paper, so she is facing away from him.

She circles her arms protectively around her stomach. *Amir, Edith, Gemma, please come now. Please.*

Hot breaths, very close, lifting the hair off the nape of her neck, raising goosebumps of panicked terror. She fights his grasp, struggles to escape it, but he is too strong. With the hand not holding her in place, he undoes the knot on her apron, his touch surprisingly gentle. The apron crumples to the floor, a yellow and pink heap beside the bouquet of red roses.

Soiled. Violated. That's how she feels.

He steps away slightly and she breathes again, inhaling the acrid scent of burning spices. Oh no, she's ruined dinner. Why is she thinking this now? When the life she thought she could salvage is shattering apart. Who knows what will happen between now and dinner . . .

He must have smelled burning too. 'Cooking for hubby, are we?' he mocks, his voice taking on that same sing-song tone she remembers and loathes and fears.

She wants to cower, scream, sob.

She will not give him the satisfaction of seeing how terrified she is.

'Yes,' she says, standing up straight, facing him. Her voice, thankfully, does not reveal that she is quaking inside.

Lord Ganapathy, help me! How will I get him out?

'I need to go and switch off . . .' she begins.

His eyes blaze, his grip on her hand tightens, nails digging into her skin, and her mind flashes to the bruise he inflicted that took six weeks to fade. 'Stop being like this. *We* are meant to be together, you and I. Don't you want to get out of this bind we find ourselves in? Let me figure this out.'

'Sanjay . . .' Now she can't stop her voice from quivering like a leaf in a storm.

'Can't you run away? Come with me today. Now. Come on.' He tugs at her arm.

How does one counter madness? What does one do?

He misinterprets her hesitation. 'I have money, don't worry.' His voice has taken on the mocking note again. He looks around the hallway and peers into the living room. 'We may not be able to afford a house as big as this at first, but when there is love, does anything else matter?'

'Sanjay,' she says, stalling for time to come up with a plan, her voice somehow steady again, 'how did you find me?'

'Oh, that.' He smiles. 'You make all sorts of interesting friends in prison. This man, he knows your husband's friend, the one you were renting from before.' An exaggerated wink. 'He got me your new address and phone number.'

He grins, and she sees the madman superimposed upon the old Sanjay — the boy who was once her friend.

She takes a deep breath. She doesn't know if this is the exact wrong thing to do. But what she does know is that it needs to be said. She should have said it ages ago, when he first stamped his possessiveness, his jealousy upon her skin. Ideally even earlier. Then, perhaps, he wouldn't be here now. 'Sanjay,' she says softly, 'I do not love you.'

His eyes widen, glitter dangerously.

Crash. His hand comes down hard on the small cabinet in the hallway. It shudders, cracks, the keys falling in a jangling heap onto the carpet. 'Stop lying to me!' he yells.

She rears back but can't move. He's still gripping her arm roughly, and she's trapped between him and the wall. 'I'm not lying,' she manages.

'Is it money you want? A house of your own? I will get it. I promise. Anything you want. Just come with me.' Tears in his eyes, even as his spittle flecks her face with each vehement word.

'I don't love you.'

She is backed up against the wall and he is upon her, pressing close. 'Don't you dare say that, don't you dare.' Hot breath sour in her face. Granite eyes flashing. He leans in close, kisses her neck. She fights him, tries to free herself from his clutches. 'Don't you dare,' he murmurs into her ear, his voice thick. 'You are mine and mine alone.'

'No,' she whispers. 'I'm married to Amir.' And then the secret . . . Cradling her belly, she looks into his eyes, the eyes of the man she has dreaded for so very long, the face that harangues her nightmares. 'I'm pregnant.'

He shoves her, hard. She almost falls but, scrabbling around wildly, she grasps the wall and regains her balance. 'Get out,' she says, her voice shaking. 'Go, Sanjay, get out.'

And he does. To her utter surprise he does.

'I will be back,' he seethes at her as he goes. 'And I will destroy you. And all this . . . all these materialistic things that you value so much. I will make you hurt just as much as I am hurting. I'll make sure you know how it feels.' And then he spits. The frothy yellow goo misses her by inches, landing with a splat on the carpet by her feet. He laughs mirthlessly and says, with one last, venom-filled glance, 'Whore.'

CHAPTER 27

Edith

Edith is making her way to the kitchen to put the kettle on when she sees a strange man carrying a bouquet of red roses knocking on the front door of Number 2 — Sapna's house. The name had come to her in bed and Edith had drifted off to sleep smiling. There was life in her old bones after all, her memory was not a goner yet.

Well, about time they received a visitor, she thinks. It's Sunday, after all. But come to think of it, didn't she see the thug of a husband leave this morning at the usual time? Well, it's none of her business, of course.

It's a glorious spring morning. The sun, having recharged its batteries all winter, is showing off. Golden rays, deliciously warm, snake into the kitchen, making the top of the cabinets shimmer and glow. Outside, her unruly grass is still wet from last night's showers. Birds twitter and a magpie lands hopefully in the garden, fooled by the glittering raindrops.

One for sorrow, two for joy, Edith thinks. *Where's the other one? Come on, Mr Magpie, where's your mate?*

The solitary magpie hops around and, after pecking away at the blades, flies away.

Ah well, sorrow it is. At her age, what else can she expect?

She's crossing back to her armchair with her mug of tea and two triangles of the shortbread she baked this morning, when the front door of Number 2 is opened and Edith sees the man gather Sapna in his arms, kissing her cheeks, her eyes.

Oh dear, it doesn't look brotherly at all, and it *is* rather intimate for a friendly peck . . .

She looks across and sees Gemma's curtains twitch. Did Gemma see the man kiss Sapna, she wonders.

The door to Sapna's house closes and almost ten minutes later — Edith has been keeping tabs — the man exits. But he doesn't leave immediately, no. He stops in front of Edith's house, right in her line of sight, and watches Sapna's house, a speculative look on his handsomely rugged face. She seems to attract these thuggish-looking men, that slip of a girl. What is the man thinking, Edith wonders. He appears lost in introspection, his hands stuffed into his pockets, rocking on his feet as he stares at Sapna's door as if it holds all the answers. Are those tears shining in his eyes? Is he Sapna's lover? Beautiful women always attract trouble, Edith muses.

She thinks of how Sapna had looked, sitting opposite her, in this very room, the couple of times she came to tea. So agitated. So lost. Her husband must be abusing her. She is entitled to a lover. But, if Edith's instincts are anything to go by, this man doesn't look like he'll take care of her either.

Stop getting worked up, she chides herself. *This is not your problem.*

Yet, the girl arouses a protective instinct in Edith.

Nobody, other than yourself, has your best interests at heart, my dear, she tells Sapna silently in her head. *Certainly not these men who appear drawn to you. The sooner you learn this, the better.*

138

CHAPTER 28

Gemma

After Sapna leaves, Gemma sleeps through Saturday afternoon and wakes as shadows steal the sun and stain the gardens
a frisky grey. She stands for a long time at Theo's window
looking into Sapna's garden. She sees nothing. She misses
Theo with an ache that manifests itself as leaking breasts.

Then she goes to sleep again. Curiously she doesn't miss
Rob at all.

In the morning she wakes with a start, her mouth dry.
It takes a while for her thudding heart to settle, the vague,
unqualified unease to pass. She goes to the landing and
watches Sapna's house. All seems quiet. She sees Sapna's
husband leave for work.

She feels responsible, she supposes, after the woman
came to her the previous day, so very shaken. And she is
guilty about her coolness at the end, when Sapna kept pleading for help. This is why she's keeping watch, looking out.

Once she's satisfied that everything appears fine at
Sapna's, Gemma goes back to bed. She wakes to a dull
pounding. 'I'm coming,' she calls but realises the pounding
is not at her door at all.

It is at Sapna's.

She sees the man enter with flowers. She sees him draw Sapna, wearing a pink apron over her colourful Indian dress, into his arms, kiss her like a lover. Then the door is shut.

Well, well, well, who would have thought that little dainty miss asking for help was harbouring so many secrets, almost as many as Gemma herself . . .

Gemma is aware of a tiny flicker of respect flaring inside of her.

CHAPTER 29

Sapna

When Sanjay leaves, she locks and bolts the door and slumps against it, cradling her head in her hands. She sits there for what feels like hours. Then she stands on trembling legs and blockades the front door with two of the kitchen chairs, and has a shower, scrubbing her face and body clean of Sanjay's kisses, his spittle, his repulsive touch, until her skin is red and sore. Afterwards, she rights the key cabinet in the hallway and scours the carpet where Sanjay spat. The scent of cleaning liquid mixing with the salt of her tears mingling with the smell of burnt spices makes her gag. She spends the rest of the day jumping at the slightest noise: the wind whipping against the letter-box flap, children laughing and joshing as they walk past on the main road, a coke can rattling down the pavement. Her resolution to be strong, an adult, is forgotten.

In the end, tired of being afraid, she decides to go outside for some fresh air and a short walk. But when she looks in the key cabinet for her keys — the new set Amir cut for her after she lost her first set — they aren't there.

A chill creeps up her spine, making her tremble. Where could they be? She scours the house for them. But they are gone.

She will not entertain the possibility — she will not — but it is there. In her head. Seizing her heart. Making her quake with dread.

Does *he* have them?

Amir comes home and Sapna serves him curd rice and pickle. 'I was cooking biryani and mughlai chicken but it got burnt,' she says. Tears smart her eyes but she swallows them down, smiling fiercely.

He is tired. There are dark circles under his eyes. And yet, he has never looked more handsome. She goes up to him, cups his face in her hands and kisses him.

'What was that for?' he says, his expression dreamy.

'For being you,' she says. And then, taking a breath, she floats the idea she's been formulating in her head since Sanjay's sudden, terrifying visit. 'Amir, I know you grew up here, that England is your home. But what do you say to moving to India? You wouldn't have to work so hard and . . .'

And I would be closer to my family. I would feel safer there.

Sanjay's visit has brought home to her how entirely alone she is here, when Amir is away, how vulnerable. It is just her, Amir — when he's home — and the defenceless new life growing within her. At least in India, she would have family; even though Baba has disowned her, her brothers would come to her aid. Wouldn't they? Even if not, *someone* would be there, on her side, at her side if she called. And truth be told, she is petrified by Sanjay's parting words. She wants to be far away, across the world if possible, in the bosom of family when he makes good his threat. And knowing him, he will.

He *will*.

In the long hours after Sanjay left, she considered coming clean to Amir about her past. But . . . then she would have to tell him why she married him. So, on balance, she has decided not to, for as long as she is able to get away with it.

She could go to the police, like Gemma suggested. She would have to do it without Amir's knowledge. But, even if she went behind Amir's back and told the police of her fears, what would they do? What *can* they do? She has no actual proof that Sanjay is stalking her. Perhaps Gemma and Edith saw him arrive, but he brought flowers, he kissed her. And after that he shut the door. They didn't witness the violence. They don't know what he's capable of. And in any case, if Sanjay can escape prison in India and come to England, he can surely evade the law here too?

All things considered, the best solution, she thinks, is to go home to India, where there are people to help.

Amir has stopped eating and is staring at her, completely befuddled. 'But I thought you wanted to *escape* India. Live here. You told me that your father was being irrational and you wanted to be far away from him.'

'I miss them, my family.' Her voice is wistful as she finally puts into words the ache that has been her constant companion since she left India, the desperate, desolate longing. 'I want to go home.'

Amir wrinkles his brow. 'I don't understand you, Sapna. Not at all. You said your home was with me. You wanted it. You wanted *this*.' He waves his hand around. 'We've only just settled here . . . And now you . . . I just . . .' He stares at her, the dreamy look of before quite gone, replaced by something like disgust. Loathing. 'You can't just change countries, move continents at will . . .'

She can't help it. The tears she has been holding back burst out of her, a veritable torrent. 'Please,' she manages in between sobs, 'I want to go home.'

She knows she sounds like a spoiled child crying for the moon. But she can't seem to stop. All the fear from the near miss of this afternoon comes flooding back. She wants to tell Amir the truth about what happened earlier today, but how, when she hasn't told him about the past? If she comes clean, then he will find out that she used him as a means to an end . . .

She is stuck. All alone. In a horrible situation. And she can't confide in her husband. This is why she wants to go home, where they know already and will help. Even if her baba shuns her, even if her brothers blame her, they will still help when she's in need. Won't they? She hopes they will. She *needs* to believe so. For if not, she's lost.

Amir sets down his cutlery on his half-finished plate with weary finality. He pushes his chair back. He doesn't come to her, comfort her, like she wants, needs him to. Instead, he turns away from her. He picks up the cardigan he discarded when he came indoors. Shrugs it on. Then he opens the front door and leaves, without another word or glance at her.

She watches him cross the road and walk away, pulling out his phone.

* * *

She stands at the window, waiting for him to come home. Finally her tears shudder to a stop, but the pain doesn't, a keening dirge within her. It's getting dark now, shadows leaching the light away. What will the shadows bring?

CHAPTER 30

Gemma

The phone rings, jolting Gemma from a dream about *him*.

She shakes her head, trying to rid her mind of him. Disorientated, she scrambles blindly for the phone, her heart thudding with alarm, with worry for her child. *Theo.* Has something happened to Theo?

The dream was so vivid. *Him.* He has no place in her new life; he should, by rights, stay firmly in the past.

But . . . how can she control her dreams? Thankfully, she doesn't sleep-talk — as far as she knows, she hasn't said his name out loud in Rob's presence. Her husband remains blissfully unaware. And she means for it to stay that way.

In any case, she hasn't dreamed of him in a long time. *That's because you haven't been sleeping long enough to dream.*

Ah. She is relieved when her fingers close around her phone.

She picks it up, her heart shrilling as loudly as the ringtone. *Please let Theo be all right.* Some part of her is convinced she'll be punished for dreaming about her past.

She fully expects to see Rob's number, hear Rob's voice, urgent, panicked, so she is unnerved when she sees *his* number, her dream manifesting before her.

She blinks, rubs her eyes.

She is not dreaming. It *is* him.

She holds the phone to her ear, heart hammering, her whole body shaking as her fantasy comes alive.

His voice. Just as familiar as always. Beloved. 'I need you.'

'I'll be right there,' she says, baby and husband forgotten in a moment. She is, once again, a young girl, head over heels in love.

CHAPTER 31

Sapna

Sapna sits in vigil by the window, wishing for her husband to return home.

Come back, Amir, please.

She should have told him the truth, come clean about her past. But she couldn't bring herself to. Like she hasn't told him about losing the second set of keys, the ones he got cut after she lost the first pair. She didn't want to see his face harden in that now familiar expression of disappointment and distaste.

And so instead she told him she wanted to go home, back to India, thought it was the lesser of two evils, and now she's lost him anyway . . .

Don't think like that. He's just taking a few moments to himself. He'll come back any minute now.

As she waits, she sees Gemma leave the house, looking smarter than she's ever seen her, in skinny jeans and a nice sweater. Her hair in a stylish updo, make-up on. A desirable woman, not a tired, sleep-deprived mum. Gemma disappears down the street in the direction Amir went just moments before.

Where is she going this time of evening? Sapna wonders, curiosity briefly piercing the carapace of hurt. It's none of her business. She thought Gemma a terrible snoop. Well, now, here she is, doing exactly what she accused Gemma of. Gemma deserves a night out; her husband is away at his mum's with their son for the weekend, Sapna recalls her saying when she visited her yesterday. Embarrassment swamps her, momentarily displacing pain, as she relives how she stole some of Gemma's precious free time with her panicking the previous day.

Sapna waits, her cup of tea going cold. And waits.

The silence in the house pulses with threat.

She goes to the loo, and while she's there, she's pretty sure she hears a noise. A door opening. The kitchen door, which emits a whine like a bleating goat.

She's imagining things, surely?

'Amir?' she calls, and her voice shakes like a sapling in a storm.

No reply.

And now, footsteps.

'Amir?'

No response.

Her teeth chattering. Her whole body shaking.

She checks with trembling fingers if the loo door is locked. It is.

And now the plaintive whine of the kitchen door again.

Someone leaving?

She thinks of Sanjay. Knocking over the cabinet in the hallway. Her missing keys, which she's sure were last in there . . .

No. No.

She waits in the loo until night arrives in earnest, creeping with blue-black fingers down the toilet walls.

She listens for noise, sound, footsteps.

But there is nothing.

Finally, finally, she unlocks the loo door and steps outside on jelly legs.

The house is quiet.

Nothing moves.

The living room is bathed in grey gloom.

Her teacup sits on the windowsill, a viscous skin of milk floating on top of the brown liquid.

And next to it are her missing keys.

Her heart stutters with dread even as she starts shaking again. The keys weren't there when she set her cup down and went to the loo, she is absolutely sure of it.

But now, here they are, drawing the eye, impossible to miss.

She stares at them until her eyes blur, picturing Sanjay having a good laugh at her expense. On trembling legs, she goes to the kitchen door. It is locked. She peers through a gap in the newspaper, at the garden. It is just the same as always, overgrown, the grass dusted with shadows. The hair at the nape of her neck stands to attention even as goosebumps erupt on her arms and her whole body prickles.

Is he out there right now, watching her watching for him?

She looks at the keys again. Are they a message? From him? *I have access to your home.*

* * *

As darkness settles, Sapna realises with a sinking heart that Amir might not return home tonight. She has never been alone here at night before. She is tempted to go to Edith — Gemma is still not back and she doesn't know any of the other residents of the houses and flats nearby. But . . .

She has already made a fool of herself with Gemma. She thought she could trust Edith, but she knows now that Gemma and Edith have been discussing her and she does not want to provide more fodder for gossip. And she has resolved to behave in a more mature way from now on, although what she just did with Amir negated all that . . .

What if Sanjay comes back today? What is she to do? She will not open the door. She will not. But what if he has keys? Was it him just now, returning her keys? Or is she going mad, imagining things, like Amir has accused her of more than once?

If it was Sanjay, why return her keys? The kitchen door was locked when she came back from the loo. How did he lock the door? Did he cut new keys and return hers?

He said he would destroy her. What will he do? These thoughts go around and around in her head until she cannot stand them anymore.

She walks into the kitchen. Amir didn't finish his dinner. He will be hungry when he comes home. She stopped cooking in the dark after she was sure someone — Sanjay — was watching her. But now . . . now her fears have been realised, the worst has happened. Her nemesis came here, he accosted her, threatened her. Cooking, doing something practical, will hopefully ease her worry, give her something to do as she waits for Amir.

She checks that the front door is double-locked and barricades it with two kitchen chairs, like she did this afternoon, taking care not to look at the spot on the carpet where Sanjay spat. She does the same with the kitchen door, using the other two chairs. Even if Sanjay has keys, he will struggle to open the doors now. She makes herself a mug of strong tea, English style, with hardly any milk, and plays the radio on its loudest setting so she won't have to listen to any knocking that may sound — if Amir returns and can't get in because of the chair barricade, he will ring the bell, she is sure, unlike Sanjay. She can still hear the doorbell if it rings. She can then peer through the window and, depending on who it is, decide whether to open the door.

She switches on the extractor fan and is grateful for the loud sound it makes, though it usually irritates her. As she cooks she sings along loudly to the radio, just in case she might hear the sound of knocking over the sound of the fan and the music blaring. If she sings, she reasons, all she will hear is the sound of her own tuneless voice.

And so, she does not hear the fire, hissing and crackling through the house. She only feels the first tendrils of unease coil up her spine when she smells the smoke, when it stings her eyes, inciting tears that are nothing to do with her bottomless, yawning pain . . .

CHAPTER 32

Sapna

Suddenly she's assaulted by a bout of coughing, abruptly aware of the thick curls of smoke crowding in from the hallway, enveloping her . . .

She rushes to switch off the hob, then realises it isn't on. The first finger of fear shivers up her spine. She wants to escape through the front door but can't enter the living room, for clouds of billowing smoke, licked with orange heat, smother her, preventing her from going further, so she rushes back into the kitchen, knocks away the chairs barricading the door and tries to open it. It's locked. Of course. She cannot for the life of her think where she put the keys — they were next to her teacup on the windowsill in the living room. Had she pocketed them? She upends her pockets. Only fluff. No keys. And then she remembers — they're still on the windowsill. She didn't want to touch them, knowing they were most likely a message from Sanjay. Oh, why didn't she pick them up? Now she can't get to them for the smoke and the flames. Is there another key to the kitchen door? She pulls drawers open haphazardly, searching desperately, even as her throat burns and fiery smoke steals her breath. She tries to

152

open the windows. They won't budge. Are they locked? Do they also need keys to open? She can't remember.

Sapna bangs on the windows, trying to make enough noise so someone will hear. She tries breaking the windows open with the biggest utensil she can find — the four-litre Prestige pressure cooker. The windows hold, not even cracking slightly. Sapna bangs the glass in the kitchen door next, using all the strength she can muster to hit at it with the pressure cooker, shouting, 'Help me, please!'

She is hot, so hot. She cannot breathe, cannot see for smoke. She hears the crackle of the flames and an agonised keening, which she realises is coming from her scorched throat. She gives up trying to break open the door and sinks against it, her hands caressing her stomach, which nurtures burgeoning life. Coughing, sobbing, pleading, praying . . .

And suddenly, it doesn't hurt anymore — nothing does. In her mind, she is far away — walking back to her childhood home along the narrow muddy path between rain-drenched fields, the green ears of paddy bending gracefully as if bowing allegiance to her, the thick curtain of monsoon rain enveloping her. She seems to have no umbrella. She must have forgotten it. But it doesn't matter.

She savours the feel of water trickling down her cheeks and pooling around her nose, the way it teases her hair out of neat plaits and plasters it in limp, wet strands around her face. She likes the sensation of being alone, invisible almost, surrounded only by a blanket of rain. Snatches of a haunting melody float up to her. She guesses it is Sumitranna, singing to his bullocks as he coaxes them to plough the last field bereft of paddy.

Her mother is sitting on the veranda with her sisters. They are chewing paan and gossiping. Tumblers of tea and a plate of freshly cooked, piping-hot potato bondas sit between them. The dog is fast asleep, mouth wide open. He is sprawled, half on her mother's lap and half on the veranda beside her. His nose twitches occasionally when a fly lands on it. Ma's eyes dart from side to side trying to pierce the sheet of rain as she nods and mumbles 'Hmmm . . .' at regular intervals to her sisters' chatter. Her mother is looking for her, Sapna realises. She walks out of the rain into Ma's dry, welcoming arms, and is enveloped by her mother's scent — the pungent yet achingly familiar smell of spices mixed with sweat, the perfume of her childhood, of security, of love.

Sapna blinks and her mother disappears in a wisp of smoke. Something is clutching her heart in an iron grip, squeezing the breath right out of her . . .

NOW

'They've caused nothing but trouble since they moved in,' we say to the detectives who come round asking questions. We're earnest, our expressions suitably grave, yet still we can't help the damning note of judgement creeping into our voices.

'They were always fighting.'

'We were warned that they would bring down the tone of the place . . .'

'Well, by *they* we mean, well . . . We're not racist, not by a long margin, if that's what you're suggesting . . .'

'Well, if you're *sure* you want us to go on . . .'

'We think he hit her,' we whisper.

'And there was her stalker,' we mutter in hushed tones.

'She used to cry at her kitchen table in the middle of the night when her husband was asleep upstairs.'

'She was covered in bruises.'

'She had strange men visit with flowers.'

'And there was the fire — terrible, that.'

'What a tragedy. Not that *this* isn't, of course, but a fire, well . . . It's so uncontained, isn't it, so wild and dangerous.' We shudder.

'We were worried our entire cul-de-sac would go up in smoke that night.'

'And now this . . . One thing after another, isn't it?'

'A real shame.'

'You can never really tell what goes on behind closed doors, can you?'

'We should have said something, done something.' We look suitably upset.

'But, well, you know how it is. We didn't want to interfere.'

'We regret it now, of course.'

'And she always assured us she was fine, that she had allergies, that she'd bumped into a cardboard box of all things!'

'We took her at face value. Wouldn't you do the same? We feel ever so bad now.'

'Hang on a minute,' the detective in charge says. 'What exactly do you think happened here?'

'Well, we assumed . . .'

'Isn't that the case?'

When we finally stop talking and listen to what the police have to say, we're flabbergasted. Dumbfounded. Lost for words.

'Well, we never,' we gasp when we catch our breath. 'We expected something like this, but not . . . No, definitely not what you've just told us . . .'

'Oh dear,' we say as the truth sinks in. 'We would never have guessed, not in a million years . . .'

PART 2

TWO MONTHS PREVIOUS

CHAPTER 33

Edith

The first Edith is aware of the fire is when she hears the sirens. She's startled awake by pulsing blue lights, keening in urgent alarm, spilling through the windows into her house. She pulls on her robe and opens the front door to eye-stinging smoke, to flaming orange heat. Fire engines spray silvery arcs of water onto the spewing smoke, the spitting embers that cloak Number 2 in an ashen fug. Then Sapna is led out on a stretcher onto the waiting ambulance. Her husband is nowhere to be seen.

Edith feels horror creep up her spine. Memories, forcibly buried, escape their internment and ambush her. For the first time she is glad her boys are not here, to witness this and relive . . . No . . .

Darkness claims her, blessed oblivion.

Edith comes to in a paramedic's arms. The gentle woman hands her a cup of tea, hot, milky, comfortingly sweet. 'This will help,' she says kindly. 'You've had quite the shock.'

Edith wraps her hands around the mug and sips, trying to push away the painfully bitter taste of the past.

'My neighbour . . . is she going to be okay?' she asks, her voice shaking, mouth tasting of smoke.

'She's in good hands, love, don't you fret. You know her well?'

'They've only recently moved in. She's so young, a slip of a thing.'

'Drink up now and go to bed. The fire's under control, so you're not to worry. Try and get some sleep.'

Edith lies in bed, hers alone now, shuts her eyes tight, and plugs her ears with her hands like a little child, hoping that by this small action she can contain and resist the images that bombard her. Images from the past and from just now. And yet, they come all the same.

She does not sleep.

CHAPTER 34

Gemma

'He's back,' Rob says. 'I saw him just now as I was coming home.'

'Who?' Gemma asks.

'The neighbour.' Rob's head jerking towards next door — Number 2.

Gemma's hands still, holding her cutlery in mid-air. She gives up all pretence of eating, nausea churning in her stomach. Not that she's had any desire for food, or anything else for that matter, recently.

She looks up at Rob. He's forking mash into his mouth, unconcerned.

For him, this is just a drama removed from him. An interesting piece of gossip.

'I spoke to him,' Rob says.

Her stomach somersaults. She sets her cutlery down, pushes her plate away.

'Not hungry?' Rob asks.

She shakes her head. 'What did he say, then?' Her voice doesn't tremble. It's only mildly curious. Thank God.

'The police questioned him and let him go. He was at the Holiday Inn that night — argument with the wife — the staff were able to confirm as much. He's been staying there these last few days while the house was being checked to make sure it's safe for him to move back in again.' Rob pauses to shove another forkful of sausage and mash into his mouth.

Gemma takes a sip of water to ease her agitated stomach. It doesn't help.

'He gave a fair impression of a distraught hubby but . . .' Rob chews thoughtfully, in no hurry to finish the sentence.

'But?' Gemma nudges after a beat, unable to bear it.

'I think he did it,' Rob says, once he's swallowed his huge mouthful.

'*What?*' Now Gemma can't keep the shock from her voice.

'At the very least he's hiding something, that's the impression I get,' Rob says.

'You're a detective now?' Gemma says, her voice cold. She can't seem to modulate her voice to sound normal. What's normal? How should she sound? She doesn't know. She's lost all objectivity.

'All I'm saying is, his alibi has holes.'

'Listen to yourself, Rob. You've been watching too much crime on Netflix,' Gemma snaps. Too harsh. *Get a grip.* But no matter how many times she's told herself this, she hasn't been able to, not really, since that terrible weekend. It's been a huge struggle to carry on as normal. It's a wonder Rob hasn't picked up on it.

'That night . . .' Rob is saying between mouthfuls, completely oblivious as ever, thank goodness . . . 'he could just as easily have slipped out after checking in to the hotel and driven here, started the fire and driven back.'

'I'm sure the police would have thought of that and checked it out,' Gemma says carefully. She takes a breath to settle her racing heart. Where is Theo when you want him to wake up and create a distraction? 'And in any case, wasn't it an accident? I didn't notice any strange vehicles. There was nothing suspicious at all, except for the fire, of course. The police did ask. Anyway, he doesn't own a car, does he?'

'I wouldn't know. Good job you called 999 when you did, love.'

'I was awake — habit I suppose, from waking with Theo — and I smelled the smoke.' The lies come easily now, although something inside her dies every time.

'My wife to the rescue even off-duty.' Rob smiles fondly at her.

I don't deserve it.

'You caught it just in time,' Rob says. 'Just imagine if it had spread here . . . We have insurance, but the personal stuff, you know . . .'

'That's not the point.' Orange flames cavorting merrily. The acrid scent of burning dreams. Strobes of blue from flashing fire engines. Keening sirens. Silver arcs of water dousing the hungry blaze. Firemen bringing out a stretcher . . .

Gemma shivers.

'I know.' Rob reaches across and gently pats her hand. 'But because of you, their house is mostly intact. They hadn't got round to buying furniture and furnishings,' he said, 'so there's not much fire damage. Shame about his wife, of course.'

'Yes, poor dear.' Her voice remains even — no hint of the turmoil within her. How is she so adept at saying things people want to hear? Skilfully playing the roles expected of her: the wife Rob expects; the capable, life-saving nurse applauded by the police; caring mum to Theo; neighbour and fellow gossip to Edith; and to Sapna and Amir . . . She shrinks away from the thought.

Rob is tucking into his sausages. Gemma shudders, the sight of the meat turning her stomach even further.

'Anyway, the man . . . What was his name again? Ah yes, Amir,' Rob is saying. 'He said he's ever so grateful to you.'

She swallows, although her mouth is dry. 'To *me?*' Her voice sounds hoarse.

'For calling 999. He's been out of his mind, he said.' Rob pauses in the act of bringing his sausage-speared fork to his mouth, a thoughtful frown on his face. 'He *sounded* upset. Although he might be faking, of course.'

'*You* sound like you don't like him much,' Gemma says carefully.

'I don't know . . . He was overegging it, I thought, and, well . . . There's just something about him that's not quite right . . . Just a feeling . . .'

Gemma manages a passable snort of laughter. 'Since when did you get *feelings*?'

Rob grins, mouth full of half-chewed sausage, waving his knife at her. A blob of gravy falls onto the tablecloth, congealing in a gloopy mess. 'I've a feeling about you, my love.' He winks suggestively.

'Theo'll be awake in a minute, Rob,' she says and he sighs, turning his attention back to his plate. 'What else did he say, then, the neighbour?' she asks, trying to sound casual.

'He was very interested in the man with flowers that you saw and told the police about. Said the police are on the lookout for him.'

'Good luck to them. He seemed unhinged, I thought. I told the police so. And I also told them about what — who — I saw lurking in their garden. Although on the night of the fire I didn't see anyone.' How she manages to keep her voice light, she doesn't know.

'Strange people, these new neighbours,' says Rob, setting the cutlery down, his plate clean. 'Makes me almost wish for surly Mr Shaw.'

'They keep themselves to themselves mostly.' She hasn't told Rob about Sapna knocking on the door, frantic, on the Saturday afternoon. She didn't tell the police either. That interview had been excruciating, but, thankfully, they didn't seem very interested either in her or the information she volunteered, having already made up their minds, she assumed, about it being an accident.

'Yes, I suppose so. Just as long as there are no more fires or anything else that might damage our property,' Rob says.

'Touch wood.' Gemma pats the table, just as the baby monitor beside her transmits Theo's wails. She's never been more grateful to hear her little boy's urgent demands for attention.

CHAPTER 35

Sapna

She's so very tired. She aches all over. She wants her mother. It's quiet — a strange humming quiet punctuated by beeps. Where is she?

Voices. Familiar. Particularly one — the one she's been longing for.

'Ma . . .' she tries, but her tongue is heavy and will not do her bidding.

'Sapna.' Her mother's voice: close, saying her name like a prayer. 'We are here in England, janu. Your baba, brothers and I.'

Baba? Does that mean he has forgiven me?

* * *

'How could you? How dare you?' her beloved baba's face contorted with rage when Sapna told him she wanted to wed Amir. 'Disrespecting your elders by choosing your own groom, a Muslim too of all people!'

'Amir is not religious. He is Muslim in name only.'

'That's even worse. He has no integrity.'

'But he . . . he's from a good family, Baba!'

'Where's his family, then? They should be coming to speak to me — not that I'd give permission for any child of mine to marry outside our caste, let alone a Muslim.'

'Baba, his parents are dead. He's not a practising Muslim. But he's a good man.'

'And you know this how? If your marriage was being arranged by us, through the proper channels, we would have done all the vetting, checked his credentials, his character. It is *not* up to you to choose. As your father, I must decide what's best for you, the man you will marry. I don't know this man — he's hardly been in the village a week and you've fallen in love?'

Love. Her father spitting the word.

'That's not how we do things in our household. You'll bring shame and dishonour to our family if you persist with this foolhardy mission.'

'But . . .'

'This man . . . this Muslim . . . how do I know what he is, who he is, whether he can provide for you when he lives so far away? I want for my daughters men who will be able to look after them, men I know, whom I have vetted. If you insist on marrying this man — not only a stranger from a different country, but to make matters worse, one from a different religion — you are dead to me.'

I have no choice, Baba. I really don't. Amir is the lesser of two evils. She can't say it, so she keeps quiet, incensing her baba further.

'You have made up your mind, I see. You are intent on dragging our name through the mud. Well, I have made up mine.' Turning away from her. 'You are dead to me.'

Baba . . .

* * *

'Your sisters, nephews and nieces send their love.' The familiar vowels, the lilting cadence of her mother's voice. So

166

longed for. So comforting. 'They wanted to come. But you know how it is. Shilpa's girls have exams, Sunita's baby's due any minute. They wanted me to tell you that they miss you very much.'

Is she dreaming? Has her yearning for her mother conjured her up? Or dare she believe that her mother really is here, with Sapna's brothers and her baba too? But how?

She tries to open her eyes, but lacks the energy to do so. She's so intensely, incredibly weary. It's easier to leave them closed and allow her mother's whispered assurances and endearments to soothe her, like they used to do when she was ill as a child, massaging her hair, singing soothing lullabies until her feverish body eased into sleep . . .

CHAPTER 36

Edith

Edith presses the button for her stop and stands slowly, joints creaking, her body swaying as the bus trundles down the road. She needs to get ready nice and early so she is standing by the door when the bus comes to a standstill — she takes an age getting off and some of these young drivers get terribly impatient.

'Excuse me,' she says to the Asian man sitting beside her. A young man, around the age of her Jamie, perhaps.

He stands, smiling at her, displaying a crooked mouthful of yellow teeth. He looks familiar somehow, something about him speaking to her, asking her to take notice. She can't quite put her finger on it.

'I am getting off here too,' he says, his accent hesitant, a soft, slow drawl like Sapna's.

Sapna. That poor girl. In hospital. Edith would bet a thousand pounds it was the husband who caused the fire and put her in there. She watched him stride briskly away on Sunday evening, merely half an hour after he had arrived home, but he must have sneaked back later. The police think it was an accident, that's what Gemma told Edith. *What do they know?* she huffs to herself.

Edith knows it was the husband. She's sure of it. She was going to tell the police, but they didn't question her. If they had, she'd have told them a thing or two about the thug. But they'd only talked to Gemma because she was the one who called 999. Edith has toyed with the notion of going to the police station to report the husband, several times. Even just now, when she was in town, she walked to the station although it was in the opposite direction to the market, hovered outside it. But in the end, she lost her nerve. For she has nothing but suspicions, her intuition telling her the man had something to do with it. No concrete proof.

And now he's back next door, as if nothing happened. The brazen lout!

The bus judders to a stop and as she tries to manoeuvre her shopper, the boy who was sitting next to her says, 'Allow me, please.'

He gets off first, carrying her shopper in one hand as if it's a balloon filled with air, and holds out his other hand to her.

She waves it away. 'I might look ancient to you, but I can manage.'

He grins, displaying that crowded jumble of teeth again. 'You *are* quite sprightly for your age.'

'Cheeky boy.' She laughs. 'Thank you, though,' she adds as she takes her shopper from him. 'I did need help with this. I always go overboard in town — bargains, you know. Can't resist.'

As they talk, the boy is joined by two others, one of them quite young, and an older couple Edith assumes are their parents. A short, squat man and a slender woman, wearing a flowing turquoise dress like the ones Sapna favours, dotted with sequins that glitter seductively in the sunshine, a matching scarf covering her head and framing her face.

Once again Edith thinks of Sapna, crying in Edith's lounge because a man in the shop had been rude to her. *I only wore the shawl around my head because I was cold.*

169

Sapna, that's who this family reminds her of. In fact, the woman looks almost exactly like her, that same haunting beauty coupled with ethereal elegance. Could they be . . . ?

Any doubts Edith might have had are dispelled as the group turn into the cul-de-sac in front of her.

It *is* Sapna's family. She hopes they take that man, Sapna's good-for-nothing husband, to task. How can he live in that house knowing what he did to his wife?

Edith fumbles in her bag trying — not very hard — to locate the key to her house as from the corner of her eye she watches the little group of people knock on the door of the house where Sapna almost met her demise. And who knows, if the fire had spread, perhaps Edith herself and even Gemma and her family — dear little Theo, imagine! She shivers. And yet, this horrid man, the culprit Edith is sure, is allowed back into Number 2. The injustice of it terribly upsets her.

She has watched Sapna's husband like a hawk since he returned after the fire. He appears thinner than he was when they first moved in, scruffier definitely, his face unshaven, features etched with a permanent scowl. But he's got away scot-free, whereas poor Sapna . . .

She wants to talk to the family, now she knows who they are, ask them how Sapna is doing, when she will be discharged from hospital. She wonders if they're here to take Sapna back to India with them — that would be for the best, given Edith's suspicions about her husband, but even so, she will miss the girl. In the short time she's known her, Edith has begun to care for her.

She recalls Sapna telling her, 'I am all alone here. All the people we know are in Hounslow and, in any case, they are friends of my husband . . .'

On that fateful Sunday, Edith heard the fight through the adjoining wall and watched Sapna's husband storm away. She kept an eye out from her living room, not concentrating on the telly, leaving the curtains open a little, but he didn't return, and when her eyelids started drooping, she finally gave up and went to bed. She briefly considered calling in

170

on Sapna but left it, thinking she'd go in the morning at a decent time. Since the fire, she's wished over and over that she had gone with her instincts, checked on the girl, talked to her . . .

She finds her key just as the front door of Number 2 is flung open and Sapna's husband appears, stumbling back a little when he sees the group gathered on his threshold.

Edith drops her key and makes a show of picking it up as she waits to see what will happen out of the corner of her eye.

The short, balding man shouts something rapidly in a language Edith doesn't understand.

'I don't speak Urdu. Or Hindi for that matter. Your words are wasted on me,' the thug says in English, putting his hands up, palms facing outward as if in surrender.

'See, not even a proper Muslim.' The disdain is clear in the father's voice as he speaks in English, the words halting but loud, spitting fire. 'If only I had chosen a husband for my daughter, none of this would have happened.'

True, thinks Edith.

'Listen,' Sapna's husband says, 'you wouldn't even be aware that your daughter was in hospital if I hadn't called you to let you know . . .'

'*You* put her there.' The man steps forward and jabs Sapna's husband on the chest. 'First you spirit my daughter away after a week — a week! — of courting her, bringing shame to my family, and then you almost kill my beloved child.'

'Baba.' The boys try and hold their father back but he's having none of it.

'Beloved child, ha!' Sapna's husband mocks. 'You said she was dead to you when she married me. How dare you come here now and accuse me of hurting her?' He's shouting now. 'I didn't hurt your daughter. I rescued her. *She* has hurt *me*. I was such a cuckold. I loved her while she was just using me.'

'What do you mean?' the father yells.

Yes, what on earth does the thug mean? Edith wonders. Interesting how he's turning it around, making it Sapna's fault. The horrid man.

She notices as she muses that Sapna's mother has gone very pale, one hand hovering over her heart.

Edith knows that she can't stand at her door all day, blatantly eavesdropping on the drama next door. Sooner or later someone will notice. As quietly as possible, she lets herself inside her house and then pulls the door closed, not fully though, just enough so she can watch the proceedings through a gap in the door, grateful that their houses are angled in such a way that she has a direct view, and even more grateful that, while her body has succumbed to the relentless wear and tear of old age, her hearing and eyesight are sharp as ever.

She looks at the little group gathered next door, shouting their business for all the street to hear — come to think of it, nobody would blame her for eavesdropping, they're practically asking for it by doing this in public. Couldn't the thug have invited his wife's family inside? Although, Edith wouldn't have heard anything then.

'She married me to escape the fix she got into with that man, didn't she?' Sapna's husband is saying.

'What man?' The father looks apoplectic, as if he will explode any minute. He takes a step forward but the thug stands his ground.

The boy who helped Edith with her shopper lays a warning hand on his father's shoulder but the father violently shrugs it off. 'What man!' he yells again, his words thundering in the evening quiet, startling the cooing pigeons and flustering the gently twittering sparrows nestled in the hedge. Over at Gemma's, Edith notices the curtains twitch. Gemma has taken up her post at the upstairs landing.

'The man who visited the afternoon of the fire. He brought roses!' Sapna's husband spits. Now his voice is rising far above the polite monotones he reserves for the general public to the angry, uncontrolled cadence Edith has heard reverberating through the walls.

'A man brought her roses?' Sapna's father's voice falters.

'Oh . . .' Sapna's mother moans. The brothers exchange glances. It's obvious to Edith that the mother and brothers

172

know more than they're letting on, while the father is completely in the dark.

'I'm convinced it was his baby she was carrying and not mine at all.'

At this, Sapna's father steps forward so quickly that Edith recoils, his hands around Sapna's husband's throat. She watches Gemma push aside the curtains, her shocked face appearing at the window, having given up all pretence of hiding. She's holding her phone in one hand. She must be calling the police.

A baby? Sapna was pregnant? This is news to Edith. It makes her ache. Especially as what the thug said sinks in: *was* carrying. Oh dear. Oh no. With trembling fingers, she roots around in her cardigan for a tissue, and when she finally locates it, she wipes her leaking eyes, blows her nose. So much unnecessary loss . . .

'What did you say? How dare you!' Sapna's father is screaming, even as he chokes Sapna's husband.

Sapna's husband does not flinch, not in the man's suffocating grasp, not when the boys pull their father back, not while the mother stands quietly, tears running down her face.

'I said that your daughter married me to escape her troubles, her unsuitable boyfriend who got her pregnant. *I* was unsuitable in your eyes, but *he* must be even more so. Or perhaps she just tired of him. It explains a lot. Why she made a play for me the moment I set eyes on her, the foreigner who would take her safely away, out of the country, why she was so unhappy here, why whatever I did was never enough, why she didn't tell me she was pregnant, why she was always pining for home . . . Perhaps she tired of him, perhaps he didn't want the baby and she thought she could trick me into being the father. Perhaps, once she was here, she missed him and wanted to run away with him, who knows?'

'How dare you!' the father shouts again, struggling in his sons' arms. 'How dare you!'

Edith cannot believe it. This is worse than *EastEnders* or *Coronation Street*. If this was a busier street, there would be gawpers all the way up and down the road.

'You must have done this to our girl, then, when you found out about this man,' the father yells. 'Or perhaps you did it for dowry. You knew we had disowned her and you thought it was not good enough. This house, it must require a lot of rent. You wanted her to pay her way. You must have pressured her to ask us, and when she refused, you decided to burn her.'

'How could you even think that? I'm not some heartless creature . . .' The thug's voice stumbles. 'I don't even believe in that antiquated system, for God's sake. How can you think I'd do that to her? I married her because I *love* her.' And now his voice breaks.

To give him credit, he does sound like he means it, Edith thinks. Framed in her window, she sees Gemma's hand at her heart, clutching the necklace she's never without. She looks dreadfully wan. Theo must have kept her up all night.

'When did you come here, by the way?' Sapna's husband is belligerent now as he addresses her father. 'You weren't home when I called to tell you about Sapna. Only your wife was. You and or one of your boys might have been here earlier for all I know. You might have been here all along. Perhaps you did this. Because she brought dishonour to your family name. You said she was dead to you when she married me. But when you found out about her other man, perhaps that was one step too far. You couldn't allow her to drag your name through the mud again . . .'

'What are you talking about? What is this nonsense you are speaking?' Sapna's father cries.

'Honour killing. You started the fire to prevent your honour from being tainted further,' Sapna's husband persists.

Does he have a death wish? Edith wonders. Sapna's father looks incandescent with rage — it takes all three of the youngsters to hold him back, Lord knows what he'd do to Sapna's husband . . .

'The police said it was an accident,' one of the brothers says.

Both Sapna's father and husband ignore him.

'I do not know about any other man,' Sapna's father spits. 'My daughter was good, meek and dutiful, until you came along and turned her mind. You are just inventing this man to—'

'I am not. He was here, ask anyone. Ask the neighbours . . .'

Edith steps back from the door just in case they turn round and see her avidly watching. She notes that Gemma is doing the same.

'. . . because he made a scene in the doorway like you're doing now, bringing flowers for my wife, kissing her in public . . .' Thankfully Sapna's family are too caught up to even glance towards either Edith's house or Gemma's.

How does this man know all this? Who told him about the other man? Edith wonders.

'My daughter is not—'

'I thought you said she was dead to you. Is that all over, then? Is she back in your fold again? Have you come to take her back once she's out of hospital?'

'I will not take her back. How can I when she is married to you? She is no longer ours to claim but yours to look after and cherish, which is where you have failed like I knew you would. If only she had let me choose a proper man for her—'

'Why are you here? To insult me? To blame me? I'll tell you one more time: I did not hurt a hair on your daughter's head.'

Lies, Edith thinks. *I've heard you shout at her. I'm beginning to believe you about the fire. You might not have done anything to harm her physically, but you have scarred her emotionally.*

'I love her. But she . . .' His voice shakes. He gulps. 'She used me and betrayed me . . .'

'No, son, she . . .' the woman speaks at last, her voice halting as she scrabbles for the English words.

But she doesn't get a chance for Sapna's father intervenes. 'I am warning you. If anything happens to her again, if she is hurt again, once she comes home to you, I will personally break every bone in your—'

175

'So you've come here first to accuse me and then to threaten me? Go away, I don't . . .'

His words are drowned out by sirens splicing the air and once again they are heading for Edith's street, their no longer quiet and peaceful cul-de-sac. They come to a stop in front of Sapna's house and two police officers get out.

'I cannot believe it. You called the police?' the father blusters.

'When did I have the time? I've been standing right here talking to you,' Sapna's husband retorts as the police officers approach.

'Now, what's going on here?' one of them says.

There's a moment of silence before both men start talking at once.

Looking across, Edith sees Gemma's curtain fall back in place, hiding her ashen face . . .

CHAPTER 37

Sapna

A humming sound punctured by beeps, strangely soothing. The cheerful voice of the day nurse. It must be morning. She should open her eyes, stop hiding behind a facade of sleep. But she doesn't want to. Because if she does, that means she has to face the real world, where the choices she's made have come back to bite her. And she's not ready to, not yet . . .

She knows she must, sooner rather than later. She cannot stay in this limbo, eschewing reality for ever. But it is tempting. And why not? She wants to get away with it for as long as she can. Pretend she's a child with no responsibilities, her mother's voice speaking to her tenderly, soothing her, doctors taking care of her. Here she feels safe.

Amir visits every single day, sitting by her side, holding her hand, telling her he loves her, apologising over and over again for leaving her alone that night. 'I'll never forgive myself, Sapna. I'm so sorry.'

She is too tired to process what she feels, too weary to do anything but acknowledge his obvious, palpable remorse.

And then he says, 'I love you, even if you don't love me back.'

What does he mean by that?

As if he has heard her unasked question, he says, very softly, hurt threading through his voice, 'I know about the man who brought you flowers.'

She shivers, hearing Sanjay's threat in her head: *I will destroy you.*

There's something she needs to know, but is afraid to ask. She tries to push the thought of it away, but it is there, always, a dull throbbing ache.

She thinks instead of her mother. She will be here soon, talking to her, telling her stories about her childhood, tales comforting in their familiarity, not like the memories that threaten to consume her, memories she has tried so hard to suppress. Her mother, in her determinedly cheery voice, will regale Sapna with stories of the home where she spent her first eighteen years. Bringing it back to this sterile room where she lies, hiding from the shambles she has made of her life. She waits for her mother, and before the bad memories claim her again, she relives a good one.

She is newly arrived in England, a shy bride, just getting to know her husband. *Her husband.* She is still getting used to the term. Amir takes her to Kew Gardens. They go by train, blessedly uncrowded and clean — so unlike the trains in India. Sapna sits by the window, looking out on people's back gardens — a trampoline, broken net flapping in the wind; an abandoned sandpit, weeds pushing through the soggy sand; a shiny new fence surrounding a tired-looking garden, scrubby grass, a pile of bricks, an awning bent out of shape. A woman is pegging washing out to dry, even though the sunlight is weak and patchy, without promise. The houses sit close together, roofs sloping towards each other as if sharing secrets. She spies a wall tattooed by graffiti, bold squiggles painted in myriad colours transforming the plain wall into something special, and is charmed and awed. It is a work of art, she thinks. It wouldn't look out of place in a museum. The English make even their graffiti look good, she muses. They pass by a cemetery, neat paths and an odd bench or two bisecting rows of graves, dotted with newly budding trees, their branches like arms waving at her to come on in and give them some company. Bunches of flowers adorn some of the graves, spots of colour among the drab, mournful grey. She thinks she spots a rabbit, floppy ears, a flash of smoky fur, gone before she can point it out to Amir. She smiles up at this man, this stranger, her husband. He smiles back, that eager, endearing smile. He's a nice man, she thinks. She's lucky, like her ma whispered, holding her close one last time, as they said goodbye: 'Count your blessings. You've married a good, kind man and are starting a new life with him, far away. A clean slate. Think of the positives. Be happy, my janu.'

Thoughts of home crowd in and she pushes them back down. No, she is not going to let homesickness ruin this day.

Amir and Sapna alight at Kew and walk into the gardens. It's a lovely spring morning, crisp, the sun playing hide-and-seek with the trees, staining the branches gold, the air fragrant with the fresh, hopeful scent of burgeoning life. The gardens are like paradise after the dull greyness outside — so many trees, such bursts of colour, the foliage reminding her of the woods at home, rife with snakes and other dangers. She feels cold and pulls her coat tighter around her. She doesn't want to go into the tropical house for fear the longing for home will overwhelm her. She sticks to the paths.

After they've wandered for a bit, Amir says, 'Let's have a picnic.' He lays the blanket on a patch of grass underneath a copse of trees, and from his rucksack takes out cartons of apple juice, a baguette, hummus — which she tasted for the first time two days ago and loved so much, so thoughtful of him to bring it along — spiced chicken wings and violet grapes the exact shade of the bougainvillaea climbing up the wall of the nuns' convent . . . *Don't think of home*. He arranges them in that methodical way he has. The rucksack must have been so heavy, she thinks, and yet he lugged it without complaint so they could have a feast of all her favourite things. He squats upon the blanket, looks up at her, standing diffidently on the path, smiles. 'Come on,' he says.

She knows better than to sit on the grass next to a bunch of trees with mossy, fern-riddled holes in their trunks, you never know what poisonous creature they might house. 'But snakes . . .' she begins.

He laughs, eyes crinkling. 'No snakes here.'

'Really?'

When he gets that particular twinkle in his eyes, they change colour, look more orange than brown. 'Really.'

She runs to him, squats beside him on the blanket, daringly leaning against a holey tree trunk. She smiles up at the man she is married to, his face soft with laughter, his eyes puckered in delight, and realises that she is beginning to like him. Very much.

After they moved to the house in the cul-de-sac, they lost their way, Sapna realises. Amir always working; Sapna bored and lonely, missing home, feeling stalked, the spectre of Sanjay looming.

But now, here, she has time to think and she sees how Amir has tried to make Sapna feel loved, to ease her transition into this new country in his own way. His working all hours has been so she can have a big house with a garden, and when she hasn't appreciated it, he's taken it personally.

When Amir visits next, Sapna resolves to squeeze his hand when he holds hers. They've both made mistakes but he's her husband and he's trying. She will tell him that the man visiting with flowers is not someone she cares for — far from it, in fact.

I will destroy you. She shivers, as much from recalling Sanjay's threat as from a thought that has just occurred to her. How does Amir know about Sanjay?

A beep. Two. A series of beeps, ricocheting into one long keen, bring her back to the room. Voices, urgent, getting closer, rushing past. The slap of feet hitting linoleum. 'Code Blue, Room 211, Code Blue,' she hears. Something's happened next door. Someone's dying.

His face distorted, ugly with rage: 'I will destroy you.'

The thing she's dreading looms. She tries to push it away.

I don't want to know.

If she doesn't know, there's possibility, there's hope.

A leer, a mirthless cackle: 'I will destroy you.'

Anger, hot as the fumes rising from dry chillies being pounded to a paste, consumes her.

No, you haven't managed to destroy me. Not yet.

I hate you, Sanjay. I hate you just as much as I loved you, once.

CHAPTER 38

Gemma

Rob reaches for Gemma in the night but she pretends to be asleep. Later, after feeding Theo, when she slips back into bed, he tries again.

'I'm tired,' she says, pushing him away. How can she be intimate with him when everything is weighing on her mind? And if he knew what she has done — please, no — would he still want to touch her, make love to her?

She was hoping he'd be asleep. She stood in Theo's room for a long time after her little boy fell asleep, watching Sapna's house, Amir standing in the garden and smoking while wiping away tears.

'You've not been yourself these past few days. What's bugging you? Theo's sleeping better. What's the matter?' Rob's tone is gentle enough.

'Nothing's the matter. I'm just tired. All those sleepless nights catching up with me.'

'I thought that's what that weekend was for. What did you spend it doing, then?' He's trying to be light-hearted but she can tell that he's serious. He wants to know, has sensed something is amiss.

She tries not to shudder. *Not now, Rob. You've always been so easy-going and accepting of me. Don't start suspecting me now.* 'One weekend isn't enough to catch up on months of sleep deprivation.' She manages to keep her own voice light.

'Why don't you sleep during the day while Theo's asleep?'

'Not that easy. He doesn't sleep for long.'

'He's been sleeping better.' Rob says again.

'Yes but . . .'

Rob leans close to her, his peppermint breath fanning her face. 'What were you *really* doing that weekend? I know you went out. You gave your good top to the dry cleaners; I saw it when I picked up my suits.'

Even Rob, kind, unsuspecting Rob, has his limits. 'I must have forgotten to collect it after wearing it to Bev's fortieth.' Her voice is steady enough although she's shaking inside.

'I asked to see the receipt. You handed it in on the Monday after the weekend on your own.'

'You're checking up on me now?' She hopes he interprets the tremor in her voice as anger and not fear, its high pitch as righteous upset and not guilty defensiveness.

'You're hiding something.'

Yes, I am. And it's been eating away at me. That's why I've lost weight. I can't eat. I can't sleep. I can't look you in the eye. I'm just about holding myself together.

'That's not an excuse, Rob. I really don't appreciate you checking up on me, going behind my back and asking the dry cleaners for a receipt for Christ's sake! What happened to trust?' She manages to inject outrage into her voice, hoping turning the tables on him will dissuade him from probing further.

She can't live with herself, with what she has done. And now . . . Rob . . . *I've pushed him to this. Turned this simple, trusting man into a suspicious, jealous spouse.*

'Yes,' Rob leers. 'Go on, you tell me. What happened to trust?'

'I don't have time for your haranguing questions, your jealous interrogation. I want to sleep.' Her voice is intentionally sharp, even as she chastises herself for being unfair. Rob is not the jealous sort. Usually. But these are not usual times.

Rob moves away from her, all his bluster gone. He sounds resigned. 'I'm not stupid, you know.'

She had hoped Rob would be, as ever, his happily oblivious self. But, like he pointed out, he's not stupid.

Rob, you and Theo are the best parts of me. You bring out the best in me, unlike . . .

I like the woman I see reflected in your eyes, although I'm undeserving of it.

But now you've seen through me to the darkness I keep hidden. I'd hoped what was within me wouldn't infect you and Theo, but it was inevitable, I see now. The venom in me befouls everything it touches, poisons all that is precious. Beautiful. Pure.

'You're still pining after him, aren't you? Did you go to see him that Sunday?' Rob asks, and his voice is very soft, thick with pain, saturated with hurt.

She's glad of the dark so he can't see her face. 'What are you talking about?'

Her heart bangs against her ribcage so loud she thinks it will burst right out of it.

'I know there was someone else before me — the love of your life. You married me on the rebound.'

Oh, the naked hurt in his voice.

'Rob . . .' All this time, she'd thought Rob *didn't* know. She'd hoped to keep the two parts of her life apart, neatly contained. *Fool.*

'I . . . I thought my love would be enough to make you forget him, bring you round to loving me like I do you. Apparently not . . .'

Her heart cleaves, shatters at the raw pain in his voice.

Her husband. Father of her child. Hurting from the wounds she has inflicted, selfishly following the heart that she thought she'd schooled into forgetting, moving on.

All it took was one call from *him* and . . . she'd thoughtlessly tossed aside everything she'd built, the life she'd carved for herself.

And for what? She has made things worse, ruined *everything*.
If what she has done gets out . . .

No.

It won't.

Please.

Will her marriage survive what she has done?

Why should it? her conscience asks. *You didn't care about your marriage when you were . . .*

Please.

Rob and Theo — she can't lose them. They are the *good* in her life. They make her better than she is. 'Rob, I . . .'

He is suddenly upon her, so close that she has to do everything in her power not to flinch, duck, move away. For the first time, she is afraid of her big but until now always gentle and kind husband.

His eyes flash amber sparks. 'Don't lie to me. Please don't.' And just like that, all the anger goes out of him, leaving only hurt, his words hollow with it. 'At least allow me the courtesy of that much.'

'Rob, I . . .'

'You still love him. And I think you saw him that weekend.'

Her mouth dry, no words coming out.

Rob stands, takes his pillow and leaves the room.

She lies on the double bed and stares at the ceiling until it undulates into fuzz, her throat thick and eyes harsh with pain and regret.

CHAPTER 39

Sapna

Sapna has heard what she was dreading. One of the doctors standing at her bed, discussing her, 'the patient', dispassionately with another, telling him casually about the smoke inhalation injury, the miscarried foetus . . .

Sapna saw a baby bird fall out of its nest from among the branches of the banyan tree once. The tree was hopelessly high and it fell on a rock, fluttering its wings weakly. She was rooted to the spot with horror, hot moisture prickling her eyes, her fingers crossed, willing for its chest to rise. It lay there, beak partly open, eyes wide, unseeing, chest stubbornly still. She watched the mother hop beside it, peck at it with its beak, trying to make it move. And she felt an ache, thick and glutinous like tar, permeating every cell of her body. She felt like that now.

Out of nowhere, a memory.

It is night time, a few days after she has met Amir and decided to marry him, although she hasn't gathered the courage to tell her father yet. She is sitting on the veranda. Crickets chirp busily and mosquitoes buzz. Night jasmine infuses the air with its heady scent. From the kitchen drift spicy aromas of the supper they've just had: tangy fish fry and boiled red rice. Snatches of voices from neighbouring houses waft in the evening breeze. Soorya stumbles home through the fields singing drunkenly. Inside the house, she can hear the low rumble of her baba's voice as he coaxes Sapna's littlest brother to finish his supper — always a fussy eater, he has suddenly declared that he doesn't like onions in his food. She listens to her baba patiently convincing him and tears sting her eyes.

Dusk is falling, the sky a warm golden pink. The crickets are singing, frogs croaking. On the far side of the hill a flickering light jumps, playing hide-and-seek with the shadows. Someone navigating the treacherous path between the fields with a torch. The first of the glow worms arrive, a series of pearly golden lights turning on and off, dancing to a tune only they know.

Sapna's mother comes out onto the veranda and sits herself down next to Sapna, sighing with exhaustion and relief as yet another day with its chores and its travails comes to an end. She slips her hand through Sapna's and together they watch the darkened world that Sapna will soon be leaving behind. Her mother knows, of course. In fact, this was partly her mother's idea.

'There's a man just arrived from the UK, a Muslim but non-practising, so I've heard. He lost both of his parents in a car accident a few years ago — they were from here and so he's come to get in touch with his roots. I think that shows a sensitive, kind nature. Those who've met him say the same, that he's gentle and modest. He's at a loose end and will be grateful if a kind soul offers to show him around,' Sapna's mother says, a few days after Sapna came to her in tears, confessing what she's done, everything she's done.

Her mother is upset but non-judgemental. Sighing, crying, but taking Sapna's side. Always on Sapna's side. 'I thought of Sanjay as one of our boys. I felt for him, poor lost soul, derided and unwelcome everywhere because of his family problems, and, ignoring your baba's caution, I invited him into our home and our lives. I overlooked the fact that of all of my girls, you were the most like me, a bleeding heart and champion of the underdog. I saw you get close to him — he was so caring and gentle with you, but I thought it was a sibling relationship. *Just* that.' Her mother sobs.

'I'm sorry, Ma,' she cries.

'I am too, child. A mother is not supposed to have favourites, but you were always mine from the moment you entered this world, smiling, I swear.' Cupping Sapna's face with her hands, looking at her as if she's learning her daughter's features by heart, committing them to memory. Knowing what is to come — the fracture of their family unit, Sapna on the outside, shunned, ostracised because of her actions — but not telling her. Sparing her the agony, the worry of it for a little longer.

Sapna will hoard this precious confidence from her ma in her heart, cherishing it, using it as a talisman in the horrific days that follow, when her father will denounce her and she leaves home in disgrace. The gift of her mother's words.

You were mine, child, Sapna laments now, mourning the babe she's lost. *My secret. My love. My favourite. My only. And now, I have lost you.*

Did Sapna lose her child because when she first suspected she might be pregnant she wished with all her heart that she wasn't? She was worried, scared and every day she wished for blood, for the child that had implanted itself in her womb to be washed away.

No, her fate — ending up here like this, losing the child she had grown to love so fiercely — was irrevocably determined when she crossed paths with Sanjay. That was when the trajectory of her life changed . . .

She thinks back to the first time she met Sanjay, then a shy gangly boy, her oldest brother's friend.

He had come home for lunch, her brother having warned all of them not to ask Sanjay any questions about his family. 'His father ran away with another woman. His mother managed to get by selling fish and cleaning houses.

188

But now she is ill and I suspect he hasn't eaten in days. Keep topping up his plate, Ma,' Sapna's brother had said.

Sapna noted how her brother's friend's eyes would not meet any of theirs; how he tried to hide the holes in his shirt by strategically placing tatty notebooks over them; how, despite his torn clothes, his fingernails were clean, his hair was combed and slicked back, and his face was washed; how he tried not to eat too much or too fast although he was obviously hungry. Her heart went out to him.

'You are the kindest of my children. The one with the softest heart,' her mother would say often.

At the end of the meal, Sapna's mother supplied Sanjay with a huge tiffin box of food and the healing potion she made with herbs that she swore worked like magic on all ailments. 'For your mother. My boy tells me she's unwell.'

His eyes welled up then, and although he tried very hard not to — Sapna saw him swallow once and then again — his voice trembled. 'I don't think she will be getting better, Aunty.'

Sanjay became a fixture in their house after that, especially when his mother died. He attended Sapna's sisters' weddings. It was almost as if he was another of her parents' children.

He was so good with Sapna's littlest brother, more patient than Sapna's own brothers, greatly understanding of his tantrums. Sanjay fixed anything at Sapna's home that needed fixing and was always so polite and gentle with Sapna's mother. He won over all of their hearts, even Baba's.

As for Sapna . . .

Sapna started off feeling sorry for him. She was kind to him, doing little things for him. He would call her 'little bird', tease her, but not as badly as her brothers, who never knew when to stop. But Sanjay would gauge exactly when her laughter at her brothers' banter was at the point of tumbling into tears and he would ask her brothers to stop.

She cannot quite pinpoint when her friendship with her brothers' friend became something more, something different. Perhaps when he started bumping into her at school, independent of her brothers. Perhaps when he started walking her home?

Or perhaps it was that time he convinced her to come swimming with him and she went, even though she knew she shouldn't — he was only an honorary brother after all. Sanjay rescued her when she thought she was drowning, and the thrill that travelled through her when his hands clasped her wet body was distinctly unbrotherly. His eyes darkening, the look in them that she knew was mirrored in hers . . .

It was then that she started doodling his name in her books, crossing it out thoroughly after, so her secret crush wasn't discovered. She ached to see him, and when his hands accidentally brushed hers, she felt that thrill again. She knew it was wrong — a good and dutiful girl should not have feelings such as these for a boy before marriage, she should save them for the man her parents would choose for her to wed — but she also did not know how to stop it . . .

Sapna and Sanjay never openly acknowledged it to each other, but it was there between them. An electric charge. That thrumming, secret knowledge that their relationship had changed, crossed a line. She cannot pinpoint when *he* changed, becoming jealous, possessive . . .

Sapna tries to shut out the images, but they come regardless, assaulting her mind, weakened by the loss of her child . . .

'Who is he? Tell me! Why were you flashing your teeth at him, huh?' Sanjay's nails dig into the soft flesh of her upper arm as he pushes her against the tumbledown wall of Sumitranna's compound, the mossy bricks in danger of collapsing.

'Let me go, Sanjay,' she hisses, a bit too loud, hoping *someone* will hear and come to the rescue — why oh why did she take the shortcut through the alleyway behind Sumitranna's house? It is always deserted at this time of day; Sumitranna is with the other men working in the fields and the women are at the market or in their kitchens. Sumitranna's compound is sprawling, and behind this wall there are only fruit trees,

190

swaying gently in the sultry breeze, mango and guava and cashew and banana, whose fruit she and Sanjay steal whenever they have the opportunity.

'Not until you tell me who he is.' His breath on her face, smelling of onions. His face, too close, contorted in rage, teeth bared. She cannot find in these monstrous features the boy who carried her gently over the stream when it was flooded during the monsoons, the boy with whom she has shared her lunch every single day.

'You followed me here!' she snaps. 'How many times have I told you not to do that?'

His fingers dig deeper, his grip becomes harder, vice-like. There will be a bruise, she knows, and he will grin harshly upon seeing it, like he did the last time he imagined she had smiled at some boy, flirted with him. 'Something to remember me by,' he will say.

The passion for Sanjay that had blossomed briefly has been crushed ruthlessly by his jealousy, its innocent radiance doused by his possessive rage. He follows her everywhere, keeping tabs, misconstruing her every action, punishing her for imagined slights. 'You are mine,' he says. It is a threat and a warning. 'Only mine.'

She knows that if she tells on him to her brothers, they will set him right. But . . . Sapna is ashamed to do so. 'You led me on,' Sanjay says often. 'You fostered these feelings I have. You are mine. You have stolen my heart.'

Her brothers would warn Sanjay not to mess with their sister, but Sapna would go down in their estimation. While supporting Sapna, they would assume their sister was at fault. She's seen them callously diss other girls who've been in similar situations. It is never the boy's fault, whatever his actions, however violent. It is always the girl who is blamed. Always.

Nevertheless, losing respect with her brothers or not, she has been tempted to go to them several times, but each time, as if sensing she's reached breaking point, Sanjay has performed an about-face, done something kind, taken her by surprise, revealed the boy she cares for behind the jealous, possessive, cruel mask. And then she dithers. When all is said and done, she reasons, this is *Sanjay*. The boy she grew up with. Although sometimes he scares her, she can handle him . . .

Now, hot tears seep from Sapna's closed lids onto the pillow as she strokes her stomach, bereft of child.

I can handle him, she told herself, until that terrible day in the jacaranda copse . . .

And then it was far too late.

'Tell me what he means to you!' Sanjay hissed, cornering her as she walked back home from the shops, the sun relentlessly beating down on her head, but not as much as this man who had once been her friend — and briefly, her crush — was battering her very soul.

He twisted her arm, and it felt like it was being wrenched from its socket. She let out a little whimper of pain. He grinned.

It was mid-afternoon, the sun at its zenith, the road deserted. Ma had started making mango pickle and realised she was out of mustard oil and so she had dispatched Sapna to Nagappa's store. As Sapna was putting the oil into her bag, she had dropped her purse and the shopkeeper's boy — at least five years her junior, only just a teenager — had kindly picked it up, handed it to her. She'd smiled her thanks, and this was what she assumed had set Sanjay off. She'd hoped he wasn't following her — that he was safely taking shade at this time of day like everyone else — but even as she did, she'd known it was futile. She was momentarily startled by his grip on her arm as she walked home but not surprised.

'Nothing,' she whispered. 'He doesn't mean anything to me.' How many times had they been through this before? It had to stop.

And then, suddenly and without warning, he was upon her, pressing his face against hers, grinding his mouth on hers. She tried to push him away but that only made him more insistent, his tongue pushing open her lips, sliding inside her mouth, a slimy, probing presence. He tasted of garlic and vinegar, making her want to gag. This had not happened before. Ever. He had always stopped short of this.

192

She was suffocating. She was . . . And then his hand, the one not twisting her arm, was on her breast, kneading it violently, and his finger had found her nipple, was twisting it.

With all her strength, she pushed him away, the bottle inside the bag she was carrying connecting with his leg.

He yelped, jumping back, loosening his grasp of her. It was enough. She ran, as fast as she could, down the road, into the fields.

She could hear him behind her, panting, calling, 'Please, Sapna, stop. Why are you running away? Don't you see? We're meant for each other. Please, Sapna, all I do is out of love for you.'

This was the next stage after he hurt her, the remorse, the apologies, the tears. She would feel sorry for him then, recalling the lost child who'd found refuge with her family, the boy who could be gentle, kind, so very loving. And she would forgive him, despite the bruises, the hurt he'd inflicted upon her.

Not anymore. Not after this. This time he had gone too far.

She was at the jacaranda copse, beside the stream, after which was the field that adjoined her house, when he caught up with her.

Again his iron grip on her arms, pinning her. He pushed her against one of the jacaranda trees. His body upon hers. Hard. Insistent. His eyes dangerously dark with something she couldn't name as they bored into hers.

She was trapped. No way to escape. Nobody about.

She had been scared of him before but now . . . she was petrified. Before this she has been able to recognise at least something of the Sanjay she had loved in the monster tormenting her.

Not now.

'Stop this, Sanjay. Let me go,' she managed to say. 'Please, Sanjay, please stop.'

'Sapna, can't you see how you make me feel?' His voice thick. 'Don't you realise just how much I love you?'

His hand under her churidar, groping.

'No, what are you—'

His other hand clamping her mouth shut; her screams as he violated her, hurt her, abused her, swallowed by its uncompromising clasp.

When the nightmare was finally over, his grip on her loosening, she had sunk her teeth as far as they would go into the flesh that had prevented her pain from being voiced and then she ran all the way home, gathering her torn churidar to her, retching on her sobs which tasted of him — fetid, rank, rotten.

And then she was in her mother's arms, her mother smelling of sweat and fried onions, pushing her hair out of her eyes, crying, 'What happened, Sapna tell me what happened?' in that soft voice she used to hide her panic, and Sapna managed to choke out between sobs, 'Make it stop, Ma, make it stop, I don't want to see him ever again.'

Her mother spoke to Sapna's brothers, asking them to make sure Sanjay paid for what he had done, but to please take care that their father did not hear a word of any of it.

Her brothers never looked Sapna in the eye again. They too, like everyone else except Ma, blamed her. This was why she had held off from telling them about Sanjay before now. For them, like for everyone else, it was, as it had always been and would likely always be, the woman's fault. She must have led Sanjay on somehow, they were thinking, she knew. She missed the easy banter she used to share with them, but in their eyes, she was now the worst kind of woman, not their innocent, beloved sister anymore.

But . . . her brothers kept their promise to her mother and they managed to get Sanjay arrested. They had friends among the police. Just as much as they had supported Sanjay before, they now made sure he was punished for what he had done to their sister.

And as for Sapna . . . She married Amir to escape Sanjay, thinking England was far enough away from his clutches. She did so at great cost, breaking ties with her family. But she did not, could not, tell Amir about her past, worried that he would blame her too, that he wouldn't be able to look her in the eye, just like her brothers.

She ran away, but she could not escape. For Sanjay had managed to get out of prison — ironically, thanks to Sapna's brothers' friendship, he too moved in the same circles and he too knew people who could be bought. Sanjay found Sapna. He came all the way here to hound her.

And yet, even after he voiced his threat she could not bring herself to tell Amir.

And now her baby is gone.

She thinks back to Sanjay's last, fateful visit.

'Get out!' she had yelled.

And surprisingly, he had obeyed.

Why? Is it because he was already planning the fire? His words: *I will destroy you.*

Meekly leaving her because he knew that the next time, he wouldn't bother with words, he'd just ignite the flames that would consume her as completely as his words didn't . . .

But would Sanjay, who professes to love her, try to *kill* her?

Or does someone else have it in for her?

CHAPTER 40

Sapna

On her last night in hospital, exactly a week since the fire and being rushed here by ambulance, Sapna dreams of her father.

Her mother has sat in vigil by her bedside every day and so has Amir, despite believing that she's cheating on him with Sanjay. But, even though Baba and her brothers travelled to England with Ma, they are yet to visit her. She takes it to mean that she is not forgiven.

In her dream, her beloved baba is pointing a finger at her and yelling, 'You're nothing but trouble. Not only have you brought dishonour to the family, now you're heaping more upon it . . .'

She wakes up sobbing, her face and pillow wet with tears. She washes them away, plasters a smile on her face when her mother comes to visit.

'We're going back home, janu . . .'

Her mother's nickname for her, janu, *my life*, almost cracks Sapna's resolve.

But she does not cry. She has shed enough tears. She's going to be strong from now on. She's going to behave like the adult she is and not the immature child who is wailing from within her: *Take me home with you, Ma.*

'Your baba says your place is with your husband.' She cups Sapna's face in her hands, tears falling down her face unchecked like mangoes during the monsoon storms. 'I . . . I wish . . .' Ma takes a shuddering breath. Then, she says, her voice firmer, 'You are strong, janu, stronger than you know. And Amir . . . he seems nice. He is good to you, isn't he?'

She thinks of Amir, how he had walked away that evening when she needed him the most. How scared she was — he *knew* she was afraid to be alone in the house after dark and yet he went anyway. She waited and waited and he did not come back.

She thinks of his face distorted by anger. How unrecognisable it becomes.

She thinks of how he has come into hospital every day from work, smelling of outdoors and tiredness and remorse, sitting beside her, holding her hand, apologising for being short with her, for leaving her alone that night, telling her he loves her, even though he believes she doesn't love him back.

She looks right into her mother's eyes. 'Yes,' she says. 'Yes, he is.'

'I spoke to your baba and he said you can call, keep in touch with me,' Ma says.

'Will he . . . will he speak to me?' She hates herself for the tremor in her voice.

Her mother does not meet her eye, fiddling with her shawl instead. And that is Sapna's answer right there.

'Maybe one day, janu,' her mother says, finally.

For her father, Sapna is still the disgraced daughter who went against the family code by choosing her own spouse, a Muslim. Sapna is still dead to him.

Her father and brothers came here out of loyalty and love for her mother — they did not want Sapna's mother to travel alone, when they were unsure of the situation here. They did not visit Sapna in the hospital. She has brought dishonour to the family, and now they have had to use up their meagre savings in order to book flights here and back. *You're*

197

nothing but trouble! her father shouts in her ears, her dream vivid and alive.

'Take care, janu. You are loved,' her mother whispers, her breath smelling of saunf, sweet in Sapna's ear, her tender kisses anointing her cheeks, her forehead.

Then her mother is gone and she is alone. In a few minutes her husband — the man she married to escape her fate, the man she tricked — will come to pick her up and take her home. The home from which he walked away that fateful night. The home where she lost her child. The home which has never been home to her . . .

CHAPTER 41

Sapna

Before Amir arrives to take her home from hospital, Sapna comes to terms with the undeniable truth: this is her life now. She cannot hanker after her childhood home; her father has made it clear she is not welcome back. Sapna has chosen Amir, she needs to make the best of her decision.

While they are waiting for the doctor to sign her off, she says to her husband, 'The man with the flowers . . .'

Amir looks at her and she notes the pain in her husband's eyes. He has lived, these past few days, with the knowledge that she loves someone else and it has hurt him terribly, she sees. And that is when she knows, without a doubt, that Amir loves her, that he cares for her, that there is hope for them yet, if they learn to trust each other and to be honest with each other.

'I don't love him,' she says.

And now the pain in her husband's eyes is pushed aside by a flicker of hope.

She takes a deep breath. And then she tells Amir the whole sorry truth.

Even after Sanjay turned up on her doorstep and issued his threat, she had been afraid to come clean to Amir about her past, worried that he too, like her brothers, would blame Sapna, would assume she was at fault, that she had somehow provoked Sanjay's actions. She had also not wanted Amir to know that she had married him primarily to escape her fate — her childhood friend turned stalker and abuser.

But now . . . her baby is gone. She is broken. And this man, her husband, deserves the truth.

'Did you ever love me?' he asks afterwards, his eyes stark with sorrow and hurt.

'I have grown to love you,' she says.

It is the truth and it isn't. She has grown to care for him, but there have been times in their very short marriage when she has loathed him too.

'I have grown to love you,' she repeats. And if it is not quite the truth, she is determined to make it so.

'Was the child mine?' Amir asks.

The child. Her baby. Was, not is. How can nothingness hurt so very much?

'I don't know,' she finally whispers in answer to Amir's question. It is the truth. She doesn't know if the baby had been Sanjay's or Amir's. All she does know is that she misses her child with her all; she wants her baby. She had loved it so very, very much — she hadn't known how much until it was too late.

Amir comes and sits next to her. Very gently, he cups her face, kisses the tears she doesn't even know she is shedding.

NOW

'Do you know anything about the baby she was carrying?' the detectives query, looking grave.

We nod sagely, we appear suitably upset, we sniff discreetly and blow our noses with the tissues they kindly offer. 'She lost it,' we say. 'In the fire.'

'We are looking into that fire again,' the detectives say. 'It was ruled an accident but there were a couple of things that didn't add up.'

'Oh?' We exchange intrigued, shocked, surprised — guilty? — glances. 'What things?'

'Sorry. We're not at liberty to say.' They don't appear sorry at all. 'So,' they prompt, after a bit, 'the baby?'

'We told you,' we sigh. 'She lost it in the fire.'

'She was pregnant when the assault and death occurred,' they say.

'Oh?' Again, we look at each other. Shocked. Aghast.

We shake our heads. All these years we've lived here and nothing like this has happened. Nothing has even come close.

In our heads we're thinking, *They moved in and brought trouble and disrepute with them.* 'A travesty,' we say, hugging our children close, holding on to our loved ones as if whatever has happened is catching. 'What an absolute tragedy.'

PART 3

ONE WEEK PREVIOUS

CHAPTER 42

Edith

They are fighting next door. Again.

Sapna returned home from hospital six weeks ago, a pale facsimile of her earlier self. Edith went round with her carrot cake and lemon squares when the thug was at work and Sapna thanked her with a wan but genuine smile. 'Just what I felt like. Thank you, Edith,' she said in her heartfelt way and Edith felt warmed, even as her heart went out for the girl and all she'd been through.

For the first couple of weeks after Sapna came back, all was quiet and peaceful next door.

And then, predictably, it started up again. Shouting. Arguments. Anger and pain tossed back and forth, reverberating through the thin walls.

Edith sits in her house with her hands to her ears to shut them out. But she can't shut out the memories. The feelings that the raised voices and harsh words thundering through the wall evoke.

When her husband died, she thought they had died with him. But all it takes is the faint echo of a voice raised in anger for everything to come back, savage and wounding. Inside she is, still, the perpetually scared girl she always was. She sees herself in Sapna. Sapna, who came back from hospital sallow and lifeless, and yet somehow grown up. What she had experienced was etched in new lines upon her beautiful face. Her eyes had aged decades in mere days, and were now haunted and carried the indelible imprint of loss.

Edith knows how she feels. She's been there. The baby she lost when she 'fell' down the stairs. The one she is convinced was a girl. The daughter she never had.

Ambulances had come in the night then too. She too had been carried away on a stretcher, the white sheet covering her rapidly turning red, her boys standing at the window, three small, pyjama-clad, shivering bodies; three little faces, pale and anxious.

Edith hears them fighting next door and she's angry. The anger builds and builds within her.

She is about to storm round and ask the thug to leave his poor suffering wife alone when, as if he had heard and acknowledged her intention, he storms out, walking away briskly, without looking back, like he did that fateful night.

He has been gone a few minutes and Edith is wondering if she should go round to Sapna with the apple crumble she made that morning — the girl could do with fattening up — when she spies that other man, the strange man who came the afternoon of the fire.

Edith has been keeping an eye out for him. There's something not quite right with him — nothing she can put her finger on, but Edith has learned to trust her instincts, and where the men around Sapna are concerned, her instincts ring sharp caution. Edith hasn't seen this man since the afternoon of the fire. He hasn't been near Number 2, Edith is sure, in the six weeks since Sapna has been home.

But now, here he is, carrying flowers again, roses once more, the pale-pink of newborn skin. He strides jauntily, confidently, to Sapna's door and knocks loudly, bypassing the doorbell.

It occurs to Edith that he must have been keeping watch, waiting for Sapna's husband to leave home before he arrived with flowers. Her hand goes to her heart, which is drumming an urgent warning, for she knows, without a shadow of a doubt, that there will be trouble. Just like last time.

Well, not on her watch.

This man hasn't reckoned with Edith. She will not stand by and do nothing again.

Edith picks up the phone and calls the police.

CHAPTER 43

Sapna

Sapna returned from hospital six weeks ago determined to be a good wife, uncomplaining and welcoming when Amir came home from a long day at work.

He has been so kind to her, unlike her brothers and father, who have condemned her and ostracised her for what Sanjay did.

But things have not been easy since she's come home. For the first few days, she tried to ignore the unease she felt in the house.

But the house . . . It creeps her out. With each passing day her fear and her loathing of it has intensified.

'I'd like to move away,' she told Amir her third week back. 'Do we have to stay here?'

'The landlord has been kind, not holding us to account for the fire or asking us to pay compensation, allowing us back in . . .'

'It wasn't our fault.'

He didn't meet her gaze and she saw that he assumed that she had caused the fire, even though the police ruled it an accident. Why was he so quick to decide she was at fault?

'It *wasn't* me.' Her voice rose in anger and frustration. Why didn't he believe her?

'In any case, the lease is for six months and if we move we'll lose the deposit.' Amir sighed.

There was nothing she could say to that. They couldn't afford to lose the deposit. They were barely getting by as it was, especially since Amir hadn't been able to work his shifts during her first few days in hospital, when her condition was critical.

But she cannot relax in this house that claimed her child. Amir is stressed about the rent. He is, once again, working all hours, and those rare few minutes when he is at home, he's preoccupied. She waits up for him, even though evenings alone in this house spook her, and when he does come home, it annoys her that he's not fully there. During her first couple of weeks, fresh from the resolve she made while in hospital, she tried to contain her resentment and upset and they'd had a good fortnight free of argument. But with each passing day since, it's been harder to maintain a smiling front when inside she's seething. It's inevitable, then, that she and Amir are arguing again, all the time, even more than before, all her resolutions scattered to the wind.

It *is* this house driving a wedge into their relationship, pushing them apart. She knows Amir thinks her feelings about the house are irrational, nonsensical. But she's convinced there's something malevolent here, poisoning them, driving them away from each other, making them unhappy.

And not *only* that, of course. There's also Sanjay.

'Your brothers searched high and low for him but it's as if he's disappeared into thin air,' her mother told her at the hospital, trying but failing to keep the worry from her voice.

Wherever he is, Sapna knows he's biding his time. But, she has decided, she will not live in fear of him. He has destroyed her life, changed it irrevocably twice now. Once in the jacaranda copse — she was so near home and yet she might as well have been on the moon — and once here in this very house, taking from her her most precious gift, her child. The police might say it was an accident. She knows differently. She also knows that it's not over, that he will come for her. And when he does, she'll be ready. He will not destroy her again.

Lately she has begun to feel watched. Again.

The previous evening she heard something in the garden, saw a shadow move, and it has been playing on her mind ever since.

She could ask Gemma if she has noticed anything, but her next-door neighbour hasn't been round to visit since Sapna got home and hasn't answered the couple of times Sapna has rung her doorbell, wanting to thank her for the flowers she sent to the hospital, and for calling 999. She saved her life. But Sapna gets the feeling that Gemma is avoiding her. She doesn't blame her. She cringes at the thought of how she behaved on the day before the fire, when, spooked by Sanjay's phone call, she had called round at Gemma's. In Gemma's shoes, she would be just as wary of opening the door to the crazy neighbour; she would keep her distance too.

Edith, on the other hand, bless her, has been round often with cake and the offer of company. But Sapna can't quite relax with her after Gemma let on that she and Edith had been gossiping about her.

* * *

'He's back,' she says to Amir when he comes home from work, weary and grumpy and in no mood to listen to her 'paranoia'. 'Sanjay is stalking me again,' she cries when he doesn't respond, her voice taut with urgent worry. *Please believe me. I'm not making this up.* 'He laid low for a few weeks but now . . .'

'Ah, Sapna, not that again,' Amir sighs. 'He came here, tried his luck. You told him you weren't interested. He left and hasn't been seen again. He must be back in India by now.'

'He's not the type to let go so easily. He came all the way here, will he give up just because I told him to leave?'

209

'The fire must have spooked him.'

'Nothing spooks him.'

Amir is impatient now. 'But you told me your brothers, who know him—'

'Knew him . . .'

'Well, knew him, then.' Amir's voice rises along with his frustration. 'The fact remains that they weren't able to find him.'

'That doesn't mean he's not around.'

'Why does everything have to be a drama with you?' Amir yells. 'You never go anywhere and yet you keep losing your keys. How many sets have you lost now? The key cutter is becoming my friend, "Hello mate, back again?" he said when I asked him to cut another set the other week.'

'What do the keys have to do with anything?' She can't help yelling too. Why doesn't he give credence to her fears? They were proved right before. They were justified.

Amir grits his teeth and closes his eyes as if conjuring up a shred of patience. 'Well, you're the one who thinks there are people coming into the house. If you didn't keep losing your keys, they wouldn't have the means to, would they?'

'I didn't say there were people in the house. I said I saw—'

'Why can't we have one quiet, peaceful evening without all these worries, theories, suspicions?'

'Why won't you believe me? Why won't you ever take me seriously?' She's screaming now.

He swings his fist hard against the wall next to her. She flinches, backs away. She can see his skin turning red where it made contact with the wall.

'Did you really think I'd raise my hand to you?' he fumes. 'Do you think so little of me?'

'Why did you do that if not to scare me?' she cries. 'And why do *you* think so little of me, pooh-poohing everything I say?'

Why doesn't he believe her when he knows what Sanjay is capable of? Why does he dismiss everything she says? How can they build a relationship when he takes her words so lightly, mocks her, dismisses her fears, as though she's making things up? Why discredit her? It *hurts*.

'I've had enough. I need some air,' he cries, and the next thing she knows, he's leaving and it's just like the evening of the fire. Amir storms off in a huff and Sapna stands at the window, watching him walk away, weaving with tiredness. Darkness encroaching, no husband, just resonating silence, seething with recriminations and Sapna sharing the horrible house with old ghosts, perpetual regrets and fresh mistakes.

And of course, just like on the day of the fire, Amir has barely left when there is an urgent pounding at the door, and even as she takes a deep breath to prepare herself and pulls it open, she knows who it will be.

CHAPTER 44

Sapna

He has brought flowers just like before.

'I'm back,' he says, smiling. 'You're looking good. I was so worried about you.'

Smiling! Worried! He really is crazy.

'How dare you?' She is shaking with rage. Her whole body, her voice aquiver with fury.

'You asked me to go away and I did. I tried to stay away, even though I was beside myself when you were in hospital.'

'Ha! You stayed away because you were afraid of what my brothers would do if they caught you.'

He ignores her, continues as if she hasn't spoken. 'I was so relieved to hear you'd recovered, although I had hoped your parents would see sense and take you home. But they left you here, with him. Your so-called husband.' His voice is thick with disdain. 'Even so, I told myself that if you were all right, I'd leave you alone. But you've been unhappy, Sapna. He isn't right for you, this man you're shackled to. He doesn't know you, care for you, like I do. If you were happy, I would have left you to your own devices, but you're sad, so I came back.' He grins, the tint of madness warping his eyes.

'And you make me happy, do you? How *dare* you show your face here after what you did?' she cries.

'What did I do?' He has the gall, the sheer bloody nerve to look puzzled.

'I don't care what the police say!' she screams, and she doesn't care if the whole neighbourhood hears. Let them. 'The fire was no accident!'

'I agree. It wasn't.' He is coolly nonchalant.

How *dare* he? 'My child died in the fire, Sanjay, do you understand?' And now, her voice breaks.

'Ah, Sapna, don't cry. I can't bear it.'

'*You* can't bear it? Listen to me, Sanjay. There is nothing between us. *Nothing*. I am married to Amir. I am not yours. I *never* was.'

He drops the flowers, covers his ears with his palms. 'Sapna, why are you saying this? How can you? We share a special bond—'

'No, Sanjay. We do not share *any* bond.' *Not now my child is dead.* 'You forced yourself upon me. You raped me. You violated me. I don't love you. I hate you.'

'Don't say that, Sapna. Please don't . . .' He rocks on his feet, his eyes shut tight.

'You're a murderer. You killed my child.'

Now his eyes fly open. 'What are you saying? Why are you lying?'

'You started the fire and I . . . I lost my baby.'

'I did *not* start the fire.' He is angry now, puffed up with self-righteous wrath. 'That woman did.'

'What . . . ?' She is nonplussed.

'The woman with your husband. They went to the hotel down the road together.'

'What woman?'

'He left you here, alone at home at night, and called her.' Sanjay spits, sounding disgusted. 'He waited around the corner and then she came.'

'No . . .' Amir, with a woman? No.

'I'm not lying!' Sanjay is indignant.

She can't process it, doesn't want to believe it. But it appears Sanjay is telling the truth. Despite what he has done, she knows him well enough to tell when he's lying and when he's not. He has a righteously angry and wronged look about him. If he had started the fire, he would have proudly owned it. She can't, *won't* think about Amir leaving her here alone at night to meet another woman . . .

'They walked to the hotel around the corner, what was it called again, Holiday something . . .'

How would Sanjay know Amir was at the Holiday Inn that night unless he's telling the truth?

'Amir checked in and then the woman went in. After a bit she came back *here*. She looked furious. She threw the cigarette she had just lit up through your letterbox . . .' Sanjay sounds upset, as if he's reliving it again.

Sapna believes him, although it sounds fantastic. A *woman* started the fire. Not Sanjay, but the woman Amir is seeing? Sapna can't get her head around it — the fact that Amir cheated on her, and that his mistress hated Sapna so much that she wanted her out of the way . . .

'What did you do?' she manages to ask, her voice trembling, a hand on her heart.

'I . . . I was shocked. I hadn't expected her to do that. I don't think *she* had either. It looked like a spur-of-the-moment thing. She was walking past your house, lighting up, and then, suddenly, as if she'd made up her mind right then and there, she walked up to your door and poked the cigarette through. And, well . . . nothing happened at first. I thought the cigarette had fizzled out. Then, whoosh! Smoke and flames . . .' Sanjay looks traumatised.

What, is she supposed to feel sorry for him? And as what Sanjay is saying sinks in, a thought occurs to her. 'I'd barricaded the door with chairs from the kitchen. They must have caught fire first.' She asks again, 'What did you do?'

And now he won't meet her eye. *Now* she knows that, whatever he says next, he's either lying or feels guilty. 'I . . . I was going to come help you . . .' No righteous tone, his voice small. 'But then I heard sirens . . .'

He cocks his ear then. Listens. 'Am I imagining it or are those sirens? Again. Heading here?'

If he expects Sapna to answer, he will be waiting a very long time. She is slumped against the door, still trying to process what he has said. The woman her husband was seeing started the fire. And this man, who was right here, watching, ran away to save his own hide while Sapna was gagging for breath, losing her — and possibly his — child.

'They *are* coming here. The bloody woman must have called the police. How dare she? *She* started the fire, she's a criminal and she's trying to frame me, I bet, now she's seen me talking to you. And the police will believe her, of course, a respectable English woman—'

'What are you on about, Sanjay? How could Amir's mistress have seen you talking to me just now? You're not making sense.'

'You believe me, don't you, about the fire? I didn't do it. But she'll tell the police I did.'

'Who?'

'The woman your husband is seeing, the one who started the fire. Your neighbour.'

CHAPTER 45

Edith

Edith watches the man run away as the sirens approach, slipping away from the cul-de-sac just as the police car turns in.

He had been engaged in intense conversation with Sapna. Edith had opened her door just a chink, trying to eavesdrop like she'd done before — well, who could blame her, she wanted to protect the girl, collect as much information as she could for the police — but they were rabbiting away in their own language. She didn't understand a word and gave up in the end, content to just keep watch and rush in to help Sapna if necessary. Edith had periodically looked across to Gemma's but all was quiet there. Ah well, she must be busy with the cherub.

The police officers — a man and a woman, the woman obviously more senior, good for her — take a statement from Sapna. She appears dead on her feet, poor love.

Even after they leave, their keening sirens just a memory, the girl stands there, slumped against the open door, scattered petals of crushed roses like discarded thoughts, a sullied dirty pink, at her feet.

Edith can't stand it anymore. The girl is in shock, small and out of place in her green dress.

She steps outside, locking her front door behind her, and goes round to Number 2. She puts her arm around the girl and she collapses into her arms. It's a strange feeling. Edith's sore hip and tired knees rise to the occasion, suddenly bearing up as she leads the girl inside, supporting Sapna's weight. She's tiny but still . . . It's like when the boys were small and needed her, and even though she was about ready to collapse, bruised and aching from the beatings Jack had inflicted on her, she still found the strength to care for them, carry them upstairs if need be, look after them, love them.

All you need to feel well again is a sense of purpose, Edith thinks. Otherwise you're defeated, old and tired. You might as well be dead.

The acrid aftertaste of smoke hovers in the musty air inside Number 2, the house bearing the scars of the abuse wreaked upon it like Edith bears the scars of Jack's abuse.

She tried to protect the boys but knows they carry them too, which is why they're scattered about the world, finding excuses not to return home for a visit with their mother.

She doesn't blame them. But she is lonely.

She *was* lonely.

Not now. *Now* this girl needs her.

Edith sits Sapna down on a stool — they've yet to get furniture after the fire, it appears. The landlord must have supplied them with these stools to replace the kitchen chairs. Burned to a crisp, so Edith heard. She makes her way to the kitchen — same layout as hers but with a variety of colourful spices in jars, the counters branded and stained with their fiery, kaleidoscopic heat. She finds loose tea and sugar and after a bit of rooting around, digging up yet more spices, she manages to locate some tea bags. She makes Sapna a hot, sweet mug of tea — three sugars plus one more for good measure.

The girl sits with her hands wrapped around the mug, her eyes huge and dark and haunted.

'Go on, drink up. Everything seems better after a cup of tea. I speak from experience.'

The girl obediently takes a sip. And another. Edith feels as gratified as if she has drunk an entire gallon of the stuff herself.

Then, very softly, Sapna says, 'He betrayed me.'

Well, of course. Edith doesn't know if she's speaking of the man who just left or her thug of a husband — they're both equally guilty of letting this girl down, this much she knows. Nevertheless she asks, gently, 'Who did, love?'

'Amir.' Sapna takes a breathe. 'My husband. He was with another woman that night, the night of the fire.'

I wouldn't put it past him, not at all, Edith thinks. Out loud she says, 'Oh?'

'I think I know who it was. It all makes sense. How she brought round his favourite cake. How he knew her name although I hadn't told him. How she looked guilty when I asked her if she knew my husband.'

'I've lost you, love. Who are you talking about?'

'Gemma. She's having an affair with my husband.'

Edith angles forward on her stool so quickly that her hip protests. '*Our* Gemma? From Number 3?'

'Yes.'

'But when would she have the time what with her bubba . . . ?' But then Edith recalls that she'd seen Gemma take off that evening too, right after Sapna's husband left. She'd looked sharp, like in the old days before she got pregnant, and Edith remembers feeling happy for her. *She deserves a night out,* she'd thought. Her heart sinks. Nasty surprises are not good for her, not at her age. 'I . . . I thought she was happy with Rob . . .'

'It *is* her, I'm sure of it,' Sapna says. She's almost finished her tea and it's brought some colour back into her cheeks, Edith notes, even as her mind churns with the thought of Gemma cheating . . . No . . .

She thinks of how she herself was during those first few months with a new baby. No time nor desire for anything except a good night's sleep. No. She won't believe it of Gemma. That

218

girl adores her bubba, although she likes to moan about him not sleeping at night. 'I'm sorry, love, but I can't see Gemma putting her family in jeopardy. She's happy now. Settled, finally, after all she went through. She wouldn't give that up easily, not Gemma.' When she met Rob she finally . . . 'Oh.'

'What is it?' Sapna looks up at Edith, a glimmer of curiosity piercing the desolation in her face.

'She wouldn't give up her family for anyone except . . .'

'Except?'

'Her ex. He was the love of her life. She never really got over him. When she moved here, she was in pieces. She managed to get herself together and move on, especially after meeting Rob, marrying him. But I always got the feeling she never really was over her ex, not completely. Then the bubba came along and I thought that finally this would make her put it all behind—'

'You think . . . Amir could be her ex?'

This woman's thug of a husband. It explains a lot. Why Edith — who's learned the hard way how to judge people, after having made a mistake that dogged her all her life — has never taken to him. The absolute brazen *cheek* of the man, moving here with his new wife, right next to his ex, who was finally getting over him, casually, blithely disrupting her life without a second thought . . .

Rage, salty hot in her mouth. 'Where is your husband now?'

'I don't know and I don't care,' the girl says, a flash of steel in her eyes.

Good for you, Edith thinks.

'I can't stay with him. Not after what he's done. Lying to me, bringing me here, with his girlfriend next door . . .'

Sapna takes a breath. But she doesn't break down, doesn't cry. The girl is growing up. Like Edith, she's had to learn the hard way. Poor dear.

'I can't go home. To my childhood home in India, I mean. I'm not welcome there.' And now a tremor fractures her voice.

219

Edith, suddenly, impulsively, says, 'You can stay with me, my dear. For as long as you like.'

Tears shimmer bright as jewels in Sapna's eyes. She sets her mug down, gets off her stool and comes and kneels down beside Edith, wrapping her in a hug.

Edith is surprised by the stinging in her eyes. She can't recall the last time she was hugged in this way, with heartfelt affection.

'You're very kind,' Sapna says, still holding her tight. She smells of jasmine and spices, a sweetly haunting scent. 'I can't tell you how much it means. But for now, I'm staying right here.' A breath. Then, her voice sparks determination. 'Amir, however, is not.'

Edith smiles at the girl, pats her cheek. 'That's the spirit, love. But if you ever need anything or want company, you know where I am.'

'I do. Thank you, Edith.' A small smile. 'You might be sick of the sight of me and come to regret your offer.'

'Never, my dear,' Edith says stoutly.

'Believe me, I would like nothing better than to be rid of this house. I . . . I've never warmed to it. But . . . for now, until I decide what to do next, I'm staying here. Why should I move when I'm not the one at fault?'

'Quite right too,' Edith beams. The girl is growing a backbone. Good for her.

'Thank you, Edith. You're a good friend.' With another affectionate hug, the girl lets go.

And Edith makes her way home feeling sprightlier than she has in years.

CHAPTER 46

Sapna

After Edith leaves, bless her, Sapna brews more tea, this one the Indian way, spiced with cinnamon and ginger and cardamom — Edith is right, tea helps somehow — and sits by the living room window, thinking things through. Before, she would have cooked for Amir, her way of making up after their fights. Food was her apology, her manner of showing care. Not anymore. Her tears are exhausted and she is clear-headed, dry-eyed. It is dark, but she is not scared. The monsters are not in the darkness, she has come to realise. They are not lurking outside. They have always been with her but she has not seen them. She has not understood. They claim to love her then betray her in their different ways. Because of Sanjay, the monster from her past, she lost her family. And, because of the man to whom she has promised her future, she has lost her child.

She sits by the window and watches Amir return to the cul-de-sac, walking slowly towards home, his head down, hands in his pockets. He doesn't look up, across at Gemma's, not once. She watches as he comes up to their front door. He hesitates in the doorway, wondering, no doubt, about the crushed petals on the doorstep, scattered like confetti after a wedding.

He lets himself in and starts when he switches on the light and finds her in the living room. 'Why have you been sitting in the dark?'

'Sanjay was here,' Sapna says. She can't bear to look at her husband. Her cheating, lying husband. She thought she'd trapped him in marriage and felt sorely guilty about it, but now she finds that he's been lying to her too. But while she's come clean to him since the fire, he hasn't. And it's because of him and his affair with the woman next door that Sapna has lost her child . . .

Gemma. The viper. Bringing chocolate cake — Amir's favourite. Fake kindness hiding a black heart. No wonder Sapna has never really warmed to her. A part of her knew. That same instinct that cautioned her against this house also warned her to be wary of her neighbour. How could Amir bring Sapna here, next door to his ex? Now she realises that it wasn't the house, mere bricks and mortar, driving a wedge between herself and Amir, it was all the lies, the secrets they were keeping from each other, the secrets hiding next door.

'What?' Amir says, looking dazed.

'He came here while you were away.'

Understanding dawns in his eyes. 'The flowers?'

'Yes.'

'You were right, then, when you said he was back. He must have been biding his time.' Amir runs a hand across his face.

'Yes,' she says.

'I'm sorry,' he says, coming up to her, hand outstretched. *You should be sorry.* She moves away.

He looks hurt.

You've hurt me. She takes a deep breath. 'You saw Gemma that day, the day of the fire,' she says.

'W . . . what!' But colour has suffused his face. He cannot meet her eye.

'You went to the Holiday Inn with her.'

'I . . . How do you . . . ? Who . . . ?' All he can do is bluster.

She lets him. Then, 'Are you having an affair with her?'

'No!'

'How can I believe anything you say?'

'It's the truth.'

Truth. Even if so, it's too late now. 'Did you sleep with her that night?'

'No, I just wanted to talk.'

'Why?'

'We . . . you and I . . . we weren't getting on. You told me when we got married that you wanted to live in England, with me, that you wanted to move far away from home. But you were so unhappy. I felt you were disappointed in me. Dissatisfied. I worried that you thought that you had made a mistake, marrying me. It made me feel so . . . impotent.' Tears shining in his eyes.

Too late.

'And then, that evening you said you wanted to go back home to India . . .'

'Perhaps I was unhappy because I sensed that you'd lied to me. Brought me to a house next door to your girlfriend!'

'She's not my girlfriend, she's my ex.'

'Whom you wanted to see after our fight.'

'She was the one who told me about this house.'

'That's why you wanted to move here!'

'No. No. There's nothing between us. That evening was the first time I saw her properly, spent time with her one to one, after we split up . . .'

'You said she told you about this house.'

'She texted me.'

'You still have her number.'

'She's my friend, nothing more. I . . . I don't love her in that way anymore. We've both moved on. She has a child! I wanted to move here because it was cheap. You can't get a house like this anywhere in London at this price, even in the grottier areas.'

223

'You didn't tell me about your history with her.'

'I didn't want to complicate matters. You were already unhappy. I didn't want to make you even more so.'

She doesn't know if she believes him. She doesn't know if she cares. The damage has been done, a wedge well and truly driven into their relationship by their mutual deceits. But nevertheless, she wants to know the truth. She deserves to know. 'Why did you call her that evening?'

'I was upset. I wanted to talk it out with someone and she's my friend.'

'You knew she would come because she still cared for you.'

Now colour once again floods into his face. She cannot feel sympathy for him. Especially when he says, in a small voice, 'Yes.'

'You took advantage of her feelings for you.'

'Yes.' And then, with a flash of defiance, 'You took advantage of me too, marrying me to escape your bind.'

'I did,' she says softly. 'And I'm sorry. But once I married you, I tried my best to be a good wife. I know it wasn't enough. But I did try.'

'Do you know why *I* married you? Because I love you, Sapna.' He is earnest, looking right at her, eyes shining with sincerity. 'I love you, not Gemma, not anyone else. You.'

She believes him. About this, at least. But what he did . . . 'You should have told me when we moved in about your history with Gemma.'

'I know. And I'm sorry. Look, we've both made mistakes. Can't we put this behind us and start again? Please? If you want, we'll break the lease, lose the deposit, move far away from here, start afresh . . .'

She takes another deep breath. How can they move on from this? 'Sanjay said Gemma started the fire.'

'What?' He is stunned. 'What are you saying? Gemma? No, no. Come on, Gemma wouldn't . . .'

'Why not?'

'She's not . . . She just would not . . . Wait. *Sanjay* said this? Your deranged stalker?'

'*Now* you believe he's been stalking me?' she cries.

'He must have started the fire himself and he's blaming it on Gemma.'

'He said Gemma threw a lit cigarette through the letterbox.'

And now Amir blanches. 'She . . . she wouldn't.' But he's not so sure anymore.

'She's done it before, hasn't she?'

'In our wild student days, once or twice. Nothing happened. I don't think you can even start a fire like that.'

'Well, in this case she did. I'd barricaded the door with the kitchen chairs, worried that Sanjay would come when I was all alone, make good his threat. The cigarette must have fallen onto the seat cushions — some oil had spilled onto one of them earlier that day, I remember, and the cigarette must have caught on that particular one . . .'

'Oh Sapna, I'm sorry . . .'

What's the use of being sorry now? 'I didn't know Gemma smoked.'

'She does when she's upset.'

Somehow this, her husband's casual knowledge of Gemma's habits, her quirks, hurts more than all that's gone before. 'She was angry with you, wasn't she? You used her — calling her when you were upset, sending her on her way when you were done sharing. She was angry that you'd chosen me and so she threw the cigarette through the letterbox as she passed the house.'

He is ashen — she knows he agrees with her that that's what happened. But still he says, 'You have only Sanjay's word for it.'

'I believe him.'

Amir's face contorts, his eyes like flinty stones. 'The man who raped you?'

'The boy I grew up with. I can tell when he's lying. He was telling the truth about this. I can also tell that you know Gemma's capable of it. That you believe this is what happened, that you're arguing for the sake of it.'

Now all the bluster goes out of him, his shoulders slump, defeated, and he slowly lowers himself onto the stool Edith had perched on before. 'I don't want it to be true.'

'Sanjay saw—'

'Where is Sanjay, by the way? What did he do? Did he . . . ?' He can't complete the sentence.

She knows he wants to ask if Sanjay hurt her. *Bit late, isn't it?* she wants to say. *Bit late for your concern when you left me here, not believing when I said he was back.* 'He ran off when the police came.'

'The police were here? Again?'

'Edith called them when she saw Sanjay arrive.'

'You told them about the fire? About Gemma?' His voice is small. He might love Sapna but he also cares for Gemma.

'I did not. I wanted to confirm it before making accusations,' she says.

She sees relief wash over his face.

'In any case, I don't trust the police. They thought the fire was an accident.'

'What did the police do today?'

'They asked after Sanjay. I told them he'd run away just moments earlier. I pointed out the direction in which he'd disappeared. They asked if he'd harassed me and I said not this time but that I didn't want him turning up again. They said they'd see about getting a restraining order against him.'

'Okay.' Amir rubs a hand across his face again. Then, in a small voice, 'And what about us, Sapna?'

'I . . .' She takes a breath. 'I need some time.'

'I'm sorry. For not believing you. For everything. Please—'

She interrupts him, wanting, needing to put into words all that has been going through her mind since Sanjay told her about Gemma and Amir. Wanting him to understand why she's so upset. 'It's because of your secret association with Gemma that we moved here. It's because you called her to talk that day that she started the fire. I know you didn't cause it, but it's because of you that I lost my child. I need some time to process that, to forgive you.'

226

He is defeated.

'Please leave.'

'Where will I go?'

'Go to the Holiday Inn. To Gemma's house. I don't care. Just leave.'

'But you're scared here . . .' he tries.

'Scared. Ha! *Now* you care, do you?'

He has the grace to look shamefaced.

'I should have been scared of the people watching the house, stalking me, and those living beside it, rather than the house itself. Anyway, since when did you start giving a damn about my feelings, my fears? You who mock them . . .'

'I . . .'

'You didn't care that I was scared that night. You walked off and left me here. Where were you when your friend set fire to this house, killed my child? Where *were* you?'

CHAPTER 47

Gemma

'She knows about us,' Amir says.

'Oh.' Gemma fingers the necklace at her throat, the one he gave her, the one she told Rob was her dead mother's.

Despite everything, here she is again. Amir calls and she answers. She shouldn't have come. Her marriage is floundering. Rob, the father of her child, who always saw only the best in her, who trusted her irrevocably, is withdrawing from her. She has broken his faith in her.

Objectively she knows the right thing to do. She knows Amir isn't good for her, that he doesn't want her, that he's using her. And yet, this man reaches out and all objectivity is thrown to the wind in the face of mindless passion, renewed hope, which trumps cold, hard sense every single time.

Amir beckons and Gemma regresses from nurse, wife and mother to the girl whose parents never cared for her, who yearned for love and who this man singled out for attention. The first man who saw *her*, loved her — or so she thought — for who she was.

Her parents were a tight unit of two, their love for each other obsessive; it contained no room for anyone else, not even their own child. She was unwanted — they had told her so multiple times. 'We didn't want children. You were an accident.' Which they showed with their actions, shutting her out, ignoring her: *You're a burden, an interruption, a nuisance.*

She found refuge in books, learning. She chose a uni as far from home as she possibly could. The look on her parents' faces when she told them she was leaving . . .

Even then, she had hoped for *something*, some small indication that she mattered, a word, an expression to show she would be missed. There was nothing but relief. *At last*, their faces said, *we're finally rid of you.*

Then this gorgeous man, handsome, charming Amir, whom everyone flocked to, had chosen *her*. And all the love in her that had so far been unclaimed went to him — all her passion, her need, her desire to be seen, to matter, validated by his singling her out for his affections, what she took to be love.

And it is that needy, vulnerable girl who responds every time Amir gets in touch — for she is *still* seeking his approval. That girl will do anything for him, although he has hurt her over and over. She will abandon the profession she loves, throw aside her family as if they are nothing.

Gemma hates that girl, greedy for Amir's scraps of affection. She wants to be the woman Rob used to see when he looked at her, the caring nurse, the loving wife and mother. Her problem is that she just doesn't want it enough — not as much as the needy girl inside her yearns for Amir's attention.

'Sapna kicked me out,' Amir is saying.

And just like that, Gemma's heart jumps. It rises, it sings. There's hope yet for them. Isn't there?

Amir looks devastated but he will come round. He loves *her* really, doesn't he? They have a shared history. What does he have with Sapna, that paranoid slip of a girl who made a play for him to get away from her obsessive stalker?

What madness is this, Gemma? There's Theo to consider. There's Rob . . .

She loves Rob, she *does*. Not with the all-absorbing, all-consuming, selfish passion that she has always nurtured for Amir. Her love for Rob is gentle, steady, mature. She is grateful to him for lifting her from the depression she had sunk into after Amir broke up with her, for loving her in his wholesome, uncomplicated way, for making a life with her. For giving her the gift of Theo.

But Amir has always taken precedence. She promised herself she would not be like her parents, that once she had a child, he or she would come first. But she is more like her parents than she thought or wanted to be. Amir has always exerted a strange, hypnotic influence on her, holding her heart in his careless possession. No matter how many times he lets her down, she still experiences this magnetic pull towards him. He calls and she answers. No matter her conscience, what she knows to be right. He overrides it all. It has always been this way.

The rational part of her sighs in exasperation, cries in despair, but the rational part has always had no hope, no voice where Amir is concerned.

'Did you start the fire?' Amir is asking.

'What?' She is jolted from her thoughts. What does he know? *How* does he know? He *cannot* know.

His eyes when he looks at her, the pain in them. He knows. But *how*?

'You're still wearing the necklace I gave you.'

'Well . . .'

'Gemma, I love Sapna. Not you. Not anymore.'

It hurts. Oh, how it hurts. She's heard these words before but that doesn't take away the sting of them, no matter how many times he says them.

He's lying. Deluded. Isn't he?

You're the deluded one.

She shushes her conscience like she does every time where Amir is concerned. His hurtful words mean nothing. He's just a besotted fool, momentarily taken in by Sapna's beauty; her fragile, vulnerable, teary, helpless act. Isn't he?

How can he love that girl when he and Gemma had — have? — such a strong bond, such a deep connection. How can it mean nothing at all?

'It's over, Gemma. We're over. We have been for a very long time. You know this. You agreed we should just be friends when we broke up. If I'd known you would be like this, I wouldn't have moved here.'

'Don't lie, Amir. You know I've never quite got over you. You like it. You take advantage of it.'

His face flushes. He looks like a little boy caught with his hand in the biscuit jar, and she's floored by the urge to take him in her arms. What is wrong with her?

'I don't love you. I love Sapna,' he says again.

He used the same horrid words when she leaned in to kiss him at the Holiday Inn that weekend and he pushed her away. She had just wanted to ease his hurt, kiss it better. His words draw her back to that night.

* * *

'She's unhappy all the time,' Amir cried when Gemma got there and asked him what the matter was.

'Amir, don't take this the wrong way, but I have to ask . . . Have you hurt her?' Gemma said.

Amir stared at her, his features stamped first with incomprehension and then horror.

'It's just that Edith saw you raising a hand to her.'

'I was wiping away the tears on her face. They were mixing with flour and becoming a mess — she'd been cooking, you see. She was upset about something, hence the tears. She's always upset. I don't know how to placate her, what to do to make her happy. You know me, Gemma. How could you even think . . . ?'

'I saw a bruise on her arm when I visited.'

'She bumped into one of the packing boxes.'

'You can't get a bruise like that from packing boxes.'

'You can if it holds a great big pressure cooker that her mother insisted she bring from India. Gemma, this is me! I would never do that to a woman. You know this.'

'You hurt me,' she said softly.

231

He recoiled. 'Not physically.'

'Not physically, no. But you hurt me all the same.'

'Ah, Gemma, I wish things could have been different, believe me. I would have been much happier with you.'

That sentence warmed her heart. She stored it away to unpack and dissect, cherish and treasure at her leisure. It resurrected hope — hope that she had never really put to bed even as she met and married Rob and had a child with him.

'But when my parents died, both at once in that car accident, I was all over the place. It took me a while to find my feet. I had to get away. I went travelling . . .'

'And you met her.'

'I met her.' He sighed deeply, his eyes sparkling with unshed tears. 'She said she wanted to go far away from home. That England was perfect, a fresh start, with me. And now . . . now she says she wants to go back home to India. I'm at a loss. She's *never* happy.'

'Perhaps because she loves someone else?' Gemma suggested softly.

'What?'

'There was a man visiting her today with flowers. Red roses. When she opened the door to him, he gathered her in his arms and kissed her in full view of the whole street.'

'You . . . you're joking?'

'You know I'm not.'

He slumped on the table, his head in his hands.

'Perhaps she wants to go back home for the sake of her baby?' Gemma said.

'What?' Amir's head shot up and he stared at her, bewildered, uncomprehending. 'Did you . . . Sapna's pregnant?'

'She hasn't told you?' Gemma was genuinely stumped. Why had that woman told *her*, the neighbour, and not Amir, her husband? And then it occurred to her why. It was simple, really. 'Perhaps it's that man's. The one who was visiting her today.'

And at that, Amir's eyes spilled over. And she couldn't resist. She leaned across, kissed him.

And that was when he had pushed her away, shocked. 'What are you doing, Gemma? I'm married. You are too. I love my wife.'

Despite everything, he loved his cheating, perpetually whining wife, who entertained other men when Amir was working and was possibly carrying someone else's baby. It made her *furious*. 'Why did you call me here, then?' she asked.

'I needed a friend to talk to. To share with.'

'You don't get to do this anymore, Amir. Play with my feelings. Use me and discard me as you like, when it suits you,' she cried.

But that's what he'd done. And she had let him, more fool her.

She was seething as she walked home, hating herself for having run to him when he called, daring to think there was hope for them. It had always been like this with Amir — she lost all sense, behaved like someone she didn't recognise and often loathed.

Since he'd moved in next door, he'd ignored her. He was working all the time — she had thought that might be why. (There she was, inventing excuses for him, making allowances for his indifference towards her, except when it suited him.) When she did spot Amir, walking to and from work, she was a mess, covered in Theo's sick, wearing her oldest, most comfortable clothes. So it was for the best that he hadn't made contact with her, despite moving in right next door. There would be time enough to meet and talk, she'd thought.

So when Amir had called her that day, serendipitously when Rob was away, she'd jumped at the chance to catch up with him, properly, for the first time since he broke up with her.

And then, when he rejected her yet again, after he'd moaned about his wife for the better part of an hour, not asking one thing about Gemma, not even how she was, and *nothing* about Theo, she was incensed. At herself most of all. *Fool.* Getting dolled up for him when all he wanted was to vent about his wife and then, when she tried to offer comfort, looking scandalised, saying, 'I love my wife.'

She had walked past the house he shared with his wife — Sapna, asleep or probably cowering with neurotic fear inside — and she was furious.

Raging.

Her weekend, her time off without Theo, was ruined — the previous day by Sapna, knocking on her door, crazed and deluded, waking Gemma up from her much-needed sleep, and now by Amir. She wanted to do something, *anything*, to get back at these two people who had used her without a second thought. And so, she reverted to being a teenager again — which was what Amir did to her, turned her into an infatuated teen with an unrequited crush — and played the silly little prank she and her friends had inflicted on people who had annoyed them, neighbours who'd shouted at them, teachers who'd been mean. Come to think of it, she'd even done it a couple of times at uni, with her friends, Amir among them. They would post lit cigarettes through letterboxes. They had fizzled out, of course, nothing had ever come of it. But the very act had made them feel better, righting in a small measure the wrongs, the injustices they felt they'd been subjected to.

And so, that evening, as she walked past Number 2, she did the same. She had a pack of cigarettes with her, she'd taken it along for old times' sake — she and Amir always used to share a fag after making love. For shame. What was she *thinking*? She *wasn't*, that was the problem. She never did when it came to Amir and he knew it. He had *used* it. She felt mortified and upset anew, and so, before she could change her mind, she took out a cigarette, lit it and posted it through the letterbox.

Unlike when she was younger, it didn't make her feel better. Then, she would have been egged on by friends and they would have run away to hide, falling over themselves laughing as they watched the irate homeowner open the door and shake their fists at the empty road.

Now she felt nothing but fury, absolutely unappeased by her act of sabotage. Until . . . flames burst upwards in a raging whoosh from Number 2, splitting the darkness with smoke-tipped orange sparklers. Then her anger was instantly replaced by panic. Bright and burning wild as the fire. She'd whipped out her phone, dialled 999, watched the ambulances and fire engines arrive and Sapna being wheeled away.

Oh, what have I done!

* * *

Now, she says, 'Why do you think the rent at your house was so cheap? It's my uncle's. I urged him to rent to you and to give you a good deal. I persuaded him to keep you on after the fire.'

This is what Amir did to her.

After he broke up with her, she'd wanted nothing more than to move on. And when she married Rob, had Theo, she thought she had. Then Amir texted her out of the blue to say he was back in the UK and looking for houses to rent. Serendipitously, her Uncle John, who owns both the house she shares with Rob and Theo and the one next door, was looking for tenants as Mr Shaw had died recently.

Uncle John had always had a soft spot for Gemma. So when Amir had contacted her, Gemma had asked her uncle if he would rent to her friend, at the same subsidised rate he charged her. And that's what Gemma told herself when he agreed: Amir was just a friend now and she was helping him. Doing a good deed. Her life was with Rob and Theo.

But one look at Amir as he moved in next door was all it took for all the feelings she had pushed away for so long to come rushing back, and then she knew she had made a mistake. But it was too late.

She takes a deep, steadying breath. 'I never stopped loving you. But you . . . you never loved me, did you? I was just someone to pass the time with . . .'

'Gemma, I . . . It was over when I told you it was.'

'Did you ever love me at all?' she asks, her voice small. Even now she is hoping, wishing . . . But at the expression on his face, the small flare of hope dies. 'You used me that weekend. It was my first weekend without Theo, and first your wife uses me and then you do. I was angry.'

And so, she had wrought destruction.

Amir is thinking the same thing. 'You could have killed her, you know. Sapna.' There is such pain in his voice when he speaks of his wife.

'I didn't know that the fire would take. It had never happened before. You know that. I thought it would fizzle out on the carpet.'

It's no excuse.

'You could have killed her,' he says again. His voice, so full of desolation and despair, cuts through her.

'I didn't, though. I called 999. I saved her.'

But I hurt her. I hurt my husband. I might lose him. And my son . . .

'Gemma, she lost the baby . . .'

She can't look at him, so she looks at her hands. These same capable hands that have nursed countless lives back from the brink of death have wilfully, mindlessly taken a burgeoning life.

She has blood on her hands, like Lady Macbeth.

She has been lying to Rob, to the police, to everyone. But most of all, to herself.

So many lies. So much subterfuge. So many wrongs. And for what?

CHAPTER 48

Sapna

Sapna spends the night by the living room window. Thinking. Drinking umpteen cups of tea.

By mid-morning, when the police car stops in front of her house, the police emerge — the same two as yesterday — and the doorbell goes, she is wide awake and pacing.

Now what, she thinks as she flings open the door.

'Can we come in?' the woman says with a solemn, determined expression, and that's when fear takes her in a stranglehold, her ire shrivelled by dread.

Amir, she thinks. *Please let him be all right.* He might have hurt her, lied to her, but she has hurt and lied to him too. He has been kind to her. He saved her when she needed saving, married her, brought her here when she wanted to escape.

Please let him be all right. The chant goes round and round in her head even as she silently steps aside to let them through, babbling, 'I'm sorry, we don't have proper furniture yet.' *We. Please.* Even as she pulls out the stools for them, she prays. Police officers are in her living room. This can only be bad news.

And then as the officers refuse her offer of tea, as they sit, grave faced, official, incongruous on the stools, she understands anew the truth that came to her after she asked Amir to leave. Despite everything, she cares for him. She is angry with him, hurting, feeling cheated and betrayed, but, at the heart of it all, she loves him.

The policewoman has started talking but Sapna has tuned her out, missed the first part of what she was saying. But her next words pierce the fug of upset . . .

'We found his wallet, his coat and one shoe, washed up near Richmond,' the policewoman is saying, her voice sombre but kind. 'We think he jumped off the bridge there. We're sorry but it appears that he most likely drowned.'

The pain is terrible. Soul shattering. *Oh, oh, oh.*

The policewoman is standing now, putting an arm around her. She smells of stale perfume and tiredness. 'Are you all right?' Her voice is surprisingly gentle.

Sapna cannot answer. She's thinking: *Drowned.* Her mind protests: *No.* He can swim. Can't he? She doesn't know. There's so much she doesn't know about the man she's married to and now she will never get the chance . . .

Oh, oh, oh.

Richmond . . . Why would Amir go all the way to Richmond? Did he have friends there? But wait, isn't it near Hounslow? Perhaps his friend asked to meet him there? But if his friend was there, why . . . ? All conjecture, of course. Amir is gone. She is truly alone in this country now.

Out of habit she strokes her stomach. She hasn't bled since she returned home from hospital. She has been feeling queasy, unable to eat in the mornings, the thought of food turning her stomach. Could she . . . ?

Stop. Why is she thinking this now?

Because she doesn't want to think about what happened.

Amir. Gone. Oh . . .

'Do you have any idea who his next of kin might be?' the policewoman is asking.

'His parents are dead. He doesn't have siblings. So it's me, I think, as his wife . . .'

The policewoman pulls back and looks at her, sharply, exchanging glances with the other officer, who sits up straighter on the little stool.

'You're *married* to him?' the policewoman asks.

'Yes.' She colours, fiddling with her shawl. 'We've been having problems, but . . .' No chance of making up now. *Oh, oh, oh.*

'How long had he been harassing you?'

'Well, I wouldn't call it harassment . . .'

'But you wanted to bring a restraining order against him?'

'Oh. *Oh?*'

Sanjay. It is Sanjay's coat and wallet they found. It is Sanjay who's drowned. Sanjay, who once rescued her while swimming in the village lake. The irony!

The shock must show on her face as the policewoman nods at her colleague and he goes into the kitchen. Even in her distress, she's ashamed of the state of her kitchen. She hasn't washed a single thing since the previous morning. The stove is sticky with boiled-over tea, the sink full of dirty dishes.

But her mind flits away from worrying about her house-keeping to processing what it's learned. Overwhelming relief that it's not Amir, mingled with a stab of sadness for Sanjay, the boy she'd cared for once long ago before his possessive violence choked the affection, curdled it into hate.

Memories flood her, alongside guilty relief that Sanjay won't be turning up here anymore. Strangely liberating grief for the lost boy in ragged clothes, her brother's friend, sharing their meals, becoming part of their family, growing into the man she slowly but surely began to loathe . . .

The policeman returns with tea — he must have found the last clean mug — and hands it to her. She gratefully takes a sip. It scalds the roof of her mouth. She welcomes the pain. It's a respite from the tumult of emotions ambushing her.

'I'm sorry, I got it wrong. I thought it was my husband you see . . .'

'So you're saying Mr Sanjay Kumar *isn't* your husband?'

'Yes.'

The policewoman nods, her expression clearing. 'I'm sorry for the misunderstanding.'

'No, it's my fault. I missed the first part of what you were saying, I tuned out . . .'

She nods again. 'Ah, it happens. We have that effect on people.'

Sapna manages a small smile.

'So, do you have any idea who Mr Sanjay Kumar's next of kin is?'

She closes her eyes, seeing, in her mind, the shambling boy her brother had brought home for lunch, his father missing, mother on her deathbed.

'In this country, I think *I* am.'

'All right.' The policewoman nods. 'You're okay to go on?'

'Yes.' She takes another sip of her tea. Strong and not as sweet as the one Edith makes, but just what she needs. 'Thank you for the tea,' she says to the policeman and he smiles, nodding his acknowledgement. His colleague obviously does all the talking in this partnership.

'We found a note in his wallet. It was in one of those Ziplock bags, so mostly intact.'

'A note?'

'A suicide note,' the policewoman says, briskly.

Oh. Sapna thinks of Sanjay yesterday, standing on her doorstep with flowers, his face morphing from hopeful to manic in seconds. She has hated him and sometimes — often — wished him dead. But now that it's actually happened, she is sad, and a part of her is grateful that she is so, that she can see past his terrible actions to the person he once was.

'We also found this. Do you recognise it, by any chance?'

'I . . .' A hand creeps up to her heart. 'I do. It's the key to the kitchen door.'

'*Your* kitchen door here?'

'Yes.' She recalls the day of the fire, finding the keys she thought she'd lost. The ones she'd last seen hanging in the cabinet which Sanjay had knocked down. The noise she thought she heard when she was in the loo — the kitchen door opening, footsteps, and then, when she finally gathered the courage to come out of the loo, her keys waiting by her teacup. A message. From Sanjay. *I have access to your home.*

Then the fire happened and she lost her baby, and this incident, so scary at the time, was pushed to the back of her mind . . .

'Do you mind if my colleague tries . . . ?'

'No. Please go ahead.' She hears the policeman try the key, open the kitchen door, a blast of fresh air smelling of apples briefly displacing the stale fug inside.

Keys . . . She hears Amir's angry voice. *You keep losing your keys.*

'Did you also find the key to the front door, by any chance?'

'No, ma'am, there were no other keys. If he took any others, they must have been in his pocket.'

That figures. Perhaps if she hadn't let him in — was it only yesterday that he was alive and well? — he would have come in anyway, which is why that key must have been in his pocket, handy, ready and waiting. She shudders. Just as she suspected, he had access to her house, *this* house, since the day of the fire — he could have come in any time he liked, let himself in either through the kitchen door or brazenly through the front door. And on the heels of that thought comes another. Freeing. Sanjay cannot come in anymore. He cannot scare her anymore — a looming spectre, a threat to her happiness, always there. He's gone for good. Now she can finally, properly move on.

She takes a deep breath of relief that Amir is not dead, that they have a chance to repair their relationship, start afresh, work on leaving all the lies and mistrust and blame and betrayal behind. When she thought it was too late, she was devastated. She cares for Amir, loves him. He has reiterated that he loves her, not Gemma. So perhaps they will be able to forgive, forget, rebuild, move on? She finishes her tea, sees the police out, watches them drive away.

Then she sits at the window and thinks of Sanjay. The boy he was. The man he became.

She pictures him, just yesterday, running from the police, the demons of his past and present haunting him. Then, standing at the bridge, hands clutching the rails, staring at the swirling water below, freezing cold at sundown, even in summer, smelling of nothing at all, so unlike the warm rivers at home — the sun-kissed water, sweet sludge. He takes a deep breath of clean air, his last — what does he think about?

And then he jumps, this foreign river welcoming him with undulating arms, frosty water wrapping icy fingers around him. He receives it like a gift, his insides burning like his unrequited love as he struggles for breath and finds only water. After a bit, he doesn't feel the cold. He's swimming in the lake at home, neatly slicing the emerald water in two, droplets gleaming on coffee-coloured skin like foil on chocolate.

A man Sapna first loved and then hated so very passionately. Now no more.

CHAPTER 49

Gemma

'Rob, can we talk?'

He turns to her. This good man who has loved her in the way love should be. Selfless. Kind. Giving.

He didn't deserve any of this.

Out of habit, her hand goes to her throat, seeks out the necklace there. She touches the teardrop locket, inside which she has tucked a photograph capturing the moment they became a family. Gemma cradling newborn Theo; Rob, his arm around her, beaming down at the child they've created together.

She's thrown away the necklace from Amir and all other keepsakes and mementos she's collected over the years. She has wrung Amir out of her heart — she hopes — and finally, at long last, blocked his number from her phone.

She sees Rob's gaze resting briefly on the necklace he gifted to her.

He looks up at her.

Does he love her still?

His eyes used to be windows to his soul — an expression she'd scoffed at until she met Rob — but now they're shuttered.

In any case, even if he does love her, once she comes clean, he no longer will.

And she will lose everything good in her life.

You deserve it. You took a life even before it had a chance to properly begin.

She takes a fortifying breath, readying herself for the hardest thing she's ever done. And then, she quietly confesses everything, finally reveals to her husband all her dark, ugly truths. It's excruciating to get the words out but she does.

He listens. He doesn't interrupt. And when she's done, he says, 'It must have been hard for you to tell me. I appreciate it.' His voice is expressionless. So very formal.

'There is one other thing,' she says, fingering the locket. 'I didn't marry you on a rebound. I loved you. I love you. The love I feel for you, it's different. Not selfish, not destructive, but good, pure, precious. I've tainted it. I'm sorry.'

He nods.

And then he turns away.

NOW

'How well did you know them?' the detectives ask.

'Well enough. They moved in just three months ago, but . . . The walls are thin. They didn't have curtains. We heard and saw more than enough to get an insight into their relationship. It wasn't a very happy one. As we've said, they were always arguing.'

'Who?'

'What do you mean, who? The couple at Number 2, of course. We thought that's who you were asking about.'

'Amir and Sapna Hussain?'

'Yes.'

'And what about Sanjay Kumar?'

'Him? Why do you want to know about him?'

'Humour us, please.'

Humour? we think. You haven't cracked a smile between you since you turned up here all grim and official, asking us the same questions over and over again. Not even as you drink our teas and polish off our freshly baked (or in some cases freshly bought) cakes and biscuits. Interviews must make for thirsty work. We know you're investigating a — what was that phrase you used? Ah yes — suspicious death, yet still, a smile once in a while wouldn't go amiss, that's our considered opinion. It would definitely make us more obliged to help.

'What do you know about Sanjay Kumar?' the police prompt, jolting us from our musings back into the present, this nightmare afflicting our dreamily peaceful cul-de-sac — well, not *quite* as peaceful since Amir and Sapna Hussain moved into Number 2.

'Well, the first we knew of him was when he knocked on the door of Number 2 fit to wake the dead the afternoon of the fire.'

'That was the first time you saw him?'

'That's what we just said. We didn't know his name then, of course. Only that he came with flowers and kissed Sapna when she opened the door in a way that was definitely not brotherly, if you get our drift.' We pause for breath. 'Then he went inside, the door closed, and when he left, some five minutes later . . .'

'Ten minutes it was, by my clock . . .'

'Ten minutes later then . . . Where was I again?'

'You were saying that when Mr Kumar left Mrs Hussain . . .' the officers prompt.

'Ah yes, he looked introspective. As if he was planning something.'

'Thank you. Did he turn up again?'

'You know he did. We called your lot at once.'

'And why was that?'

'Sorry?'

'Why did you call us when he turned up? Did he ring alarm bells? Did he behave suspiciously? Were you worried about what he might do to Mrs Hussain?'

'Well . . . he seemed not quite all there, if you get our drift. And to be honest, she appeared frightened of him. And after the fire the evening of his previous visit, a tad too coincidental by our reckoning . . . Well, better safe than sorry, we thought.'

'But he brought flowers. And you said he kissed her that first time?'

'Are you trying to trip us up here? You lot must know better than anyone that one thing doesn't necessarily pre-clude the other. You can kiss one minute and hit the next.'

'Very true,' the officers agree solemnly.

'You were actioning a restraining order against him, at Sapna's say-so, weren't you? Is it true that he stole her keys?'

'Where did you hear that?' the officers ask.

'We have our ways.' We're cagey, playing them at their own game.

'Now, what more can you tell us about Sanjay Kumar?'

Why are they so concerned about Sanjay Kumar? 'Well . . . Sapna thought she had a stalker. We wondered if it was him.'

'Oh?'

'Some of us did see someone prowling in Number 2's garden — but we weren't *sure* about it. But if he had the keys to the house, then it couldn't have been him, could it?' Again, trying to play them at their game, see if they'll inadvertently reveal something.

But they know better than to fall for it, of course. 'When did you think you saw someone in the garden of Number 2?'

'Before Mr Kumar turned up for the first time.'

We pause. The officers wait patiently.

'Then last week, he came again with flowers, as you know.'

'And right after that she kicked her husband out.'

'That's all we know. Mr Kumar ran away when you lot came.'

'And that's the last you saw of him?'

'Yes.'

'You're sure?'

'Positive.' We know, of course, when to press our advantage. 'And why would we see him again? He died didn't he, the day after you lot were called out here because he was pestering Sapna, so the restraining order was moot . . . We heard his body washed up in Richmond?'

'Who said anything about a body?' the police ask sharply.

PART 4

TWO DAYS PREVIOUS

CHAPTER 50

Edith

They're arguing over at Number 2. Yet again. Will it never stop? What is it with these men who can't take no for an answer?

Edith knows that Sapna kicked her thug of a husband out. He must have come back. Ignoring Sapna's wishes. Paying no heed to her request, thinking he knows better, riding roughshod over her will.

They don't know that she can hear most of what goes on in Number 2 — not the exact words they're speaking, but she can guess from the pitch and resonance what's happening. After Jack died she moved into the boys' bedroom; it shares a wall with Number 2's master bedroom. It was peaceful during Mr Shaw's time as he'd moved downstairs by then; they set up a hospital bed in the living room as he couldn't make the journey upstairs. He'd had one of those stairlifts for a while but then eventually that too became difficult for him to manage.

Since the thug and Sapna moved in, Edith has had no peace. She could do with a good night's sleep — well, as much as her sore joints allow — unhampered by yelling and shouting into the small hours. She's considered moving back into the bedroom she shared with Jack, but there are too many unhappy memories there; she'd rather not.

When Sapna finally saw sense and kicked the thug out, Edith had cheered. But now he's back and causing hell again, this man who's messed up not only Sapna but also Gemma before her. Strong, wonderful Gemma, a nurse, a lifesaver — he reduced her, destroyed her when he broke up with her. Edith lost count of the number of times Gemma sobbed into her shoulder during those early days. She celebrated when Gemma met and married Rob, and cheered when Theo came along. But as if sensing Gemma was happy without him, just when that poor girl had finally moved on, he swanned in, the thug, upsetting the life Gemma had managed to fashion for herself.

How *dare* he?

Sapna tried to send him away. But here he is, causing mayhem, back again like a bad penny. Like Jack, who did not respect Edith, who bullied her. And she . . . she had let him. She was young and vulnerable, just like Sapna.

Edith has had enough of controlling men, men who don't take no for an answer, men who think they know best, men who abuse their women, subjugate them, wound them with words and fists.

Sapna needs help. The poor girl needs to be left alone.

She's lucky Edith is here. She's gone through it all before. She knows what's what.

I'll look after you, love. Too late for me. But not for you.

She puts on her coat over her nightdress, takes the key she 'borrowed' for just such an emergency. She spotted it in the cubby when she went round that first time with cake and surprised the thug in the process of hitting his wife. Now too, just like that first time, Edith lets herself in, but unlike that time, when the door was open and she had called out as she entered, now, she unlocks the door herself and she doesn't announce herself first.

CHAPTER 51

Sapna

'He's gone, finally. You did good, Sapna. He was making you unhappy. You're better off without him. I'm here now. I'll take good care of you, my love. We'll be very happy together,' Sanjay whispers. 'You love me really. We're soulmates, bound by destiny. And now we'll never be apart again.'

Sapna jerks awake, heart thudding, her mouth dry and acrid with terror.

It was a dream. Very vivid to be sure, but just a dream. Because he's dead.

Isn't he?

They never found a body.

And . . . *Oh God. Oh God, oh God, oh God.*

There's someone in bed with her . . .

She opens her mouth to scream but he clamps her mouth shut, his hand sticky with sweat.

'Shhh . . . only me, my love. Nothing to be afraid of.' His sour breath in her ear. His unwashed body, rank with body odour overlaid with the musty scent of the damp outdoors, pressing into hers. 'I didn't mean to startle you.'

Not a dream, no. This is *real*. He is here.

Is he? Or is she seeing things, imagining things? Please let it be so.

But she can feel, smell, taste . . . A frighteningly realistic nightmare, that's all.

Isn't it?

'You . . .' She speaks into his hand, which he has relaxed somewhat. The taste of him fetid in her mouth like that terrible day in the jacaranda copse when he raped her, ruined her. 'You're dead?'

It comes out a question.

He laughs. She shivers.

'Obviously not, my love, don't you worry. Police everywhere are the same, although the ones here like to think they're better. Ha! They're stupidly easy to fool. I learned a few tricks in prison, as I said before.'

She cannot believe it.

But he *is* here. In her bedroom. How?

The key. The front door key that the police couldn't find among his things.

Nevertheless, she asks, 'How did you get inside the house?'

'I stole your keys the first time I visited.'

'You knocked over my key cabinet in a rage.'

'I meant to do it,' he says, and she can hear the happy chuckle in his voice.

'But you returned them,' she says, recalling the afternoon of the fire, finding the keys she thought she lost beside her teacup.

'After I'd cut myself copies,' he says cheerfully.

'And yet you kept knocking on the door.'

'I liked startling you, announcing my presence. But I also liked having a set of keys, knowing I could come here any time I wished.'

He let himself in the front door, bold as anything.

'Sanjay . . .' She cannot get her head around it. She is numb with fear, shock, distress. *Oh God, oh God, oh God. This can't be happening.* But it is. It *is.* Here she is in her own home, in the middle of the night, all alone with the madman who raped her, whom the police think is dead.

'Sapna, my love.'

Her eyes have adjusted to the dark and she sees that he is smiling fondly at her, his gaze quite mad.

'I have money and the means to get more. We'll leave here — too many nosy people around, quick to call the police. We'll start our life together anywhere you like. I'll treat you like a queen. You'll be happier than you've ever been with that fool you married.'

'How . . .' She swallows, takes a breath. 'How do you have money?' Of all things, that is the only question she manages to ask.

'I met a few people in prison, did a few jobs and did them well. So I'm in demand.'

His hand on her mouth has relaxed, so she takes the opportunity to scream, 'Help!' Hoping Edith hears. Gemma. *Someone.* 'Please help!' she cries again before his hand comes crashing down on her face, grinding her teeth together in a jarring crush.

'Are you mad?' he yells, his other hand twisting her arm violently, nearly wrenching it from its socket. 'What's the matter with you?' he screams, slapping her cheek so hard her ear rings out a protest and she tastes blood. He shakes her hard, her head whirling like a dervish. 'I've come here to rescue you. I'm planning a wonderful future for us. I'm willing to overlook the fact that you married someone else, got pregnant with him. Ungrateful bitch.' Another resounding slap.

More shaking.

How long does it take to die? Please. Please let this be over soon.

She will not see Ma, her brothers, her sisters again. She will never make peace with Baba.

She will never go home. She will never again dance barefoot in the rain, mouth open, catching drops flavoured with earth and sun in her mouth. She will not breathe in the scent of freshly ploughed fields, sink her teeth into the

254

pale-pink flesh of a perfectly ripe guava. She will never again lie down under the mango tree in the courtyard, breathing in the spicy, fragranced air, listening to the cows mooing in the field below and the crows cawing in the branches above. She won't ever drink tea from a stainless-steel tumbler, sickly sweet with a thick layer of cream floating on top.

Now his hands are clasped around her neck, choking, stealing the breath from her.

She sees stars.

Then . . . she is floating. She is dancing, her bare feet kicking up dust which swirls in red clouds around her. She is home, where she belongs. She is home with her family and all is well. The neighbourhood dogs that circle for scraps bark in excitement, nipping at her nimble heels, and her mother, braiding jasmine on the kitchen veranda, laughs. 'Here,' she says, handing her a fragranced loop, 'for my dancing princess.' She sits between her mother's knees as her mother oils and kneads her hair, as she ties it in a knot and coils the jasmine around it. The breeze that drifts in from the fields below and caresses her cheek carries the earthy tang of cow manure. Her littlest brother settles next to her, his head in her lap. Crows chatter on coconut fronds, and from the kitchen comes the angry clatter of dishes that can only mean her sisters have had yet another one of their habitual spats. She wonders idly what it's about this time. She hears the sizzle of oil and breathes in the heady aroma of frying goli bhajis. She giggles as her brother inadvertently tickles her while twitching his nose and shaking his head in his sleep. Her mother hums softly, a much-loved lullaby. Her eyes close. She rests her head against her mother's bosom, breathes in the warm, sweet smell of her — fried onions and mangoes ripening in the sun — and smiles.

CHAPTER 52

Edith

Edith lets herself in with the key she stole for Number 2 envisioning just this eventuality and pauses for breath at the bottom of the stairs. As opposed to the shouting of moments ago, all is quiet. Suspiciously, ominously so.

Dread swirls, inducing nausea. She hopes desperately that it is not too late for the beautiful girl Edith has come to care for, with her whole life ahead of her. The girl who reminds Edith of who she was before Jack stole the innocence, the light and the laughter from her.

After all this she *cannot* be too late.

She rushes up the stairs as fast as her sore hip and knees will allow — not fast enough.

Come on, old girl.

Once she's at the top of the stairs, she tucks herself into the shadows just at the verge of the banister and screams with all her might.

More ominous silence, but this quiet is different from before. Stunned.

One beat. Two.

Please let it not be too late.

She's just about to scream again when the door to the master bedroom bursts open and he rushes out. The thug.

She stands poised. Ready.

As he approaches the top of the stairs, she reaches out and with all the strength, the anger, the rage, the hate within her, she shoves him down the stairs. Just like she did with Jack, finally having had enough. Just as Jack had done to her, many years before, murdering the child she was carrying, a girl, her daughter. Edith pushes the man hurting Sapna with all her determined might — interesting how strength floods into old bones when they have a purpose. 'When a woman says go away, don't come back, she means just that.'

NOW

'Oh dear,' we say, helping ourselves to the flapjacks we offered the detectives, needing the comfort of sugar to process what they have shared with us. 'We definitely didn't see that coming.'

'What did you think happened, then?' the detectives ask.

'Why would you like to know?' we parry back.

'Just curious,' the detectives shrug. Too casually, perhaps?

We decide to indulge them. Truth is, we finally feel seen, our opinions heard. We feel like we, the residents of the cul-de-sac, looked down upon by those living in the big, detached houses on the main road, are finally coming into our own. Not that we wanted this to happen, of course — first fire, then violence and death. But now that it has, well . . .

'We thought it was Sapna,' we say, and some of us shed a tear, of which at least one is genuine.

'Why?' the detectives ask.

'There was just this . . . helplessness about her,' we say. 'A melancholic air.'

'She gave the impression of vulnerability.'

'A victim,' one of the more straightforward of us snorts decisively.

'And the men she attracted . . .' We shiver.

'Go on,' the detectives prompt.

'Thuggish rogues, one and all,' we declare.

'There were many?' the detectives query, eyebrows raised.

'Two that we know of.'

'Two?'

'We're including the husband, of course. They conducted their marital spats on the street for all to see, as we've told you before.'

The detectives wait (we wouldn't say patiently, as such; at least one of them is looking at their watch), knowing we've more to add.

'Well, and that Sanjay Kumar. Always looming about the close. We sensed he was crooked. There was just something about him . . .'

'Didn't I say, when he arrived bearing flowers, "Here comes trouble"?'

'Well, we hope the trouble is well and truly in the past now, and we can go about our lives without more soap operas playing out in the street.' We sigh; we feel just a little deflated at the thought. 'Our cul-de-sac can go back to normal now,' we sniff. 'Or at least what passes for normal nowadays.'

The detectives nod briskly. 'Let's hope so.'

'Goodbye, thanks for your cooperation. You've been very helpful,' they say, standing up, raining flapjack crumbs on the carpets we'd hoovered in anticipation of their visit, pocketing their notebooks, their grim expressions still fixedly in place.

Are they taught that at police school, we wonder, as we have several times during their investigation — to sport that impassive expression that somehow also conveys firm disapproval?

Now that they're leaving, we don't want them to go.

We quite enjoyed being the centre of attention.

The more meticulous of us note that they haven't thanked us for the tea (builders for most, green for some, camomile for one) and cakes (a varied selection including vegan and gluten free) we've supplied them with, not to mention juices and biscuits, pastries and flapjacks. Our cul-de-sac might have been a crime scene in recent weeks, but the detectives have not been in danger of going hungry or thirsty here, at least.

'Just one thing . . .' The most strident of us volunteers to ask the question hovering on all of our tongues.

'Yes?' They pause at the door, the more impatient among them once again checking their watch, not bothering to be discreet about it.

'How will this affect our house prices?'

To give them credit, they maintain their impassive expressions, although we see the youngsters among them raise their eyebrows ever so slightly. 'That's a question for the estate agents, we're afraid,' they say, and then they're gone, taking the adrenaline and excitement of a live investigation with them, and our cul-de-sac is quiet again, not a leaf stirring.

Not for long, though.

Curtains twitch and doorbells ring as we visit with our neighbours, comparing notes as we munch on cake, enthusiastically praising the others' baking while quietly deciding that there are too many raisins, too little sugar, that it's not moist enough, even as we wonder what will happen next in our supposedly peaceful cul-de-sac.

'It just goes to show,' we say thoughtfully, taking a sip of our tea — too weak, not brewed for long enough — 'you never know what goes on behind closed doors.' We pause, wondering whether we should say it, then deciding we might as well. We're among friends, aren't we? We're behind closed doors ourselves. 'Especially with *that* lot . . .'

EPILOGUE

Sapna
Three months later

'Sanjay's death has been ruled an accident,' Sapna says. 'When you heard my cries through the adjoining wall, you let yourself into our house with the key I had given you for emergencies. You called up the stairs. Your call startled him, he stopped strangling me and came out of the bedroom to see who was in the house. He misjudged the stairs in the darkness and fell down them. An accident. Unfortunate or otherwise, depending on how you would like to see it.'

'*Another* accidental death?' Edith sighs, raising an eyebrow at Sapna, face deadpan, only the twinkle in those butter-wouldn't-melt eyes giving her away. A stooped, little old woman. Gentle, harmless, one might think. Underestimate her at your own peril.

Sapna is very glad indeed that Edith is on her side. Her fiercely loyal friend. Sapna is extremely fond of her, and not only because she bakes the most wonderful cakes she's ever tasted.

'Quite a few nasty accidents in our cul-de-sac. My miscarriage. Jack's fall. And now Sanjay's. Oh, and the fire too. The police looked into that again, didn't they?'

261

'Yes, but they stuck with their original verdict.'

On the main road outside their cul-de-sac, a motorbike revs up and speeds away. The sputter of the engine becomes softer and softer until it dies down completely. Birdsong and snatches of conversation float in through the open windows. Somewhere, a woman laughs. A tinkly sound, like wind chimes.

Gemma and Rob and Theo have moved away, to Wales, Edith said. 'Rob has family there. Gemma thought he'd leave her, but he's a good'un, a family man, so he's sticking by her. They're going to try and make a go of it.'

There have been rumours, Edith reports, that a Polish family with three primary school-age boys is moving in soonish.

'It'll be just like old times, when my boys were little,' Edith said, when she relayed the nugget of information, a wistful note to her voice. 'They used to play on the road out front with the Shaws' littl'uns. Got up to all sorts, they did. Such a long time ago now. My boys were all so close together in age and yet so different in temperament.' Edith sounded nostalgic.

'How do you find out all the news before everyone else?' Sapna asked.

'Oh, you hear all sorts if you keep your ear to the ground,' Edith said, mysteriously.

'You would have made a good spy during the war, Edith,' Sapna said.

Edith giggled, a surprisingly girly, infectious waterfall of mirth. Lovely to hear.

'That I would. Oh, the lives I could have led.' Again Edith sounded wistful.

'You still have a long way to go, Edith. The best is yet to come.'

Edith chuckled, raising her teacup in Sapna's direction. 'You know love, I'll drink to that.'

* * *

Sapna didn't report Gemma for arson in the end.

She came to visit Sapna in hospital, where she was being treated for the injuries Sanjay had inflicted upon her. She apologised profusely for starting the fire, then added, softly, 'I will understand if you go to the police. But Theo . . .' Her voice broke then. 'I . . . I'm sorry for what I did to you. I will always be sorry.'

Sapna couldn't do that to a mother, wrench her away from her child, that angelic little boy she'd cooed over, not even when Gemma's actions had stripped her of *her* child.

'I will not go to the police,' she said stiffly, cradling her stomach where, her doctors had told her, a new miracle had spawned and was growing healthy and well, despite the trauma Sapna had endured.

Sapna had thought in those terrible moments when Sanjay was choking the life out of her that she was ready to die. But, especially now that she knows about the babe growing inside her, she is beyond grateful to Edith for coming to her rescue when she had — she saved two lives that day.

Edith also came to visit Sapna, with her trademark carrot cake and lemon squares: 'I couldn't decide which one to bring, and anyway you need fattening up, especially now you're eating for two.' She waved away Sapna's thanks and said, briskly, 'Now, I know that you won't fancy going back to Number 2 when you leave here, considering what happened there . . .'

'Yes,' Sapna shuddered. 'I . . . I don't think I could stomach . . .'

'Which is why I'd like to invite you to come and stay with me. For as long as you like.'

'But I . . . I don't want to troub—'

'You'd be doing me a favour, love. I get very lonely, you see. I'll be grateful for the company.' She smiled fondly at her. 'I've taken quite a shine to you, my dear. You'll make an old woman very happy indeed.'

And so that was that. Sapna's relationship with Amir, the father of her child, was on shaky ground. She cared for him, but . . . he had broken her trust and that would take some time to rebuild. In the meantime, she moved in with Edith when she was discharged from hospital and she's been here ever since.

* * *

'Mrs Snooty-So-and-So is ignoring me since you've moved in,' Edith says now. 'She snorts audibly at me and, not to be outdone, I snort even louder in response. She'll have to come up with more severe means of showing her disapproval when the Polish family moves in — I'm sure she'll have something to say about that.'

'Bah humbug,' Sapna says.

Edith laughs gleefully. 'Bah humbug indeed.'

They've just watched *A Christmas Carol* on the DVD player that Edith has had for ages but didn't know how to use and which Amir set up for them, taking a perverse joy in watching the Christmas movie in the middle of summer. Edith was shocked when Sapna confessed she hadn't seen it. She's made a list of the classic movies that Sapna 'must watch', and they've been going through them, one by one, Sapna rating each out of ten.

Amir and Sapna are repairing their relationship — after all, he is the father of this miracle child in her womb, and if she's perfectly honest, she does care for him. She realised that, if she didn't know it already, when she thought he was dead.

But, she's taking it slowly this time round. She rushed into marrying him before, wanting to put Sanjay behind her. Now, she will get to know him again, at her own pace. Amir is completely on board with this.

'He has no choice but to be; if he wants you he has to fall in line,' Edith declared, severely.

As for Sapna, she's falling in love anew with the man to whom she also happens to be married and whose baby she's carrying.

'I'm learning to be strong,' she said to Edith the other day.

'My dear, you *are* strong,' Edith said firmly. 'You've endured challenges that would faze most people and come through smiling.'

I'm strong, Sapna tells herself several times a day. And I'm soon to be a mum. I will do anything for my child, protect him or her with my life if need be.

Edith interrupts her thoughts. 'You look like you found the pot of gold at the end of the rainbow,' she says as Sapna hands her a cup of tea.

'Well, not quite,' Sapna grins. She can't stop smiling. 'But what I got is even better.'

'Even better! Go on,' Edith prompts, smiling in return.

'When I called my ma, just now, my baba asked to speak to me!'

'Now that does call for a celebration,' Edith beams. 'I think I'll bake my walnut and coffee cake — you loved it last time, said it was your favourite.'

'Oh, every single one of your cakes is my favourite,' Sapna giggles. She is so very happy. 'And Edith, there's more.'

'There's more?'

'Baba asked me to visit once the baby's here.'

'That is just wonderful, my dear. I know just how much you miss your family.'

'Not as much since I moved in with you,' Sapna says, and Edith beams even more, her eyes shining.

'I've longed to go home but knew I wasn't welcome. But with my baba's blessing, I can start planning the trip. Now I have not only meeting my baby but also going home to look forward to.'

'I'm so happy for you, love,' Edith says.

'Edith,' Sapna ventures, 'will you come with me?'

'Where to, love?'

'To India, of course. To my childhood home. I can't wait to introduce you to everyone. They've heard so much about you over the phone.'

Edith is staring at her, unblinking. 'You mean it, don't you, love?'

'Of course I do. And don't you blame your hip or your knees, Edith. I know for a fact that they work very well when they need to.'

Edith cackles at that, and she and Sapna share a look as they remember that night at the top of the stairs.

Outside, the sun plays peekaboo with the clouds. A pigeon hovers, perches on the fence, looks around and then flies away in a swooping fluster of wings.

'Well, I always did want to see the world out there,' Edith says softly.

'And now we will. Together,' Sapna says, and Edith smiles fondly at her, her gaze moist. 'We'll start with India — I can't wait to introduce you to Ma. I just know the two of you will get on like a house on fire.' She stops, wincing. 'I didn't mean to put it quite like that.'

'No,' Edith says. 'But I do know what you mean. I think I will like your mum very much. I did see her when she came here with your brothers and father, you know. Your brother was very kind, helping me off the bus, carrying my shopper for me.'

'Yes, you said.' Sapna smiles. 'So, you, me and the bubba —' she strokes her stomach — 'will go to India. And maybe Amir. I bet, Edith, you'll come back armed with recipes for Indian sweets to add to your repertoire.'

'I must say that sounds wonderful indeed.'

'And after India, we'll see. Perhaps a trip to Australia to see your grandchildren?'

'Oh, my dear, I'd love that. I better make sure I'm fit and well then, eh?' Edith's eyes, her whole face, glows.

'You've many years to go yet, Edith. My bubba needs an English nana to educate him or her on classic movies.'

'Ha! You'll be an expert by then.' Edith laughs.

They sit companionably together drinking their tea and eating the raspberry tart Edith baked that morning. It's moist and springy, deliciously zesty with just the right amount of sweetness.

After a bit, Sapna says, 'And I was thinking . . .'

'Yes?'

'I . . . You know I have nightmares often and that I'm still having trouble feeling safe, especially at night.'

'Yes, my love. It's a shame, but give it time. It will get better, I promise,' Edith says.

'Yes, but I was thinking . . . What do you say we get a rescue dog? That way we'll be warned if there's someone prowling about. And in any case, I've always wanted a pet. It will be good for the bubba too, I think.'

Edith is silent, so Sapna, who was staring out at the garden, turns to look at her.

One gnarled hand rests on her heart while tears silently weave tracks down Edith's weathered face. She makes no move to wipe them — it's as if she's unaware of them.

'Oh Edith, what's the matter? Why are you crying?' Sapna asks, concerned.

'Am I?' Edith touches a hand to her cheek, stares in surprise at the moisture there. 'Happy tears, my love. I've always wanted a pet.'

'There you go, then.' Sapna laughs, delighted. 'Now that's decided, let's start looking, shall we?'

THE END

THE JOFFE BOOKS STORY

We began in 2014 when Jasper agreed to publish his mum's much-rejected romance novel and it became a bestseller.

Since then we've grown into the largest independent publisher in the UK. We're extremely proud to publish some of the very best writers in the world, including Joy Ellis, Faith Martin, Caro Ramsay, Helen Forrester, Simon Brett and Robert Goddard. Everyone at Joffe Books loves reading and we never forget that it all begins with the magic of an author telling a story.

We are proud to publish talented first-time authors, as well as established writers whose books we love introducing to a new generation of readers.

We have been shortlisted for Independent Publisher of the Year at the British Book Awards three times, in 2020, 2021 and 2022, and for the Diversity and Inclusivity Award at the Independent Publishing Awards in 2022. We won Trade Publisher of the Year Award at the Independent Publishing Awards 2023 and were shortlisted for Publisher of the Year at the RNA Industry Awards in 2023.

We built this company with your help, and we love to hear from you, so please email us about absolutely anything bookish at feedback@joffebooks.com

If you want to receive free books every Friday and hear about all our new releases, join our mailing list: www.joffebooks.com/contact

And when you tell your friends about us, just remember: it's pronounced Joffe as in coffee or toffee!